Chapter 1: December 1917 - March1918

S ometimes he did not know where the dreams ended and the real world began. He would awake with no recollection of who he was or where he had been and he would lie there, in the smooth sheets, in the soft bed, head full of nothing.

The sheets felt wrong. The comfort made him itch. The hospital smell of soap and sick did not quite drown out the other smell that crowded his dreams, a damp, mildewy smell like wet washing that had been left too long. It got into everything; the tea, the food, his clothes. Now it seemed bound to his skin. He did not just remember this smell, it was stored in him. Sometimes it faded into the background but it never went away. This, more than anything, brought back the memories. The real memories.

He could only put the pieces together slowly, in between the fever and the dreams. He was hurt. He had been shattered and bits of him were all around. In his waking moments he tried to gather them together, but they would not all fit.

From the outside it was not so bad. He was still in one piece from the outside. A nice Blighty one, that's what Frannie had called it. He'd left him at the station in Poperinghe with a wink and a pat on the shoulder and congratulated him on his luck. The perfect wound. Not life-threatening, not enough to leave him permanently maimed but enough to get him home, to England, to a comfortable bed in a hospital far from the noise and the chaos and the drowning, choking stink of fear.

He was in another hospital, the last in a long line. He'd had a fever, but it was fading. He was winning, the sister said when they brought him in.

"Bear up, corporal," she said. "You're mending well. We'll soon have you on your feet."

Her cheerfulness made him wince, though she was gentle enough in helping him onto the bed. Sister Barnes, that was her name. He'd quickly shut his eyes, pretending fatigue. Now it was dark but it had been morning when he'd arrived. Had it been morning? Light, anyway.

The day it happened, it was just after first light. They were rushing to beat the dawn that day, the grey, battered dawn. Following the railway line north of Zonnebeke, sodden and mutilated by shell impacts, lined with gravel and the remains of rusted-up track. Where there had been an impact the track rose up crazily in wild curls. He was quite taken with it. Yes, that was it; they had a break on their way back from the line and he sat, staring at the deformed track. That was just before. He looked at the track as if admiring a work of art while the men in his section pissed and smoked and complained and Frannie paced up and down, twitchy with apprehension, eager to be moving.

They had been on a working party that night, revisiting the sodden landscape they'd struggled to take just two weeks previously. It was a desperate place, a scatter of flooded craters, and the troops holding the line had to squat in the muck and make the best of it without hope of rations or even water. They were supposed to be making improvements, but it was stupid work. That night they tried to dig down, clear the water, and reinforce where they could. The ground was saturated like porridge and the sandbags they used to build up the parapet simply sank into the mire. It was hard to dig properly because the holes were often too shallow to stand up in without being picked off by a sniper. They bent over their spades and grovelled in the stinking water. It was hopeless but they kept at it all night, only stopping when the flares went up, flooding the ruined plain with a light that burned the backs of their eyes. In those brief moments of illumination they froze like statues, aching with tension and fatigue. Then he would stare out across the flatland and up the gentle rise toward Passchendaele, only a couple of miles away but as distant as the South Pole.

Through these long nights his awareness contracted into a tiny, focussed space just sufficient to perform the task at hand. The wet had long since penetrated his boots and the earth was pulling and sucking at his feet. He could feel the thick wetness softening the skin between his toes. Sometimes he thought that if he stood still long enough, he would simply dissolve into the ground. Work was the only remedy. He felt like a troll at these times, a creature without thought or reflection, and he had to admit there was a kind of comfort in it.

The approach of morning signalled the end of their shift. Mr Church, the new lieutenant, glanced at his wristwatch and gave Frannie the nod. Frannie moved down the line with a word to each man, a joke here, a "chin up" or pat on the back there. He never seemed to tire; the worse the conditions, the more his eyes gleamed bright gold against the dark streaks of

3

mud on his face.

It was a three mile walk back to Ypres and they all wanted to be well away from the line by daybreak. He picked his way carefully, feeling the slippery duckboards beneath his feet. Two weeks earlier, as they'd walked this route for the first time, laden like mules with a full pack, he had seen how men had fallen from the narrow path to a watery death in one of the endless flooded holes. He'd had to walk past several of them, abandoned at the wayside to sink or swim. Once he had seen a live one, an arm protruding from the water flailing weakly as it sank below the surface.

He concentrated hard on the feet of the man in front, taking each step carefully and deliberately, not looking up, for he knew what the gathering dawn would reveal. The long, twisting paths of duckboards, the smeared remnants of white tape slung through spiked pickets, and on either side a world of churned ground and green, viscous water, lumpen shapes coated with gruel-like muck; dead mules, dead men, cast in various attitudes of struggle or surprise, the half-light bestowing on them an unnatural beauty. Better to keep one's eyes on the path ahead. Best not to inhale the heavy, sickly smell of putrefaction.

As they walked, the occasional shell sent up a muddy shower, falling back to earth like dark rain. These were far behind and not a threat, not enough to make one break stride. Once, overhead, came the familiar high, shrill whine, falling an octave, perhaps two, and fifty yards to their left the earth erupted.

He could not help the twitch of his body in response and he lost his balance, falling to his knees, slithering, gripping the wooden boards beneath to stop himself from pitching into the mire. He felt splinters cut into his hand as he held onto the wood, rough beneath it's coating of wet. He felt a brief downpour around him, and a heavy clod of earth hit the top of his helmet, almost knocking him off balance again. He heard the sizzle as hot fragments of shell casing hit the ground, a more deadly shower that could cut through you without warning like an invisible blade.

He got up, balanced his rifle and pack, and began walking again. The others did the same. No-one spoke.

When they reached the railway line they were able to leave the duckboards behind and follow a straight course plotted by fluttering white tape. It was only natural to slow down a little, to relax and breathe. There was the illusion that the drier ground, slightly less mangled by shellfire, was safer territory. But he knew how dangerous an illusion this was. Frannie knew it too, because in response to the slackening pace he began walking up and down the line, urging the men on.

It was at this point that Mr Church, contrary fool that he was, decided to stop for a break. Frannie, almost beside himself, followed him into the lee of an overturned cart and talked in low, urgent tones. He leaned on a broken wheel as the lieutenant turned away to do his business, his broad frame intimidating the slighter man. Mr Church's face began to redden as Frannie persisted. He buttoned his fly and turned back towards the men, his voice rising sharply for all to hear.

"That's *enough* sergeant! Just concentrate on doing your own job properly, then you won't need to interfere with mine." With that, he withdrew further behind the cart, his hand straying to a flask slung across his chest.

Frannie looked down at his feet for a second. That was a bit rich. No-one was more dedicated that Frannie. A minute

5

later, Mr Church reappeared and chivvied the men to move on as if the previous exchange had not happened. His eyes were red-rimmed, and not just with fatigue. A miasma of cheap whisky drifted behind him as he passed by – pickled at six o'clock in the morning.

Then, out of nowhere, came a disturbance in the atmosphere that made his eardrums crack. He heard nothing, but there was a bright, fiery flash and a brief moment where the air seemed to have been sucked out of the world. There was no pain, not at first, but he had the sense that he'd been split from his body, as if a giant had lifted him up, taken a knife and gutted him like a fish. He heard singing like a chorus of a thousand insects, then a brief, warm fall of rain, then nothing. He thought for the longest moment that he had died.

When he opened his eyes he was face down, mouth and nostrils filled with grit and viscous liquid. He might have screamed, he wasn't sure. His ears seemed to have imploded. He could hear a distant blur of voices rising and falling, echoing from the end of a long tunnel. A hand held him firmly by the shoulder and turned him on his side. His back and legs prickled as if a whole nest of wasps were stinging him.

A voice: "Are you all right Dan?"

Then another: "He'll be fine. No hope for Mr Church, though."

"Oh god!"

"Come away now Fred, don't look."

"What a fucking mess. I'm covered in it!"

He blinked. Something liquid had got into his eyes and it stung. The prickles in his back became stabbing knives and he screamed again.

"Careful, he's got shrapnel in there."

A rough cloth was wiped across his face. He couldn't hear properly. The voices kept drifting in and out. The explosion still hummed and vibrated inside him.

"Dan, can you hear me?"

"Frannie?"

"Good lad. You'll be all right."

"Yeah, lucky sod."

"Shut up. Get the field dressing from my pack."

He felt a pair of hands exploring gently along his arms and legs. When they got near his left knee, he reacted with a convulsion that almost lifted him off the ground.

"You're all right," said Frannie again. "Just a bit of something behind the knee, and a few scratches on your back. You've the luck of the devil, you bastard."

He was shaking. For that brief instant when he'd raised his head, he'd glimpsed a body that did not seem to belong to him. His arms and back were coated in blood and straggling, glistening lumps of liver. He began to tremble. Even his teeth shook.

"What happened?"

"A direct hit," said Frannie. "I can't believe you've only got these few scratches. Someone up there must like you. Mr Church is gone though."

"Dead?"

"As a teetotaller's funeral."

"Where – where did all that blood come from?"

"Don't worry, it's not yours. You were lucky it didn't happen further up the line, or we'd never be able get you back." Frannie bit the top off an ampoule of iodine. "Brace yourself. This might sting a bit."

But he felt nothing, only a pulsing numbness. Frannie began

to apply a field dressing, lifting his knee slightly to bind the tapes around his leg, and he must have passed out.

He woke in a cave. Water dripped from the ceiling, making the candle stub by his head hiss and splutter. He was still lying on his side and he could hear low voices and a chorus of groans. Not a cave, a dugout.

"Its no good, I can't get to it," a voice said. "But I've got most of the stuff out of his back. I'll wrap him up and they can have another go when he gets to the dressing station."

"How long will that take?" Frannie's voice again.

"Well, if you fancy carrying him sergeant, you can take him yourself. But it's a long walk."

He could hear the voices well enough, but he couldn't see.

"Can't you give him some morphia?"

A laugh. "If I had any, I wouldn't waste it on him. He'll be fine."

He felt a hand on his shoulder, turning him onto his back. There was a pricking sensation in spots along his lower back but no pain. He couldn't seem to focus his eyes. Funnily enough, the roof of the dugout appeared to him in precise detail; the earth shot with fibrous roots, the wooden planking green with mildew here and there, alive with burrowing creatures. But the muttered words and stuttering cries did not seem attached to the vague, shadowy forms that heaved about him. There was a slight pressure on his leg as the doctor redressed his wound. The pressure seemed to trigger a delayed reaction and a spasm of pain penetrated the numbness, knifing along his leg like ice. His mind drew away, stretching up into the damp of the dugout roof.

He was jolted awake, back in the open air. In front of him were the hunched shoulders of a man, yoked by straps to a stretcher – his stretcher. The man's head was wrapped in a balaclava, covered by a helmet, and it was like he wasn't a man at all, just a collection of odd bits of uniform. Above him the sky swirled and he was pitched and tossed like a boat in a storm. They passed clumps of men, talking and smoking. A few looked down at him with pity, more with envy. Some laughed and waved. It was still day. Was it the same day?

Later he woke to find himself being lifted onto a bed. He was in a large, noisy place that had the acoustics of a church. He could see a beamed roof, and from some of the iron beams hung chains with hooks attached. Other beams supported strange-shaped braces, and here and there the beams were stained orange with rust. Around him a cacophony of voices was augmented by other, more basic sounds; groans, whimpers, and a faint, regular wheezing that seemed to come from close by his head. It might have been his own breathing. A face appeared above him, haloed in white.

"Corporal? Can you hear me?"

A woman's voice. He nodded, and the slight movement of his head made his ears buzz as if some infernal insect was trapped in his cranium. He tried to ask for water, his tongue thick in his mouth. She must have understood for after a few seconds he felt a hand slide under his head and he was lifted slightly, a bottle brought to his lips. He drank compulsively and coughed, spilling water down his neck. He shivered, sending another electric wave down his leg. He could not focus on the nurse, only the white and grey of her uniform. She spoke, soft and coaxing, but he could not hear her for the

9

buzzing. When it quietened, there was a different voice, a man:

"We'll take the shrapnel out of your leg first, corporal, then dress the cuts on your back. The shrapnel's buried deep so it may hurt and I'm afraid we've nothing to give you. We're going to turn you over now. You might want to brace yourself."

Before he had time to object, the two of them rolled him over quickly like a piece of bread dough. He had no impression of the man but he could remember as clear as day the instrument that he used. A bright claw of metal, arcing to two fine points, razor-sharp. The doctor said something to the nurse and he felt a hand on the back of his calf, then the cold metal bit into him. At the first probe he cried out, kicking reflexively with his good leg.

"Hold him down, nurse."

She was surprisingly strong and he felt a flicker of outrage as she pinned his arms. The doctor continued to dig. His mind raced away, up into the rafters, but again and again he was pulled back down by the excavation of his leg. The doctor was a sadist, he must be, and just as soon as the pain subsided enough he would get up and kill him.

"Got it! At last. Thought I was never going to reach the damn thing." The metal instrument came into view, and between its teeth was a small, dark ball coated with blood. "There's the source of your trouble, corporal."

It was dark now and very cold. The sweat that had poured off him during the operation had congealed into a damp glue. He had no idea where he was, but it was so cold he knew he must be outdoors. Unfocussed shadows detached themselves from the dark and he could just make out a long rank of stretchers alongside his, funnelling into the distance like rungs on a ladder. He heard the hoot of a train and realised he must be at the station in Poperinghe. Strangely, he thought he could hear Frannie's voice again.

"Come on, put him on the train, sergeant. The field hospital's full. We can't just leave him here."

Yes, it was Frannie. He was talking to a fat RAMC sergeant with a purple nose and a bad case of the sniffles. Frannie stood over him in his customary friendly-intimidating manner while he blew his nose on a stained bit of rag.

"His ticket says he's supposed to go to the hospital in Boulogne," said the sergeant, balling the rag in his fist. "This one's going straight to the port."

"But there's not another one until tomorrow," said Frannie. "So what's he supposed to do?"

"Lump it, like the rest of us."

"Do him a favour, sergeant. Do us all a favour. Put him on the train, let him get the boat home. I'll sign for him, if you like. Then you won't have any bother from the brass hats."

It seemed the matter was settled because Daniel felt hands at his chest. Someone was fumbling for the label that had been tied onto him. He heard, as clearly as though it were right by his ear, the hissing of pencil on paper – something being crossed out, something added. He was a redirected parcel, moved around at the mercy of others. Not that he wasn't well used to that. He looked up to see Frannie bending over him, hatless, his cropped red hair catching glints of moonlight.

"Dan? Want some water?"

He managed a nod and Frannie supported his head just as the nurse had done, bringing a flask to his lips. He gulped the water down until he'd drained the bottle.

"What happened?" His voice was still an ashy croak and it hurt to speak.

"You were hit. Don't you remember?"

"No."

"You were bloody lucky, old pal. A nice Blighty one. Want some more ?"

"Yes."

"I'll have to fetch it then. Might take me a little while. In the meantime," Frannie slipped a tiny, smooth pellet into his mouth, "this'll help things along."

The pellet slid around his tongue and stuck at the back of his throat. He swallowed and felt its progress down his gullet. Then it was gone and Frannie was gone too, and he was moving again in the dark but this time the movement was regular like the rocking motion of a cradle. He could hear the grind of metal against metal, the regular coughing of an engine. A train.

Time began to stretch as the morphia took effect. The train moved, stopped, and moved again at random. There was a deep silence when it stopped, broken only by the tick, tick of contracting metal and the breathing, the groans, sometimes the cries, of his fellow passengers. Occasionally an orderly would pass by, or a nurse, and he would hear their low tones as they attended a patient.

He was racked up on a stretcher. Close above him there was another stretcher, and another below. He could not have sat up even if he'd wanted to. In his drugged state he began to imagine his confinement to be that of a tomb.

The train lurched and jolted. The compartment began to fill with the sludgy grey light of dawn. There was a creaking coming from somewhere close by. He looked up and noticed a convulsive, rhythmic movement in the fabric of the stretcher above, accompanied by a regular, high-pitched gasping as if someone were trying to blow a whistle. The man must be having a fit. He tried to call for an orderly but could manage only a whisper. The convulsions became more violent, and he swallowed and tried to call again. No-one came.

He could only watch as slowly, impossibly slowly, a small, irregular patch of blood grew in the fabric of the stretcher. As the convulsions diminished the stain spread like a contagion. The convulsions ceased and the blood saturated the webbed fabric, gathered itself at the lowest dip of the stretcher and began to drip on him.

He must have screamed then because an orderly appeared straight away. And he must have kept on screaming, for the man in the bunk below prodded him in the back and said:

"For goodness sake, pipe down will you? There's some of us here trying to sleep."

The rest of the journey was a confusion of temperatures. He could not recall the hospital ship, only the damp chill of the channel wind. He remembered nothing of the trains that carried him north except their stuffy heat. And each intermediate stage of the journey was marked by the changes in climate as they took him in and out of the open air. The fever made him hypersensitive and the feeling of cool air on his face set off a violent shivering. But the confinement of the trains was intolerably hot and he was perpetually soaked in sweat.

Once he reached the military hospital in Dover he realised that he had gangrene. Even in his fevered state he could not help but be aware of the overpowering sweet stink of it when they changed his dressing. This they seemed to do constantly. Every couple of hours a nurse would apply a piece of lint soaked in some infernal icy liquid that smelled of chlorine. Then she would bind his leg again, covering the dressing in a waxy material so that he would not wet the sheets.

The procedure was repeated every few hours for days, perhaps weeks, before the doctor said that he was clear of it and that he would keep his leg. He supposed he should have felt pleased but feeling anything was beyond him. That night the nurses left him alone and he fell into a deep, black sleep, the first proper sleep he'd had in months, and when he woke the next morning the world had come back into focus. He was able to sit up and eat some breakfast and it tasted better than any meal he had ever eaten in his life.

It had been good at first, to see colours, to taste, to feel, even if most of what he felt was pain. But at least now the pain was only pain, not a huge, monstrous thing that filled the whole world. It was good to be clean too, and feel the soft, white sheets against his skin. The wonder of sleep, proper sleep, whole nights of it, and whole days of blankness, of nothing but food and rest and clean sheets and warm, soapy water.

But this hospital paradise did not last. As his body recovered, his mind emerged from its fugue and like blood to a frozen limb, the memories flooded back. There were gaps, true. Great yawning cracks and patches of deep shadow. Some of them filled, but not all. Some he would have preferred to remain dark.

Chapter 2

The light faded quickly at this time of the year, and already the trees were gloomy skeletons, their ink-blot shadows spreading across the lawn. Feeling the cold, Elissa Church gave up her half-hearted attempts at weeding and found a sheltered spot on the back porch. She shivered, pulling her shawl close to her neck. She relished the grey dusk; the stark exposure of the nuts and bolts of things matched her mood. It was her porch now, her house. Her garden too, long and straggling with its twisting path and its cherry trees. Of course in every important way, the house had always been hers. She had chosen it, filled it, occupied it. To Harry it had always been a place of passing and he had never made any secret of his disdain.

She'd moved in the week he left for officer training, six weeks after they'd married. Home on his first leave, he had stepped into the hall, took one look and said: "Elissa if you must live like a peasant I suppose I can't stop you, but you don't expect me to actually live in this squalid little hole do you?" And off he went, back to his mother's to be fed, watered and fussed over.

She'd known for nearly a month, but she still could not quite believe that he was dead. Now there was no need for a separation or a divorce that would scandalise the town and embarrass their families. The war had done the job nicely, conveniently disposing of a husband that she no longer loved and could not bear to live with.

She walked down the garden, twisting her wedding ring. Try as she might, she could not feel sorrow. The premature ending of her marriage left her with only a dull sense of waste. In their three short years they had hardly lived together, thanks to the war. Instead, they had progressed, from one leave to another, through unease to irritation, to anger, and finally, an intense dislike that had bordered on hatred.

She sucked her finger, then pulled the ring up over her knuckle. It came off easily. On the last night of his last leave, six months ago, he had staggered home drunk at four o'clock in the morning, smelling of whisky and cheap perfume. She hadn't felt the slightest jealousy, just relief as he collapsed onto the bed next to her and started to snore. At least he would not be bothering *her*.

And now he would never bother her again. She looked at her wedding ring, resting dully on the flesh of her palm. Now it was off she wanted it gone. She looked down towards the far end of the garden. It was almost dark now, but she knew that behind the shed, by the cherry trees, lay a compost heap.

She crunched her way across the frosted grass and felt her way along the side of the shed, breathing in the mingled bouquet of grass cuttings and rotted food – even through the cold of December the odour persisted. She edged as close as she could so that there would be no mistake and with a quick, jerking motion threw the ring. It flew in a silent, glittering arc then disappeared into the compost.

Along with her ring, the heap seemed to swallow what little

light was left. She stared into it, a black hump, a dark void that had opened at her feet, and massaged her denuded finger. Her elation gave way to a formless anxiety.

"Mrs Church?"

A thin beam of light filtered across the garden and Janet stood silhouetted in the kitchen doorway.

"It's all right, I'm coming."

Elissa found her way back to the path. She had thrown away her wedding ring. What on earth had possessed her?

"I was worried you might miss your train," said Janet. "You've only about ten minutes you know. Don't want to be late for your shift."

"Janet, I've done something very foolish."

"I'm sure you haven't Mrs C."

"Yes I have. I've…lost my ring."

"Oh dear."

"My wedding ring."

"Don't you worry, Mrs Church. I'll get the hurricane lamp and have a good look. If I don't find it we can have a proper search in the morning."

"No. There's no point looking. In fact, I don't want you to."

"Are you sure?"

"Yes, quite sure. It's in the compost heap."

Janet cleared her throat. "Mrs Church," she said, fiddling with her keys. "Excuse me for saying this, but I think I understand."

"Do you?"

"Let's say no more about it, shall we?"

"No, let's not. Thank-you Janet."

Just after midnight, Elissa had a few minutes alone at the

nurse's station. The evening chores were done, the sister was on her break, and Jo had snuck out into the grounds to smoke a cigarette. Garrett Hill could be an eerie place at night, but she liked these quiet moments, surrounded by the breathing, shifting, sleeping men. During the day, the hospital was bustling and cheerful and a brave face was *de rigeur*. But the night shunted away this bright façade and quietly revealed the true face of the suffering so deftly hidden by both nurses and patients. She preferred it – at least it was honest.

The hospital had been a hunting lodge in peacetime and retained some of its old elegance in the long, green sweep of the grounds. There were some reminders inside, too; the mangy stag's head that hung in the entrance hall, the narrow, glass-fronted gun cupboards that lined one side of the ward. The glass doors had been covered in hessian and the beds pushed up against them. Sometimes if a patient had a bad night and moved about too violently, the bed frame would knock against the glass, making it rattle. It had given Elissa a terrible fright the first time she'd heard it.

The patients often had bad nights. It had surprised her at first, this nocturnal torment, this sweating and sleepwalking and blind terror. It moved her far more than the endurance of physical pain because it was an unseen and unrecognised pain, and the battle against it was fought in secret. These night-time struggles brought to her a fellow feeling for men that were otherwise as distant as the moon. Sometimes she even convinced herself that she helped them.

She checked the patients' notes, running her finger around the inside of the stiff, white collar of her uniform. Nearly three years, and she still hadn't got used to it. There had been two new arrivals today; one had a shrapnel wound behind the knee that had gone deep, almost to the bone. The other man had lost three fingers and fractured an arm. He was young, only nineteen, and earlier in the evening he had joked loudly with the other patients while trying to write a letter with his left hand.

She walked over to his bed. He lay on his back, corpse fashion, right arm trussed to his chest. His face in repose was smooth and untroubled, although he had displayed a pronounced facial tick when awake. It had looked as if he was repeatedly trying to smile.

The leg wound was on the far side of the ward. She had not spoken to him yet, and he had not joined in the jocular exchanges after dinner. Now his hands were restless, plucking at the edges of his sheet. As she approached, she realised that he was talking, muttering to himself in his sleep. He was pale and his skin seemed stretched thin over the strong, prominent bones of his face. He had dark hair, soaked with sweat, forming claw-like curls against the pallor of his forehead. There was a damp stain on the pillow beneath his head. His eyes were open but he did not see her. He had the darkest eyes – grey, almost black – that seemed to soak up the light. He was all contrasts; skin and bone, dark and light.

His movements with the bed covers became more agitated and his hand got caught, twisted in the sheet. She crouched down by the bed to free him and as she tugged the sheet away, he grabbed her wrist. She bit back pain as his fingers dug into the soft flesh on the inside of her wrist. He was staring at her, or seemed to be, and she could not tell if he was awake or asleep. She tried to prise her hand free, wrench his fingers from her, but he held on tight. She made an effort to relax. Fighting him would only make it worse.

"It's all right," she said, keeping her voice low. She placed her free hand over his. He was entirely rigid, holding onto her wrist like a lifeline. He had long, broad fingers and bitten-down nails. Slowly, the frozen look went out of his face and his grip relaxed. She uncurled his hand from her wrist and after a minute she could tell by a flicker of the eyes, a tightening in his facial muscles, that he was awake.

"Feeling better?" she said.

He blinked, said nothing.

"You were having a nightmare."

He looked down at her hand over his and then back at her.

"You were caught up in the sheet," she said, removing her hand. "I was trying to free you."

"I'm sorry," he said, then immediately closed his eyes and fell back to sleep. She wondered if he'd really woken at all.

Back at her station, she pretended to tidy some papers. Her wrist was throbbing, and something about the man had made her uneasy. It wasn't the obvious distress he had felt or the pain he had inflicted. Nor was it the physical contact – she was used to that. She had held plenty of hands, soothed and comforted away many nightmares. The patients did not care who changed their dressings or bathed them or cleaned their bedpans, as long as it was done. A hand to hold in times of distress, physical or mental, was not a matter of individual contact. She was merely a stand-in, a replacement for an absent wife or mother.

She risked a glance to the other side of the room. He was still sleeping, peacefully this time. It was the force of his feeling that had alarmed her. His terror had hit her full square, like an icy wind in the face. He had been drowning and he'd clung to her for rescue, and all she'd wanted to do was get free. She felt ashamed of herself – so much for being a caring angel. She examined the inside of her wrist. A trinity of red weals followed the line of her veins; she would have some handsome bruises in the morning. Suddenly she wanted to know this man who had caught her out and exposed her pretence of mercy, even if it had been inadvertently.

She ran her finger down the patient list. The youngster with the lost fingers was called Alex, she remembered. There he was: Private Alexander James Kemble, 19. And next on the list was her mystery man: Daniel Charles Earnshaw, Corporal, 22. Harry's battalion, she noticed. She looked back over his notes. He had been treated at a casualty clearing station on the same day Harry had died.

"Found something interesting?"

Jo had crept up on her. Elissa resisted the urge to conceal what she'd been reading.

"Not really. Just checking the new arrivals. The leg wound was getting a bit lively in his sleep."

Jo fixed her with a beady stare. She had dark eyes too, like the corporal with the nightmares. But Jo's eyes did not radiate a terror that sucked up all the light in the room.

"He looks peaceful enough now. You must have worked your magic."

Elissa found herself blushing. "I just talked a little nonsense, calmed him down."

Jo raised her eyebrows and reached over Elissa's shoulder for the patient list. "Local boy by the looks of it. Wonder if he's happy to be home."

With her glossy black hair she reminded Elissa of a blackbird, hopping from one thing to another with equal amounts curiosity and relish. Elissa was furious with herself; she thought she was beyond embarrassment. She'd been a VAD for nearly three years now, and if she hadn't been in France like Jo she'd worked in a military hospital and knew the ropes.

"Look out, here comes Barnes." Jo slid the patient list back onto the desk.

Sister Barnes emerged from her office at the end of the ward and bore down on them with her customary determined gait.

"Miss Kenyon," she said, holding out a piece of paper to Jo, "please fill this list from the dispensary. You'll find the trolley in my office."

"Righto – I mean, yes sister," said Jo. She pulled a face at Elissa behind her back and scuttled off down the ward.

Sister Barnes was a small, thin woman with cold blue eyes, a wiry strength and an implacable will. Elissa had even seen it work on the MO, Dr. Stevens, when he'd tried to declare a lame man fit. Barnes just fixed him with a gimlet eye and said that he was obviously a doctor with long experience so he must know. Of course she meant exactly the opposite. He had only been qualified two years and had never served overseas, unlike Barnes, who had been a nurse for twenty years and done a stint on a hospital ship in the Boer War.

She marginally softened her expression as she turned to Elissa. "And Mrs Church, I know it's been a hard few days for you, but do you think you could stop daydreaming for five minutes and fetch some clean sheets from the laundry? Mr Kemble is prone to nighttime accidents and it'll do no harm to be ready."

"Yes sister," said Elissa. She didn't dare slack as she followed Jo out of the ward, but as she passed Corporal Earnshaw's bed she risked a quick glance over. He was sleeping silently, but his eyes slid back and forth beneath their lids and she wondered if he was dreaming Harry's death.

Chapter 3

Daniel remembered the dream clearly enough, though he wasn't quite sure where it had ended. The girl had been real, he was certain of that, but she had also been in the dream. When he tried to recall her face all he could conjure was a pair of soft brown eyes, disembodied in a pale blur. He hoped she was real – she had seemed kind.

He looked out for her during morning rounds. The tall, fair-haired VAD changing the beds might have been her, but she disappeared when the day shift came on and he didn't get chance for a proper look. He fell asleep, snatching an hour or two in the dull time before lunch, only to be awoken by Sister McKinley to have his dressing removed.

"It's looking much better now, corporal," she said, after she'd ripped off the muslin pad. "I don't think you'll be needing this much longer."

"I'm so pleased," he said, wincing.

"Have you tried those crutches yet?"

"Once."

"Well it's time you got on with it. Practice, that's all it takes."

"Really, that's all it takes is it?"

Sister McKinley tied on a fresh pad then pulled the bedcovers back up with unnecessary brutality. "My mother always told me that sarcasm was the lowest form of wit," she said. "So let's have less of the smart remarks and get on with it, shall we Mr Earnshaw?" She raised her eyebrow towards the two wooden crutches propped against the head of his bed.

McKinley was a broad, powerful woman with an astringent Edinburgh accent. She had a bracing charm and more humour than Barnes, the night sister. In any other circumstances, Daniel would have enjoyed sparring with her. She reminded him of his mother.

Philip Harker, in the next bed, waited until the sister had stalked off then leaned across to whisper theatrically. "Oh dear, what have you done to upset sister?"

"I couldn't possibly imagine."

"You mustn't be rotten to her, she's from Scotland. Give her a wink, pretend she's pretty and she'll do your bidding quick enough."

"Why don't you mind your own business?"

Harker's eyebrows disappeared into the swathe of bandages that covered his head. "Come on, cheer up old thing. Be nice to the girls and they'll be nice to you."

"Are you hard of hearing?"

"Well, if you must act like a bear with a sore head." Harker reached for his newspaper.

"Looks to me like you're the one with the sore head."

Harker opened the paper with a snap and hid himself behind it. Daniel wished he could bite back the words. He had no idea how bad the man's injury was. He kicked his good foot against the covers. He always went too far. He did not have the knack of pleasing like Frannie. Frannie could get anyone to do anything and make them feel cheerful about it at the same time, whereas he only seemed to be able to spike them

25

with their own weakness.

He looked at the crutches propped against his bedside cabinet and tried to feel some enthusiasm for moving. In truth, he would have been happy to lie in bed forever. But then again, on crutches he might get a better look at the mysterious nurse when she came back, find out who she was. He didn't know why it seemed important; it wasn't as if the girl was pretty. He couldn't even remember what she looked like. But it gave him something to think about, a focus for his flailing mind.

It took him a full minute of struggle to haul himself onto the crutches, but once he was up and going he didn't want to stop. He spent the rest of the morning lurching up and down the ward and even managed a trip to the bathroom. The simple joy of being able to urinate and wash in privacy, albeit with painful slowness, cheered him out of all proportion. He ate his midday meal sitting in a visitor's chair by his bed, and made plans for an afternoon trip in the grounds. This was too much for McKinley, who forcibly returned him to bed when she found him struggling with the doors into the conservatory, flushed and sweating.

"Really, you mustn't overdo it Mr Earnshaw," she said, enclosing his upper arm in an iron grip. "I didn't think you'd take what I said quite so much to heart. Moderation in all things, that's the trick."

She helped him back to the ward and he fell into bed and slept immediately. By the time the night shift came on at six he was wide awake again, aching but alert. He watched as McKinley and Barnes, the night sister, talked in the office, then realised that one of the night-shift girls was standing by his bed. It was the fair-haired one – she did have brown eyes. She was also slender and tall, with wavy hair the colour of set honey. Pretty after all, though not really his type. She was looking at him curiously.

"Sister McKinley thinks we should take your crutches away for the night," she said. "She's worried that you'll overdo it."

"Perhaps Sister McKinley thinks I should be tied to the bedpost too. That would keep me in my place."

The girl bit her lip. That had thrown off her nurse act. "You must be careful," she said. "If you open up the wound, there's a risk it'll get infected and that would be a shame. You've healed up so well."

"Please don't take them away," he said. He hadn't meant to implore and he cursed his own weakness. "That is, I'd rather you didn't. If you don't mind."

"I wouldn't dream of it."

She did have kind eyes. She looked as if she understood. Of course she understood nothing, but he wanted to believe that she did.

"I need them in case I need to use the, ah, facilities."

"Of course you do. But remember there's always the bedpan if you can't manage."

"Yes, there's always that."

She brushed the bedcover lightly with her fingers. "The best thing is to build it up gradually. Start with five times up and down the ward tomorrow, and then increase it to ten the next day, and so on."

"That sounds like a good plan," he said.

She patted the bedcovers. "Yes. Well, just give me a call if you need anything."

He sensed she wanted to ask him something, and it had nothing to do with crutches. She half-smiled, a brief, furtive turning up of the mouth, but then McKinley hove into view through the ward doors and she backed off quickly, walking away at a stiff clip. His eyes were drawn to the point at the small of her back where the apron ties crossed and knotted.

"Who's teachers pet, then?" said Harker, who had been hanging on to every word. "The delectable Mrs Church. She could help me with my crutches any time she liked. If I had any."

Daniel glanced at Harker. "Did you say her name was Church?"

"Yes, that's right," said Harker. "Know her do you?"

"I'm not sure." Daniel watched her sit down at the nurse's station and begin writing with slow care onto some chart or other. There was a chime of connection, but he couldn't quite get it.

"Didn't think so. Not in that league, are you old chap? She lost her husband last month I heard. Seems to be bearing up well."

That was it. "What was his name, the husband?"

"Can't remember. But he was John Church's son and heir. You know, of Church's Mills."

"I think I knew him."

Harker sat up straight. "Did you now?"

"Well, I can't be sure. If it was him, he was my CO. I was there when he – when he was hit." Daniel pointed to his leg. "That's how I got this."

"Ah. She doesn't know, I take it?"

"Shouldn't think so."

"Well, I'd keep quiet about it if I were you. She won't want to hold your hand and mop your brow if you keep reminding her of her dead husband."

"You're a veritable font of advice, aren't you Harker?"

"I do my best. And remember, if you need any more help with Mrs Church, I'm your man."

He'd had the same dream every night since the hospital in Dover and although it varied in its details it was mostly, monotonously the same. He would be back in the dank, sandy waste of East Dunkirk, biting on sand at the bottom of a pit.

It was a real place this pit, a reedy cleft just short of the beach at Nieuport, where they'd spend most of the summer. Frannie liked to joke that they were the last men on the Western Front as they huddled amidst the sand dunes listening to the hiss and suck of the sea. He and Frannie had discovered the pit together, out on patrol one day. It was an old advanced position, long since abandoned to the elements, but dry and sheltered. A good place to take cover amid the flat, sodden landscape of the coastal plain.

In the dream, the corpse would be there just as it had been in real life, legs drawn up, a bony scrawn of fingers resting on top of knees. The head was canted at a slight angle, the drawn-back flesh around the mouth showing the characteristic sunken grin of the not too recently dead. The level of decay would vary. Sometimes there were simply bones draped with sodden cloth. At others there would be a distinguishable face, and one that he thought he recognised. He would stare at it and struggle to remember. It seemed very important to remember.

At some point it would come to him that if he did not get away he would be trapped in the hole forever. He would scrabble up the loose, powdery sides only to fall back down again and again. Then he would wake up, gasping and sweat-soaked.

29

This time when he woke he was sure that he'd actually cried out, but Sister Barnes sat unperturbed in her office, face uplit by a halo of lamplight, and there was no-one else in sight. He desperately needed to urinate and he sat up, reaching for his dressing gown. He winced as a bolt of pain arced up his leg.

"Moderation, in all things," he whispered.

The hardest part was standing up, he knew that. He was tired and aching now, and it took a good couple of minutes of ungainly struggle. At any moment he expected to see Barnes bearing down on him, but she was either oblivious or had decided to leave him to it. He shuffled towards the door, leg and arm muscles aching. The bathroom was only a few yards down the corridor, but it felt like miles. How much easier it had been only this afternoon! Eventually, he managed to lever his way into the cold, windowless bathroom and pressed the light switch. It never ceased to amaze him that Garrett Hill had such modern conveniences as electricity, yet in its remote corners could still be depressingly barren and old-fashioned. The bathroom had been converted from an old scullery and the walls were brown and murky. He slumped in front of the sink, rinsing his face in the icy water. This made him feel better until he saw his grey, unshaven reflection in the mirror. Never mind the dream, he was the one who looked like a corpse. He turned away in disgust and heaved himself over to the urinal.

Once he'd done the necessary, he found that he didn't want to go back to bed despite his fatigue. His mind was jumpy and restless and he didn't want to join those sighing, shifting forms in the dark of the ward. The dream was still too close. If only he could find somewhere to sit for a while, until the corpse had retreated to a safe distance. He remembered the conservatory from his morning explorations. It was at the back of the house, at the end of a long, cabbagey-smelling corridor. Perhaps he could sit there for a while, get his breath back and have a smoke. He felt in his dressing-gown pocket and realised his cigarettes were on the cabinet by his bed.

"Damn."

"Mr Earnshaw, what are you doing out of bed?"

"What?" He nearly fell over. She was standing right behind him, wearing that hesitant little half-smile.

"Mrs Church, you really oughtn't to creep up on your patients like that. Unless you actually want to kill them off, that is."

The smile dropped away. "You know who I am?"

He had used her name without thinking. She looked most alarmed – she couldn't know, could she?

"Yes, um…Harker told me who you were," he said. "I thought I would take an evening stroll and visit such scenic highlights as the lavatory."

"Well, I wish you would let one of us know if you leave the ward. We were worried."

"As you can see, I'm fine. I was going to sit in the conservatory. I hear there's a very nice view of the grounds."

"There is, but I don't know what you expect to see at this time of night. And you were going in the wrong direction anyway." She glanced away down the corridor, then back towards him. "I can help you if you like."

He had expected her to order him straight back to bed. "Is it allowed?" he said. "I wouldn't want to get you into any trouble."

She took his arm lightly. "You won't, don't worry."

Her complicity made him suspicious. He hadn't decided yet

31

whether to tell her he'd known Church. Now it seemed she might already know. Perhaps he should keep quiet, as Harker suggested, and hope she would be too reticent to ask. It would cause him the least embarrassment and he could always tell himself he was doing it for her sake. What was he supposed to say after all? That her husband was a drunken sot that had not only got himself blown up but risked the lives of the entire company?

The conservatory was a long, low room at the back of the house with narrow, louvered windows. Rows of cane easy-chairs were turned to face the windows as if arrayed in worship and the window frames threw bars of shadow from the rising half-moon. The floor was stone-flagged and his feet were chilled after the warm oak floors of the house.

"Would you like some help sitting down?" said Mrs Church.

"If you wouldn't mind." He shuffled over to a wide, deep-cushioned chair and she manoeuvred to one side of him.

"If you rest your weight on me then I can support you while you lower yourself into the chair. Try to keep your weight on your good leg. I'll be there to help you balance."

She took one of the crutches from him and then hooked his arm around her shoulder.

"Something tells me that you've done this before," he said.

"More times than I can remember."

He teetered slightly and felt her muscles strain as she took his weight. It should have been humiliating, but it wasn't. Her apron smelled of fresh laundry and suddenly he was two feet high, clinging to his mother's skirts in the kitchen, laughing at something, at nothing. It was the same smell, the same feeling – a sense of being utterly safe and secure. He had not even realised he craved it. He found himself close to tears and was glad of the dark. She crouched down with him as he lowered himself into the chair.

"Thank you," he said. He imagined how it would feel to curl up in her lap and sleep like a baby.

"That's quite all right."

He was desperate for a cigarette. He wondered if he dared ask her to fetch them.

"I'll have to go back to the ward soon," she said. "I'll let the sister know where you are."

"You really are most thoughtful. This is not in the least like the place I was in before."

"Well, this is a convalescent hospital, so we try to give the patients a little more leeway."

"And the nurses, do they get a little more leeway?"

"I would say so. Though I'm not really a proper nurse, just a volunteer."

"You seem to know the ropes."

"I've been here a year and a half. And another hospital for a year before that, so yes, you could say I'm an old hand."

He thought that she would leave then, but she didn't. She was repeatedly rubbing at the base of one of her fingers. It was an odd, compulsive gesture, as if she were trying to erase a non-existent stain. All at once he couldn't help himself – he wanted to know if she knew.

"Was there something you wanted to ask me Mrs Church?"

The rubbing stopped and she clasped her hands together.

"Phillip Harker – he's in the bed next to mine – he told me that you're Lieutenant Church's widow."

"Yes," she said, biting down on her lower lip. "I am."

"I'm sorry. It's just that I realised who you were, you see, when Harker mentioned your name."

She leaned forward, a steely glitter of moonlight in her eyes. "You *did* know Harry then?"

"Not very well. He was my CO for a short while."

"And you were there when –?"

"Yes."

"I would like to know what happened…at the end. If you can bear to tell me."

If it hadn't been for his leg and the crutches he would have got up and run away. Instead, he lied. "The thing is, Mrs Church, my memory's a bit shot. One minute I was right as rain, the next I woke up in the casualty clearing station."

"Oh." Her head went down. "I'm sorry. It must have been horrible for you."

That made him want to laugh. What did she know about horrible?

"Not as bad as it was for your husband."

There it was again, the viper hiding under his tongue. Why did he say these things? But she restrained herself admirably and did not rebuke him, but smoothed her apron with exaggerated briskness. She probably wanted to slap him and he wouldn't blame her.

"Perhaps I'd better leave you alone for a while," she said. "In peace. I'll be back to check on you later. Or someone will."

And then she was gone in a whisk of starched skirt and he was alone with the cold floor, the darkness and the moon. Serve him right.

It was the same moon, the same sky. He imagined the flares breaking up the darkness with their red, green and white, but really it was just the dim twinkle of street lights from the road.

The night before Harry Church's death they'd found him dead drunk and flat on his face in the middle of Poperinghe.

Daniel had been having a night of it with Frannie and Fred Charnley, drinking rough *vin rouge* and shovelling down egg and chips at an estaminet until they'd gagged. On their way back to billets they came across him sprawled on the cobbles in the town square, pawing the ground in a helpless funk.

Frannie took charge as usual, ordering them to haul the lieutenant onto his feet. He was covered in grit and mud from the road and there was a brownish lump of something smeared across his chest that might have been horse manure. They all cursed – they'd only been to the bath house that afternoon. Frannie put his hands on either side of the lieutenant's head, and lifted it, almost tenderly.

"Do you know where you are sir?"

Church's mouth formed a circle and his lower lip quivered. "Don' know."

"You're in the square. Seems you had a bit of a fall."

His eyes moved from side to side, blinked, then rolled upwards, back into his head. "Is that you, Dwyer?"

"It is indeed, sir."

"You're a good man. Always thought so." With that, the lieutenant's head dropped forward and he vomited onto the cobbles. Once the worst was over Frannie pulled up his head by the hair, picked up his dangling arm and used it to wipe a trail of spit from his face.

"There you go, sir," he said. "Right as rain."

Church smiled beatifically.

"Now, come on, let's be having you." Frannie hooked an arm around the lieutenant's back and pulled him up by the belt, gesturing Fred to take the other side. "Do us a favour, sir and use your feet. We can't carry you all the way."

The walk back to Ypres took nearly two hours. They

followed the straight, flat road through clusters of tents and hutments that hung off the town's edges, dodging horse-drawn wagons and motor ambulances, threading their way past marching columns of men, black figures unmanned by the dark. There was a brief stretch of what had once been open farmland, lined with long, twisted shadows of splintered poplars spilling across the road in a distorted echo of the columns of men.

By the time they reached the outskirts of Ypres the moon was up, a fingernail curve of white veiled with sickly-looking cloud. They were quartered in the ramparts down by the canal, the old earthworks looming over them like giant grave-humps. Mr Church perked up as they approached the town and he managed to walk the last quarter-mile unaided. As they reached the hut that served as the officers' billet he suddenly started talking about his wife.

"She's wonderful," he said, flinging his arms out for emphasis and nearly falling over. "So good to me. I'm a lucky man, everyone says so." He grabbed the front of Frannie's coat. "Aren't women wonderful?"

"Aren't they just," agreed Frannie.

"Do you want to see a picture?"

Frannie rapped on the door of the hut, but the lieutenant was already ferreting in the top pocket of his tunic.

"Hope it's not buggered."

"Let's get you inside sir." Frannie tried to take his arm.

"Get off. I know what I'm doing." The picture appeared, and Daniel noticed that Fred couldn't help peering at it over Frannie's shoulder.

"Isn't she a peach?" he said, flapping the photograph about.

"Lovely!" said Fred.

36

Frannie shot him a warning look as the lieutenant kissed the photograph with some passion. "My perfect bloody wife. Wonder what she's doing now."

"I'm sure she's missing you, sir," said Frannie.

He stopped dead, staring at the image intently. "Stupid bloody bitch."

Frannie glanced over his shoulder at Daniel. Dangerous territory. Better to get him off their hands pronto. Daniel pushed open the door to the hut. It was empty and dank inside.

"We can't leave him in there on his own," said Frannie. "Stay here, and don't let him wander off. I'm going to find his servant."

Daniel took over nursemaid duty and removed the photograph from Church's grasp. "You'd better put that away sir. You wouldn't want to get it dirty, would you?" He slid it inside the man's tunic. He had tried to ape Frannie's way of speaking, but didn't have the knack. The lieutenant looked at him sharply, then noticed Fred, standing at his shoulder.

"What are you two doing here?"

"We helped you back from Pop."

"Yes. Of course you did. Well, I'm fine now. You can go."

"We're just waiting for Sergeant Dwyer to come back."

The lieutenant looked around him wildly. "And where's he gone?"

"To find your servant, sir."

"Well I can bloody well find him for myself. Bugger off, both of you."

With that he promptly walked into the doorframe, rubbed his head and cursed, then staggered into the hut. The door slammed behind him and there was another muffled impact as he collided with his camp bed. Daniel wondered if he should go in, make sure he hadn't knocked himself out, but on balance decided it was safer to leave him be.

"Come on," he said to Fred. "We've done our bit."

They sat down on a crumbled stone wall to wait for Frannie. Miles ahead of them the front line was a cauldron of light, the flickering arcs of flares and the white haloes of star shells illuminating the low curve of the ridge. He could see the skeletal outline of the Cloth Hall tower, a crooked finger pointing skyward amid gap-toothed ruins. The light from the flares and from the guns' muzzle flashes burst and expired, punctuating the dark in short exclamations, one after the other. It looked impressive. Beautiful, even.

Fred rummaged in his tunic pocket for cigarettes. "Well that's gratitude for you. Just 'what are you doing here?' then 'bugger off', if you please."

"You didn't seriously expect thanks, did you?" said Daniel. "Just pray he doesn't remember any of this in the morning."

"Why not? Maybe he'll recover his manners when he's sobered up a bit."

"No he won't, you dolt. He'll be mortified that we saw him like that. And he'll make us suffer for it too. We'll be shovelling shit for a month."

"Did you hear him? Going on about his wife like that!"

"I'd forget I heard that if I were you."

"No fear. Did you get a look at her? She was a bit of a corker."

"Fred, it's dark. How could you possibly tell?"

"He couldn't." Frannie emerged silently out of the night. "He's just dreaming, aren't you Fred?"

"No I'm – "

"Where is he?" interrupted Daniel, noticing that Frannie

was alone.

Frannie shrugged. "Nowhere to be found."

Mitchell, the lieutenant's batman, was an even bigger drunk than his master.

"I'll check on the lieutenant in a minute, don't worry. Make sure he's tucked up all cosy. With any luck, he won't remember a thing in the morning."

Chapter 4

E lissa rubbed her eyes to erase the gritty feeling of lack of sleep and clattered another pair of teacups onto the tray. The kitchen was steamy and bustling as the volunteers served afternoon tea to the patients' families, getting under the feet of the kitchen staff who were starting dinner. Changeover days were always the worst. The three days off in between the switch from night to day shifts were never enough to adjust. She was still lying awake half the night, her body twitchy with energy because it expected to be hard at work. She had been groggy all morning and the long tail of the afternoon dragged like lead.

"Well? Have you got it out of him yet?" Jo put down her empty tray next to Elissa's and proceeded to make a great show of wiping it clean.

"No."

"He seemed to be softening up nicely the last I saw. You should try again." Jo was convinced that Corporal Earnshaw knew more than he was letting on about Harry's death, and secretly Elissa agreed with her.

"Jo I..." She lowered her voice. "I don't feel quite right about mentioning it again. What if he doesn't want to tell me for a reason? I don't want to rake it all up for him again. He has terrible nightmares you know."

Jo was unmoved. "So do half the ward. They'll pass. And they might pass more quickly if he gets it off his chest. And who better to be his confessor than you? It'll do him good."

Elissa pretended to rearrange the cups on the tray. "I'm not sure I want to be anyone's confessor."

"You want to know don't you?"

Elissa gripped the handles of the tray. "I'm not sure." She was suddenly, alarmingly close to tears.

Jo stopped her wiping and reached across to take Elissa's hand, one damp, rough palm against another. "I'm sorry. Have I put my great big foot in it again?"

Elissa had to keep reminding herself; she was a grieving widow and a certain amount of tearfulness was allowed. She squeezed Jo's hand.

"You haven't upset me, honestly," she said. "If he wants to tell me he will, but I'm not going to push him into it."

"Well you're far more patient than I could ever be." Jo began loading cups onto her tray. "And watch out, here comes Barnes with the teapot."

Daniel watched the woman tucking the rug around Harker's midriff. It didn't need tucking, but she was making a meal of it anyway, giggling as he took the opportunity to whisper in her ear. The feather in her hat bobbed flirtatiously as she laughed, and he blew on it gently. She gave him a look of pure adoration. She was immaculately dressed, this one, in a dark suit with the skirt cut up above the ankle. The nurses were madly jealous of her clothes and always discussed them at length after she went sweeping out on a cloud of jasmine. She even wore make-up, they whispered, although Daniel had never noticed. She rarely stayed more than an hour and always fussed ostentatiously over Harker, bringing him ridiculous presents – great sprays of flowers, cavernous baskets of fruit – which he shared around the ward as soon as she'd gone.

Harker appeared to have two women on the go. The other one was quite different; her dress simple, her accent betraying a background that was more public house than country house. She alternated days with the jasmine-scented one and stayed much longer. She would sit with Harker for hours, talking quietly, but occasionally she too would burst into great peals of laughter, bringing a halt to the conversation around them. She brought newspapers and books instead of flowers and out of the two she was definitely the more interesting.

"I think I've managed to persuade your MO," his mother was saying, "and I'm going to see your Commanding Officer tomorrow morning."

Daniel tried to make a show of listening. His mother was resplendent in a brand-new maroon gabardine suit, her best cream lace blouse pinned with a cameo brooch that he remembered trying to chew when he was two years old. Her dark hair, shot with streaks of grey, was looped in a simple twist under the capacious brim of a black hat. Beneath its shadow, her eyes sparked with their usual ferocity.

"What's his name?" she said. "Porritt. Wretched man. Used to own Clough Mill, do you remember? Never the man his father was. Always tried to palm me off with barrel scrapings, that one."

He had been hoping to get outside today, but it had been raining all morning and he could only sit and watch as great, fat drops of water spattered against the conservatory windows. The air was humid with the weight of too many bodies and it made him heavy and tired, but his mother's energy was undimmed. She patted at an illusory loose hair.

"Anyway, I think they'll let you out for Christmas if I can get you declared fit. They might even allow you to stay the week."

"Well then," he said. "I'd better start packing."

"Is that all the thanks I get? I've gone to a lot of trouble for you, you know."

"Thank you mother. I simply meant I had no doubt you'd get what you wanted.."

Mrs Church appeared with a tray and he watched her circling the room, serving patients and visitors. Now she had switched to the day shift there were no more opportunities for a late night chat. It had grown into a habit the last week or so; he would shuffle off to the conservatory in the early hours and at some point she would find an excuse to join him. She had quickly forgiven him for the lapse about her husband and seemed eager to talk. Often she stayed only a few minutes, but sometimes it was longer – once more than half an hour.

He knew what she wanted; he had no illusions about that. Nevertheless, he found her company restful. It was not so much what they talked about, which was nothing of consequence, but rather the quality of her presence. The dreams and the memories seemed to lose their power when she was there and he'd come to think of her as a talisman. Perhaps it was time to tell her. He felt obscurely that he owed it to her, though he doubted she would thank him for it in the end.

"While we're on the subject of Christmas," he said to his mother. "I wonder if you'd do me a favour."

"*Another* favour?"

"I'd like you to invite Mrs Church over for tea. This Sunday, if I'm home by then."

She blinked at him, folded and refolded her hands on her lap. "This Mrs Church, this is Harry Church's widow? The one you told me about?"

"The same."

"Friendly with her now are you?"

"Don't insinuate. I need to talk to her about something that's all, and the hospital is not the place for it."

His mother's eyebrows disappeared under the brim of her hat. "You're not going to tell her how her husband died?"

"Yes, I think so."

"Are you sure that's wise?"

"No I'm not mother, but as I told you, she wants know."

His mother glanced around to make sure that Mrs Church was out of earshot. "D'you remember Janet Deacon, who used to help out in the shop? Well she's a char for Mrs C these days. Apparently the family won't have anything to do with her now the boy's dead. And they say she wasn't very well provided for in the will either. Not that she's exactly on poverty row. She's probably still got more than I'll ever see in my lifetime, but considering they've all that money – "

"Are you going to invite her or not?"

At that moment Mrs Church reached them, her tray almost empty. Daniel struggled to his feet.

"That leg's looking much better," she said. "How are you feeling?"

"Very well thank-you, Mrs Church. I don't think you've met my mother?"

His mother unconsciously tugged at the collar of her jacket and gave her best-customer smile. "I'm Hannah Earnshaw. It's very nice to meet you dear." She held out her hand, moderating her sparkle from fierce to friendly.

"It's good to meet you too, Mrs Earnshaw. Would you like some tea?"

"That would be lovely dear."

Daniel sat down again, and Mrs Church served up the last two cups of tea, laying them on a side table next to him. She tucked the tray under her arm.

"We're hoping to get Daniel home for Christmas," said his mother. "So he'll be off your hands for a few days."

"Oh? That's nice. Though he's absolutely no trouble really."

She slid the flat of her hand up and down the edge of the tray, and he noticed that she was not wearing a wedding ring.

"And I know that you're busy, but I wondered, we both wondered, if you'd like to come over for tea this Sunday? As a Christmas treat. A thank-you for all you've done for my son."

"Well I haven't really done – "

"Would about four suit you?"

Mrs Church glanced around the room as if searching for a rescuer, but none came. "That would be fine. You're most kind."

"Daniel will give you the address."

"Until Sunday then." She made off across the room before his mother could extract any more promises.

"Satisfied?" said his mother.

"Perfectly. Thank-you." He wasn't. She obviously didn't want to come. It would be humiliating, especially when she saw where they lived.

"Now then, how about a walk?"

"In this? Do you want to drown?"

"Not outside, silly. Why don't you show me around the hospital?"

"It's not very interesting. Lots of corridors. Rooms with beds in them."

"Come along," She gripped his arm and helped him up, none too gently. "It'll do you good. And while we're at it, you can tell me the real reason you're so keen for Mrs Church to visit."

As usual, he couldn't sleep. His leg itched and the heavy fatigue he'd felt all day had gone. Now it was midnight he was full of vim. The sister's office was empty and the girl at the nurse's station appeared to have dozed off. An ideal time to make his escape if he wanted a late-night promenade. But first there was something he wanted to do.

Right on cue, the ward door creaked open and Harker slipped silently through into the ward. He'd disappeared off to the bathroom fifteen minutes before – and had a smoke while he was at it no doubt. Daniel lay back and closed his eyes, pretending to be asleep. He waited until Harker was in bed, turned away from him, then he leaned over and whispered:

"Hope you remembered to flush."

Harker jumped and let out a gratifyingly high-pitched squeak. The nurse at the desk stirred but did not wake.

Daniel laughed. "You know how those ciggy stubs float like the devil."

"Well you're a bloody comedian all of a sudden, Earnshaw." Harker thumped his pillow into shape. "And I don't need to ask who's been whetting your blade. Can't say I blame you though. She is delightful."

"Harker," Daniel said, still laughing, "You do talk a lot of nonsense sometimes."

"Oh don't be so coy. Everyone's noticed. Wouldn't mind having a go at the merry widow myself, but I'm rather occupied on that front as you have probably realised."

Daniel sat bolt upright, his laughter draining away. "You really are the most foul-minded little troll. Her husband only died two months ago. Do you really think – ?"

"Why not?"

"Even if I wanted to."

"Of course you want to."

Daniel made a supreme effort to keep his voice low. "Actually I don't."

"My dear chap, you may be a charmless oik, but I never took you for a complete fool. It's clear that she didn't give a fig for the husband, so there's no point in wasting your noble sentiments there. She doesn't even wear a wedding ring. Haven't you noticed?"

"We've talked a few times, that's all. She just wants me to tell her how her husband died. There's no more to it than that. Good god, why am I trying to explain myself to you?"

"I've no idea," said Harker, "but it's very entertaining. Part delusion, part hypocrisy."

"You're a fine one to judge. I've seen the way you carry on."

"I'm merely being practical," said Harker. "And you should do the same. Why waste time with all the humbug?" He leaned over. "Haven't we had enough of all that – that tired old morality?"

"That's all very well," said Daniel, "but unlike you I'm not interested in dalliances with silly women."

Harker laughed soundlessly. Daniel could see the bedcovers shaking as he tried to contain his mirth. "You're priceless, Earnshaw, really. Please keep it up. I'll remind you of what you just said next time I see you trailing around after her like a lame puppy."

"I don't – "

"The strange thing is, she does seem to have a soft spot for you. Perhaps she likes common clerkish types. Perhaps she needs a bit of hybrid vigour to heat up the old blood, eh?"

"You're disgusting. And I'm not a clerk. I was never a clerk."

"What were you then?"

Daniel sighed. He should have let the comment pass. "A musician."

"Ah! The artistic type. Well, that explains the chip on your shoulder."

"I haven't got a…oh never mind. Anyway what right do you have to look down on me, *Corporal* Harker."

"None whatsoever, but at least I have no illusions about who I am. I *chose* to be the lowest of the low. The view is better from down at the bottom don't you think? I was a solicitor in peacetime. I could have easily got a commission, but I didn't want the responsibility."

"I think you'd have made a very good officer. You'd have a fine time, snooping about, interfering in everyone's affairs."

Harker snickered. "Too true, can't deny it. And as we're back on the subject of affairs, I'd take what you can get with your darling Mrs Church. She'll never consider you as a serious prospect, so there's no use mooning about after her. You'll be a pet, an interesting diversion, that's all. Divert her while you can, that's my advice."

"I think I've had just about enough of your advice Harker."

Chapter 5

Weir Street, a ribbon of ironclad respectability, branched off the main road out of Calderby and climbed the steep side of the valley, the two sides of the street forming up like rival parades. In the tiny, railed-in front yard outside number eighty-two was a rose bush that would frame the house perfectly in the summer, but now it was pruned back to a clutch of naked stubs. The gate was freshly painted a shade of dull sage that reminded Elissa of khaki and the front door had a gleaming, brass knocker, polished within an inch of its life. Mrs Earnshaw was obviously a woman with standards.

She had never visited a patient at home before. She knew, of course, why she'd been asked to come – Daniel Earnshaw had finally decided to tell her the truth about Harry. She could hardly tell him that she had changed her mind and didn't want to know. She rapped hard with the knocker and within seconds he came to the door, opening it awkwardly with one hand, the other leaning on a walking stick. He had smartened up his hospital blues with a stiff collar and badly-knotted red tie, his hair was parted and combed down flat. He looked trussed up like a chicken and ill-at-ease.

"Hello, Mrs Church."

"I hope I'm not late."

"No, you're bang on time. Do come in." He shuffled to one side. He had graduated rapidly from crutches to the walking stick, but negotiating the cramped hall was clearly awkward for him. She pressed herself against the wall as she stepped past him. His walking stick was an ancient-looking thing, almost black, the wood irregular and knotted, polished smooth with the years.

"That looks like a family heirloom," she said, as he helped her out of her coat with his free hand.

"It is. Belonged to my grandfather." He turned away to hang up her coat. "Who'd have thought I would find a use for it? Funny how things turn out."

He struggled to drape her coat over the crowded coat stand, but something about the set of his back shut out any possibility of help. He was often offhand, almost rude, without any reason that she could fathom and she wondered why she bothered with him. But then there were those night-time conversations at the hospital, that short series of clandestine, almost accidental moments when they had run up against each other and she had found herself telling him things, all sorts of things, without actually meaning to. He had drawn her out effortlessly and afterwards she found herself wondering why on earth she had divulged so much to him. She had realised only gradually that he never said anything about himself.

Finished with her coat, he opened the door to the front parlour. Mrs Earnshaw was putting the finishing touches to a table laden with mince pies, sandwiches and fruit cake. The bread looked fresh and smelled like the real thing, not the sawdusty stuff they sold at the bakers these days.

"Oh there you are," said Hannah Earnshaw. "Come on in."

Her hair was done low on her neck, a surprisingly modern style for a woman her age. She was handsome rather than beautiful, but the gleam in her dark eyes – so much like her son's – drew the attention as they drew the light. Elissa wondered why she hadn't remarried.

"You really shouldn't have gone to so much trouble," she said.

"Nonsense dear, it's Christmas. When else am I going to go to any trouble?"

The parlour was as cramped as the hall and dominated by a large, upright piano. The fire was piled high and glowing red, and every free space on the table was crowded with food. The effect was both cosy and claustrophobic. The piano had elbowed the heavy drop-leaf table into a corner by the window, and when Daniel offered her a chair she had to squeeze past it to sit down. He took his place next to her and she found herself hemmed in between him and the instrument's bulk.

Mrs Earnshaw disappeared into the kitchen and silence descended. Elissa cast around for a topic of conversation.

"Do you play?" she said, nodding towards the piano.

"I used to. Not much now."

"Why not?"

He laced his fingers together. "You might say I've been otherwise engaged."

Elissa could not tell if he was embarrassed or just being sarcastic. She was groping for a reply when Mrs Earnshaw reappeared with a large brown teapot.

"He's having you on, Mrs Church. My son has a special talent, though he pays it no consideration." She thumped down the pot on a tile stand and the table vibrated. Daniel winced

51

"Please *don't*, mother."

"Why not? It's true. It's a crying shame by anyone's estimation. It's not just that I'm your mother and naturally biased. Before the war, Mrs Church, he was a musician. Or training to be one, at any rate."

"Really?"

"Oh yes. A proper musician, mind you, not one of these cheap, honky-tonk, bang-and-clatter types. Who knows what would have happened if he'd persisted? But no, he had to go and join up, fritter away his talent."

"Try a sandwich Mrs Church," said Daniel, offering her a platter of pale, neatly-cut squares. Elissa took one.

"Do you think you'll go back to it, after the war?" she said.

"I hadn't thought about it."

"I'm sure the academy would take you back," said Mrs Earnshaw, "If you showed an ounce of interest."

"Well, we'll have to see, won't we?" he said, glaring across at her. "Now am I the only one here who wants to eat?"

He piled up four of the sandwiches on his plate before passing it to his mother, then set to with gusto. Elissa was full of questions, none of which she could ask. It was clear that he didn't want to talk about his past. In all those conversations at the hospital, he'd never once mentioned music.

She glanced at the dark, gleaming piano, so out of place in this little room. Of course. This was the instrument of a serious musician. There were two neat piles of paper on the top, one of thin manuscript books, and a second, larger one of sheet music. On top of the manuscript was a pair of glasses and a pencil, perfectly in line. Elissa imagined Mrs Earnshaw dusting the piano, rearranging the piles of music, moving and realigning the glasses and the pencil, hoping that her son would return to them. There was a silent, determined struggle in those orderly piles. She imagined them both, equally implacable, fighting this quiet battle of wills. She turned back to the table to find Daniel watching her, chewing the remains of his second sandwich.

"Everything satisfactory with your tea?" he said.

"Lovely thank-you," she said. "Would you mind passing me a slice of fruit cake?"

When they had finished, Daniel stacked the plates and helped his mother clear the table. Elissa fidgeted in her chair, watching them. She had become accustomed to fetching and carrying at the hospital, but that was probably not how they saw her. No doubt they thought she never lifted a finger at home.

Mrs Earnshaw loaded a tray with crockery and took it out to the kitchen, and silence descended again. Daniel began fiddling with the edges of the tablecloth, looking uncomfortable. She wondered if he was building up to tell her about Harry. She surveyed the room, searching for something to distract him. The piano, by sheer weight of its presence, drew her attention.

"It would be wonderful to hear you play," she said.

He looked as if she'd asked him to slit his wrists.

"Would you mind terribly? You see, I've never heard a real musician before. Just the honky-tonk type, as your mother would have it. It would be a real treat." He said nothing, and she ploughed on. "Of course I'd understand if you didn't want to. I know it's a bit of an imposition but –"

"No," he said, biting out the word like a curse. "It's not."

But clearly it was.

Mrs Earnshaw had obviously been listening in the kitchen, for at that moment she appeared in the doorway clutching a tea towel. "Ooh you are privileged, Mrs Church. He's scarcely touched the thing since he's been home."

"I played only yesterday morning."

"Yes, but only to see if it was in tune. That wasn't *proper* playing."

"And what, in your estimation, is proper playing?"

"You tell me, dear," she said, draping the towel over the fireguard to dry. "You're supposed to be the musician. At least that's what you've been telling me since you were knee high to a speck of dust."

Daniel reached for his walking stick and levered himself up. "Very well, you asked for it. You'll get what *I* consider to be proper playing. Just don't blame me if you don't like it." He lurched the two steps across to the piano. "Now, what shall it be?" He picked up the glasses and perched them on his nose. "Something noisy and modern I think. That will teach you both." He leafed through the pile and selected a flimsy booklet then made a great show of fiddling with the stool to make sure it was the right height.

He sat down and opened the piano lid. The keys were cream, not white as Elissa had imagined. He ran his fingers over them lightly and it was as if he were reintroducing himself to an old friend – or a lover.

Prevaricating, he rubbed his hands along the seams of his trousers, adjusted his glasses, smoothed back the pages of music. "I'm very rusty, so it might end up a terrible noise. Remember, you asked for it."

She had thought it was a simple thing; he could play, so why shouldn't he? Watching him now she realised that there was more to it than that. She felt nervous for him, and responsible. He laid his hands on the keys again and she held her breath.

When he began, she could tell at once that he really could play. It was not just the way he sounded the notes, but the spacing, the holding on between one phrase and the next. The sound wove around her like a web, a bubbling, not-quite melody, elusive and enchanting. At one point, he smiled at something that gave him particular pleasure and his face lit up. There was such nakedness in his expression that it made her feel like a voyeur. She hadn't understood. She thought it was just a nice thing that one did. Now she saw how he dredged down inside himself for each note. It was moving and a little frightening. No wonder he had been so reluctant. When he finished playing he said nothing, just sat quietly, staring at the page.

"Well, I thought that was very pretty," said Mrs Earnshaw. "Weren't you supposed to be horrifying us with your modern noise?"

She meant well, but Elissa felt the jarring weight of her comment. She noticed Daniel briefly closing his eyes to shut it out. Now she understood; this woman knew her son but she did not know him at all. She knew he had talent, but her lack of understanding rode roughshod over him in a way that she could never comprehend.

"It was quite lovely," she said, feeling keenly the inadequacy of her words. "What was it?"

"One of Debussy's *Images*. I'm afraid I managed to botch it completely."

"It sounded perfect to me."

"He always says that dear," said Mrs Earnshaw. "Take no notice."

"How about another?" He picked up another manuscript from the pile and flicked through the pages quickly, impatiently. "Ah, here we are. This used to be one of my favourites. *Le Cathedre Engloutie* – The Sunken Cathedral. Let's see if I can still manage it."

He did not wait for a response but simply launched in. This one was more dramatic. As it went on, Elissa could hear the sound of church bells in the chiming, strident chords. Yes, it was like a cathedral. She realised that he had stopped reading the music and had begun to play from memory. He was looking down, apparently at his hands, but she could tell that he wasn't really seeing them. He had forgotten all about her and his mother. How wonderful to be so captivated. At the final chord, the note was sustained as he leaned on the pedal, and she felt it vibrate in the pit of her stomach. She could not take her eyes from him.

It was Mrs Earnshaw, again, who broke the silence.

"That one was nice too. A bit loud though. My ears are still ringing from those bells!" She was already on her feet, oblivious to the waves of sound that still rang in Elissa's ears.

"Would you like some more tea, Mrs Church?"

Elissa bit her lip. Why couldn't the woman be quiet? "Yes, please, if it's not too much trouble." Anything to get her out of the room.

Once she'd gone, Daniel took off his glasses and polished them on the corner of his jacket.

"So what did you think?" he said, quietly so that his mother would not hear. "Did you like it?"

"It was beautiful," she said. "Truly. And I'm not simply being polite. Your mother is right, you do have a special talent. Even I can tell that and I know nothing about music. You mustn't give up, that would be awful. Like a betrayal."

He rubbed the piano keys gently with the tips of his fingers. He seemed nonplussed. She hadn't meant to sound quite so forceful, but she wanted to get through to him. She wanted to take hold of him and shake him, and say, don't you dare stop.

"Don't worry," he said. "I have no intention of giving up. But thank you for what you said." He looked at her, unblinking. "And no, I wouldn't dare stop."

It seemed that he had read her thoughts and she wasn't sure she liked it.

"Be careful," she said. "It's slippery underfoot."

The dark had sucked up what little warmth was left in the ground and patches of ice were forming on the narrow, uneven pavement . They picked their way slowly down Weir Street, Elissa trying not to make it obvious that she was monitoring him in case he slipped. She had not wanted him to come, but he had insisted on seeing her onto the tram.

"If you hurt that leg again, you'll be straight back into hospital and your Christmas will be spoiled."

"You sound just like my mother," he said, tightening the long woollen scarf around his neck.

"Good. Your mother seems a very sensible woman."

"It's no use," he said. "I'm coming with you. I need fresh air. You don't know what it's like, being cooped up in that hospital." He paused. "Or perhaps you do."

"At least I can go home at the end of my shift."

As they turned the corner at the bottom of the hill she looked back along the main road. The white flame of the street lamps reflected off the tramlines, giving them a bright sheen like liquid mercury, and there were patches of ice glimmering in the cracks of the cobbled road. There was no sign of the tram and she wondered if this was it, the moment he would tell her about Harry. This was his final opportunity, after all. She clapped her hands together against the cold.

"I'm glad you played for me," she said. "I'm afraid I rather cornered you into it."

"You did," he said, "but I'm glad you did."

"I'd hate to think that I forced you to do something against your will. I know how horrible that is. I know that when I –" She looked away down the road, pretending to look for the tram.

"When you what?"

"Nothing. It doesn't matter."

She had been about to confide in him about the last time she'd seen Harry, when he'd been drunk and she'd told him she wished he was dead. She could not believe she had been about to tell him that. She'd wanted to offer him an intimacy, an exchange for what he had given her with his playing. But that wasn't at all what she'd planned.

They reached the tram stop and she hopped from one foot to another, trying to keep the cold from penetrating her boots. How badly she wanted to confess something, anything to him.

"What a terrible coward I am," she said.

"I don't think you're a coward at all."

"I am. I know the real reason why you invited me today."

He stood up straight as if coming to attention, the icy light reflected in his eyes.

"You wanted to tell me what happened to Harry."

He gave a short, mirthless laugh like a bark. "Was it so obvious?"

"Why else would you have wanted me over?" They were

standing close now, the intimacy of truth, the warmth of another body in the iron-hard cold stripping away her reticence.
"But I'm going to save you the trouble. The truth is, I don't
really care to know what happened, not any more."

"I see." He shifted his weight from foot to foot, leaning on
his walking stick.

"You must think I'm completely callous."

"No," he said. "Of course I don't. I know it's not that."

He sounded relieved. He must have been gathering himself
up to tell her all evening.

She gulped the cold air. "But I would like you to know what
it *is*."

She had his full attention now. The intensity that had been
focussed on his playing was now directed onto her. She sensed
that he could read every inch of her, root out every secret. She
opened her mouth to speak but nothing came out. If only she
could make him understand without actually saying it.

"The tram's coming," he said. Sure enough, here was a
metallic shriek in the distance. He placed his hand gently
on her arm, just above the elbow. It was the first time he had
touched her voluntarily, deliberately.

"Tell me," he said. "Quickly."

She could see the lights of the tram, hear its hum. Her throat
closed. She wanted to tell him very badly. Why was it so
important all of a sudden that he should know?

"I can't. Not now."

"Then when?"

"I don't know. I'm sorry," she said. He had been so honest
with his playing, and she could not meet him halfway. He
let go of her arm and she could feel the heat disappearing as
quickly as it had come.

59

"I will tell you," she said. "I promise."

But her voice was drowned by the clank of the tram and she wasn't sure if he'd heard.

Chapter 6

The cold snap ended three days after Christmas, the same day that Daniel was due back at Garrett Hill. It had rained all morning, turning the ice to gritty black slush on the streets. He sat alone in the parlour, surrounded by piles of manuscript, fidgeting, waiting for the motor ambulance to pick him up. He could have walked easily– it was only half a mile – but the hospital insisted on sending the ambulance and in this weather he was not about to protest.

He ran his fingers over the piano keys and said his goodbyes. He had reason to be grateful to Elissa Church. He remembered the way she had looked at him that day when he'd played, her wide-eyed expression of wonder, as if everything in the world were a source of amazement and delight. It had ignited a spark in him and he'd practiced until his fingers ached. His mother had been driven to open the shop early just to get away from his noise.

He could not pinpoint exactly when he'd lost his love of music. The malady had grown slowly and invisibly, like a tumour. As he had struggled with his studies, with form and theory and structure, the essence of music had receded. He had been intimidated by the sheer scale of what he did not know and could not do, and it had closed him up like a clam.

A voice he had heard all his life had been silenced.

And this was hardly the most convenient time for it to start up again. The short hop to Garrett Hill was only the first part of a longer journey that would take him eventually to Raistrick barracks, then by train to London, Folkestone, Boulogne, Etaples, then god knows where.

He was afraid. No way around it. He thought that numbness had won the day, that the machinery of war had stripped him down and pared away everything vital until he was merely one of the walking dead. But now he had met Elissa Church, and he had started to play again.

He tried not to think of the friends he'd left behind, still in harm's way. Of Frannie, who'd saved his life, and Fred Charnley, who dreamed of opening a painting and decorating shop at Garton Moor. He wondered what had become of them. He had checked the papers, the casualty lists. He had done that much.

He knew that Marlow was dead. Frannie had written to him just before Christmas, a typically brief, scratchy note. Marlow had been ripped open by shrapnel just like Harry Church, and at almost the same spot.

He wished he could forget it all. He wished he could wipe it from his mind like a piece of dirt, but the memories only strengthened with time. As the days and nights drew him further away in time, the memories grew like a cancer. He was not dreaming as much, but his waking moments were disturbed by sudden images of things that had been, and occasionally things that had no right to be. He was sure, for example, that the enormous, sleek rat he'd seen yesterday in his mother's kitchen was not real. All in all he thought he preferred the nightmares. He never imagined he would miss that damned corpse.

The cough of a motor engine announced the arrival of his ambulance and he hobbled to the front door. The orderly who came out to help him was the cheery type, unfortunately.

"You're a lucky fellow," he said, shouldering Daniel's kit bag. "Getting to spend Christmas at home. I was on shift at the Durnley all last week. Many's the lad there who would gladly have changed places with you."

He reminded Daniel of the sleek rat in the kitchen. "Yes. I am truly blessed."

The orderly squinted at him and gripped his arm none too gently. "Right then. Let's be having you."

He shook off the orderly's hand and climbed into the back of the ambulance unaided. There were two other patients, one with his arm in a sling, the other with a leg missing. He nodded a good morning to them both. The sling smiled, the missing leg just stared. As the ambulance pulled away, a sense of desperate paralysis gripped him. His life no longer belonged to him. Before, it hadn't mattered.

The driver ground the gears as they began to climb the hill out of Calderby. With an exhalation of black smoke, the ambulance laboured to the top of the rise, slowing for the turn-off to Garrett Hill. The gate was kept open during the day and there were War Office signs pinned to the iron railings along with a large red cross. They crunched into the gravelled drive and passed two other ambulances parked on the grass. The drivers huddled between their vehicles in mackintoshes, smoking and shivering. As the ambulance reversed towards the main entrance, two nurses swung open the heavy doors and pushed out a wheelchair. One of them was Elissa Church. She went to the driver's side to speak to the orderly while the other girl, Miss Kenyon, opened the doors. Daniel heaved himself out onto the gravel. He must snatch a few moments with Elissa before they went in – it might be his only chance. He hobbled across to intercept her as she came to help Miss Kenyon with the wheelchair.

"Good morning," he said, ignoring the twinge in his leg. "As you can see, Christmas has retarded my recovery. Now I have to be driven about in an ambulance."

"It doesn't seem to have retarded your wit, though," she said. "And as you're obviously able to help yourself, you must excuse me for a minute. I have to help the other patients."

She turned to the orderly who had lifted the private with the missing leg into the wheelchair. "Thank you, Mr Holroyd, I can manage now."

"Right you are then," said Holroyd, all deferential politeness. Daniel half expected him to doff his cap.

"I'll come to help you get settled in later," she said to Daniel when she realised that he wasn't going away. She lowered her voice. "We can talk then if you'd like to."

He knew that he should leave her be, but still he loitered, trying to think of something else to say. The private in the wheelchair looked up at him quizzically.

"Can I push the wheelchair for you?"

The private smirked.

"It's kind of you to offer," she said, "but I'd better take him in myself."

The private's smirk grew wider.

"Now please go in, it's starting to rain."

Back in the ward he looked around for Harker, but there was no sign. He lay down on his old bed, fully clothed, and watched as Elissa and Miss Kenyon helped the private while Barnes gave him the usual lecture about crutches. The private looked duly chastened and Barnes soon had him teetering up and down the ward. Elissa came over to speak to him while her back was turned.

"Did you have a nice Christmas?" she said.

"Yes" he said. "Very nice. Did you?"

She nodded, smiling. "Quiet."

When she smiled her eyes had a melting quality that seemed to draw the sting from his thoughts. He searched for something to say to keep her there.

"Would you come over again?" he said. "For tea? I can play for you again if you like. I took your words to heart. I've been practising all over Christmas."

"Won't it be difficult?" she said. "You're still a patient here, after all. I'm not sure they'll let you go home whenever you please."

"Don't worry. I'm to be released in a few days. I'll be home for a while, but then it'll be back to barracks and no more piano. You'd better take your chances while you can."

"So soon?" The smile faded. "You're not well yet." He was sad to see it go until he realised what it meant. She was sorry he was leaving.

"My mother convinced them she can look after me until I'm fit. She knows the MO here. Got something on him, probably. Will you come on Saturday?"

She hesitated. "Yes, all right then, I will. If you really are home by then."

He had not given her much opportunity to refuse, but he didn't care. He glanced across, expecting the inevitable sarcastic comment from Harker, but the bed was still empty.

"Where's Harker?" he said. "You know, the man with that ridiculous bandage on his head. In the next bed to mine."

"You don't know?"

"What?"

She swallowed, her eyes darting around. "It's…he died. Yesterday morning."

He heard the words but could not make sense of them. "He can't have. There was nothing wrong with him, just that silly scratch on his head. He was right as rain. We are talking about Harker, aren't we? Phillip Harker. You know, he had those two women who came to see him all the time and –"

"Yes, it was him. I'm sorry. I didn't know you were friendly with him."

"But there was nothing wrong with him!"

That earned him a disapproving look from Barnes.

"Please keep your voice down," said Elissa. "You're scaring the other patients. I'm afraid that there *was* something wrong with him. You can never tell with head wounds. It did seem as if he'd recovered, I know, but it was always going to be touch and go. He might have lived for years, but – "

"I didn't know."

"He had a seizure in the night and died a few hours later."

"This morning then?"

"Yes. Early."

"Were you on duty?"

"Yes."

He looked down at his hands. They were doughy and unreal. A scarecrow's hands. He had been restored to life just as Harker had been abruptly removed from it. The arbitrary symmetry of it made him want to retch. While he was sitting there at the piano, early this morning, embracing his gift with a gusto that bordered on bloodlust, poor old Harker was here all alone, being stalked by his own demise.

Sister Barnes loomed, fixing Elissa with a beady eye. "Come on then, Mr Earnshaw, lets get you ready for bed," she said. "And Mrs Church, shouldn't you be helping out in the dispensary?"

"Yes sister."

"I don't want to go to bed," he said. "I'm not ill. Not any more."

"Nonsense," said Barnes. "You've gone quite pale." But she did not scold. "At least take off your boots. We've just changed those sheets."

Chapter 7

The road rose steeply out of Luddenridge and Elissa had to stop to recover her breath. Daniel seemed unaffected, and she watched him stride on ahead, swinging the picnic basket with careless ease. His limp had vanished. He paused to wait for her where the road flattened out along the top of the moor and she saw the house, nestled in a slight dip a hundred yards or so back from the road. It was bigger than she had imagined and darker, the stone weathered by dirt and time. Neglected certainly, but not quite the tumbledown ruin he'd described.

They had met each Saturday since he'd been released from Garrett Hill. She knew that there was gossip at the hospital – Jo had told her in no uncertain terms – but she didn't care. He would be gone soon and she was not going to forego his company because of idle talk. If she was on a night shift, he would wait for her at the gates and they would walk together down the hill into Calderby. He would cook her a late breakfast, and she would linger for a while and listen to him practise. Last week she had fallen asleep by the fire and not awoken until lunchtime. She had been very embarrassed and he had teased her mercilessly. He'd persuaded her to stay for lunch that day, making them both a pile of rather disgusting meat paste sandwiches, and they had gone walking down by the canal. It had been a good day, and she was sorry to leave him and eager to say yes when he suggested another walk the following week. He wanted to show her his grandparent's old farm, up on the moors. She did not know why, and she did not quite know how to ask.

They turned off the road and followed a rough track to the house. It was long and low, of grey stone with wide, slatted windows masked by shutters. The garden had run wild, flower beds overtaken by scrubby grass and weeds, and the whole place had a forlorn, closed-in look. She imagined that it was lonely, stuck up here all on its own.

"What a shame no-one lives here," she said.

"Yes, I suppose so."

"Did you used to come here a lot?"

"Every week when my grandmother was alive. Sometimes for days, especially when I was little and my mother was running the shop on her own. In summer I practically lived here. Only went home for piano lessons."

They made their way up the overgrown path to the front door. He put the basket down on the step and ferreted in his pocket for keys. "Gran died about ten years ago, and I inherited the place. I planned to move up here before the war. Had this romantic dream about living here, doing the whole bohemian thing. Silly really."

"It's not silly at all. Perhaps you'll do it one day."

"Perhaps."

He thumbed through the keys, avoiding her eye. She knew she'd said the wrong thing. She knew that he thought about the future, but any allusion to it would shut him up. It dug into the hidden undercurrent of fear he kept so well hidden.

It must be a huge effort of will, she thought, to concentrate so determinedly on the present moment. In that way, he was just like Harry had been in the end.

He eventually found the right key and shouldered open the door. The lock had been kept oiled, but the door was warped in its frame and squealed in protest. Inside, the air was close and musty but not as damp as she had expected. The house smelled faintly of rosemary; she'd noticed a bush gone wild growing up against one of the front windows. There was no mildew, though the distempered walls were faded and the wood on the stairs and banisters looked rickety and friable. She followed him through the hall to the back kitchen, where there was a suspicious scratching coming from behind the range.

"I'll need to check the place," he said, "make sure there's no leaks. It won't take long. Then we can have our picnic and take a walk if the good weather holds."

"Anything I can do to help?"

"Not really. But why don't you come with me? I'll give you the grand tour."

She followed him from room to room, helping him pin back the shutters and watching as he checked the walls and ceilings for damp. She imagined him here as a child, playing in the front garden or running up and down the stairs. And she could picture him in some indistinct future, painting the walls and practising the piano. He had even marked out a music room, he told her, across the hall from the kitchen. It was the last room he took her into, and he proudly pointed out the view across the moors and down the deep cut of the valley to Luddenridge.

"You can see my house from here," she said.

He stood next to her at the window.

"There, through the trees. The last house in the row."

"I didn't realise you were so close." Although he was looking out, she knew he wasn't really seeing the view. A deep frown puckered his brow and he drummed his fingers mechanically on the window sill.

Perhaps she should not have accepted it so calmly (indeed, with something bordering on relief) when Hannah had complained of a headache and declined to join them. She wondered if it had been just an excuse to leave them alone.

"Will your mother be all right?"

"Oh she'll be fine. In fact, I think she was just inventing an excuse not to come."

"Really?" This was so much an echo of her thoughts that she blushed.

"She grew up in this house, and I don't think she remembers it with fondness. She sees it as backward and primitive."

"Well, I think it's charming," said Elissa. "Though I can see how it might be lonely for a child."

He pressed his fingers down on the sill until his knuckles were white and took a sharp breath. "I'm sorry Elissa," he said abruptly. "There's something I have to tell you. I've been putting it off all morning."

She had known there was something.

"There's a new draft going out to France this week and they're lumping me in with it. Back to the old battalion. I have to be in Folkestone on Tuesday morning. Which means I'll have to leave tomorrow."

"So soon." She'd known it was coming of course, but still she wanted to say, *don't go. Not yet.*

"I wanted to tell you earlier."

"I wish you had."

"Will you see me off at the station? I'll be on the seven o'clock train from Calderby."

"I don't know…I'm on the night shift." She didn't want to go. She had no appetite for fond goodbyes at railway stations, but it would be her last chance to see him for a long time. Possibly forever. "I'll do my best."

They ate a cold lunch of ham sandwiches and lemonade in the dusty kitchen. He was silent throughout, constantly looking out of the window. He seemed at first agitated, then gloomy, and she wondered if he was angry with her for being non-committal about seeing him off.

After lunch, he suggested a walk down into the valley. She agreed, hoping that the exercise and the unseasonal good weather would improve his mood. He led her out across the moor to a line of trees that marked the edge of the valley.

"At the bottom of the valley there's a lovely spot," he said. "A big flat rock that sits right out over the water. Bit of a steep descent though. Do you think you can manage it?"

"Of course," she said. "And I know exactly the place you mean. I've been there before, many times."

"Good. Let's get on then."

She hadn't realised that the incline on this side of the valley was so much steeper. The path was muddy too and she had to hitch up her skirt, inching her way down with painful slowness. He waited for her, patiently, and offered her his hand, but she waved him away. She needed both hands to balance.

As the path levelled out by the stream they joined a wider, gritted track and passed a crossing of flat stepping stones.

She knew where she was now. The stream would soon curve around to the right and not far beyond that was the rock.

"There's a small side path coming up," he said. "It's a bit overgrown, so watch out."

A minute later, he ducked off to the left, plunging straight into the undergrowth. He hadn't been exaggerating; the path was woven over with brambles that caught at her feet and ripped her skirt. This time she did not refuse the offer of his hand, and he guided her through the maze, prying thorns from her clothes.

At last they emerged onto the rock. The sun had burned off the mist and she welcomed the warmth after the dank, tangled woodland. They were high above the stream on a broad, flat summit. Below them the water surged and hurried, causing a fine steam to rise up and coat the surface of the rock in tiny, shimmering drops.

She found a reasonably dry spot near the edge and sat down, tucking her skirt around her ankles. "I haven't been here for such a long time," she said. "I'd forgotten it was so lovely."

He squatted next to her. "I haven't been up here for years either. Walked the valley from Calderby last week to test my leg and found it again. Odd, really. It's so close to my grandparent's place, I don't know why I forgot about it."

In less than twenty-four hours he would be gone. She felt harried by lack of time. There were things she wanted to say to him.

"Do you know why I spoke to you that first time?" she said.

He took off his cap and scratched the back of his head. "You wanted me to tell you what really happened to your husband."

"That's not quite all of it." She examined her ring finger. The soft space vacated by her wedding ring had now been assimilated into the general spread of reddened, rough skin. No amount of cold cream could mitigate the effects of constant immersion in hot, soapy water. Her mother said she had the hands of a scullery maid.

"You see, I was trying very hard not to be relieved he was gone," she said. "I didn't love him, that's the truth of it. In fact, towards the end I began to hate him rather a lot. So I thought that if I could find out how he died, I would feel sorrow. I would have some kind of suitable feeling and I wouldn't be so ashamed. That's why I asked you. I thought that if I could not feel grief at least I could punish myself with guilt, especially if his death was terrible. It would bring his suffering home to me. But it didn't work, you see, because when it came down to it, I didn't really want to know. So now you know. I'm a selfish person. I didn't love my husband, and I am glad that he is dead."

She had not meant to say it like that, so coldly, all in a rush. Now he would despise her.

His chin rested on his hands. The tension had gone out of him and he seemed almost gleeful. "I know you didn't love him."

"Was…" Her voice cracked. "Was it so obvious?"

"Not immediately. It took me a while to see, but once I did –"

"It was obvious."

He stretched out his legs. "Elissa, I didn't know Harry Church well," he said, "but I didn't find him a particularly good or likeable man. Not that he deserved to die, no-one deserves that, but I don't think you can torment yourself for thinking what you did about him. Thoughts are just thoughts, after all. *You* didn't kill him."

"You must think I'm hateful."

"Not at all. Far from it."

The sun disappeared behind a cloud and the temperature dipped. She shivered. The rock beneath her was cold, but she didn't want to move and break the spell. He shifted and she felt the warmth of his arm, inches away from hers.

"It might surprise you," he said, "but I do know how you feel. I don't know if you've ever heard anything about my father. The gossip still goes the rounds every now and then."

"I assumed that he'd died. You never mention him."

"Well, he didn't die. He left, when I was about eight years old. Abandoned my mother and me without a word."

He said it flatly, as if he were describing something that had happened to a stranger, but she felt the twist of the knife in his words.

"Did you ever find out where he went?"

"No. There were rumours that he married again, has another family somewhere, but my mother never went looking for him. She was too proud."

"Have you ever thought of tracking him down?"

He scuffed his feet at a clump of lichen. "I used to. I used to imagine confronting him, teaching him a lesson, beating him to a pulp. It made me feel better. But I did nothing. I bring this up because when I think back and remember the times when my parents were together, I know that they weren't happy. That's one reason I spent so much time with my grandparents. My mother sent me away so that I would not have to witness the war between her and my father. My mother does not tolerate fools gladly, as you may have noticed, and in her eyes my father was a fool. He disappointed her I think. I don't remember him well enough to know if the weakness she saw in him was wholly his. I used to think so. Now I'm not sure. But I don't think I'll ever stop wishing him dead for leaving us. So you're not the only one you see. And I don't think you are bad, or selfish. Quite the opposite."

The sun came out again and made her skin tingle, as if she had been frozen for a long time and was only now beginning to thaw. Despite the tenderness of the season, she could almost pretend that spring had come. She began to cry and found that she could not stop. After a while she felt him shift closer, very quietly. Close, but not quite touching.

The afternoon was well advanced by the time they started back. Returning through the brambles, he led her by the hand and when they rejoined the wide path by the stream he did not let go.

Elissa was aware that some boundary was being crossed, but she was blind to everything but the feeling of his palm against hers. It was a simple thing really, an obvious thing. People did it all the time.

As they walked on and the silence lengthened, he rubbed his thumb gently against the centre of her palm. It was the tiniest of caresses, the gentlest, but it had a shocking intimacy that reached much deeper than the small space of skin on her palm. It was an awareness of something more than simply holding hands which, after all, could be dismissed as an innocent gesture if she were truly determined. After a while, he led her away from the stream onto a narrow, grassy side path. The trees closed in on them and they reached an old, thick-trunked beech tree that blocked the path. He turned towards her.

"We seem to have reached a dead end," he said.

She hadn't dared to look at him for the longest time. She was surprised at how nervous he seemed. She had imagined him all calm and control, but she could see his apprehension, the fear of going too far and chasing her away. She knew it was only the imminent threat of separation that had driven him to act. But it was she who crossed the final gap between them.

He tasted faintly of the lemonade they had drunk at lunchtime, sweet and sharp, and he was hot, sun-warmed like the ground. He settled against her, closing his arms around her back. Yes, it was a relief after all this time, she saw that now. She felt, without knowing quite how it had happened, that her back was against the tree. The ridges of bark dug into her back, the rough fabric of his jacket chafed her skin, the unexpected softness of his hair brushed her fingers. Her lips skimmed the slightest trace of bristles on his face. She closed her eyes to absorb it all. He was whispering something in her ear.

"Elissa," he said. "I love you."

She felt his hands, slipping up and down at her waist. "Please don't – "

"It's damned inconvenient I know, but I can't help it."

"Don't say it, please."

"What do you mean? Don't you love me?"

"I – I don't know."

He laughed. "How can you not know?"

"It's too soon. I just – "

"But it's not too soon to come here with me, to kiss me like that. Or am I flattering myself?"

"I can't be sure. Not yet. Please don't be angry"

She felt him tense against her. "Am not good enough for

you? Is that it? You can dally here in the woods where you won't be seen, but it wouldn't do to really love me would it? That would be too public."

"Don't be ridiculous. It's not that at all. You know – "

His hands dropped from her waist. "Oh I'm ridiculous am I? Well I'm so sorry. Too much of an oik for you, I expect."

"Why are you being like this? You know it's not that. It's nothing to do with that."

How could she say to him that she had been wrong before, that once she had believed herself to be in love and it had been the worst mistake of her life? This time she was certain it was different. It felt utterly different. But what if she was wrong?

"Please understand. I have only known you such a short time," she said. "You must be patient."

"How can you not know, Elissa? Either you love someone or you don't. You're just too scared to say it."

"Don't tell me how I feel! Haven't you listened to anything I've told you? About Harry? About my marriage?"

He backed away from her, his face set hard. "Oh so you think I'm like him do you? You think that I'll turn out to be a disappointment, just like he was. And then you'll probably hope that I don't come back either, and I may well not so that will solve your little problem, won't –"

She hit him hard across the face. "I hate you for saying that!"

He gripped her arm. "Ah, an emotion at last. You hate me, at least that's something. Give me an honest feeling any day."

He kissed her, this time without tenderness, and she was caught between wanting to fight him and embrace him. The closeness of the wood bore down on her. She struggled out of his grip.

"You have no idea what you're saying," she said. "You know

nothing of me and you don't want to listen when I try to tell you. You just see what you want to see then grasp it. That's not love."

He shook his head. "You're wrong," he said, "you stupid girl. I know you and I know exactly what I feel. It's you that knows nothing, of love or of yourself. I'm not surprised, mind you. How else could you have married an idiot like Harry Church?"

"Don't you *dare* speak to me like that." It was all very well for her to criticise Harry, but this was too much. What did he know of her marriage apart from the little she'd confided in him? A whisper at the back of her mind told her he might know a lot more than he let on. The idea mortified her. "You're impossible," she said. Without realising it, she was moving away from him, inch by inch. "You'll never understand."

"Oh that's right. I don't understand." He opened his arms in a mocking gesture. "Go on then, run off. I know you want to."

She tried to match him, glare for glare. She could see the certainty in his eyes and beneath it, the reproach. She turned away, almost tripping on a loose stone.

"That's it," he said, "Do what you're best at!"

"Oh be quiet," she said. "I'm tired of listening to your stupid, arrogant voice. Go and get on your train and leave. I hope I never see you again."

Chapter 8

Elissa stood outside the station café, which was tucked between two arches that fronted the concourse. He was not on any of the platforms so this was the most likely place. She stopped for a moment to smooth her hair. There was a sense of unreality to the bustle of the station, as if she were not really present at all but still sitting on the ward, rehearsing the scene in her mind one last time.

It was five minutes to eight and she had little more than half an hour. There would be no other chances and she did not want to have to reproach herself forever with the memory of something unfinished, a frayed thread that would rub and worry at her forever.

She pushed open the café door and was assailed by the smell of frying bacon. She spotted him immediately sitting in a far corner with his back to the wall. He had finished breakfast, pushed his plate aside and was writing something with great concentration. He had not noticed her come in and she stood for a moment watching him, her nerve failing. There was a clock on the wall and each forward movement of the minute hand brought an asthmatic click. It's already eight o'clock, it seemed to say. Did you know?

He looked up, saw her. His hair was barbered short

and stuck up in spikes on top. He had lost some of his characteristic pallor, no doubt the effect of yesterday's fresh air, and he was wearing his glasses to write. His eyes were red-rimmed – perhaps he had not slept either. He stood up as she approached the table and she could not help notice the brief expression of alarm before he composed his features into an appropriate neutrality.

"Do you mind if I join you?" she said.

"Please." He indicated the chair opposite.

She noticed how he turned over the piece of paper he had been writing on, concealing the movement in the act of sitting back down.

"I didn't expect you to come," he said.

"I was angry." She looked at him pointedly. "And I still am, but I couldn't not come. I couldn't let you go with bad blood between us."

"Blood is blood. It's neither good nor bad."

"What do you mean?"

He removed his glasses and rubbed the space between his brows. "Nothing. I don't know."

"Where's your mother? I thought she'd be here."

"She likes to say her goodbyes at home. Coming to the station upsets her."

"Is that why you asked me?"

"No. I don't know...perhaps. What do you want from me, Elissa? You've already told me what you don't want."

"What I said to you yesterday was unforgivable and I'm sorry. You're my friend and I don't want to lose you."

"Friend."

She felt tired, and exasperated with him. "I can't offer you more than that. I told you, I need time."

81

"As you see," he gestured at the clock on the wall, "that's the one thing we don't have."

"Daniel, I have tried to be honest with you. Would you rather I played the hypocrite, pretend feelings that I am unsure of, pretend that I have no doubts? Is that what you want, the dream of a happy ending? I'm sure there are countless other women who would be happy to oblige."

He leaned across the table. "I don't want other women. Yesterday, you led me to believe we might have a future...then you made it clear that I was mistaken. Your behaviour is very confusing to me, Elissa, and I don't have much tolerance for confusion at the moment. I have to fix my mind on what I have to do and I have no spirit left over for anything else."

The waitress arrived, and Elissa ordered tea that she did not want. He lit a cigarette.

"Why did you come," he said, "if you had nothing new to say?"

"I told you –"

"Oh yes, that's right. You want to be friends. Very well, Elissa. Let's write each other polite letters and pretend that nothing has changed. I have told you the truth, in good faith. Why can't you do the same? If my...if what I said to you yesterday was so repulsive, just tell me and we'll part with no hard feelings. At least pay me the compliment of your honest opinion."

"But I *have* been honest, that's the –" Her voice rose in spite of herself, and heads turned. His face was closed and blank beyond the pall of smoke. She didn't know how to get through to him. The clock beat its slow tattoo. Ten past eight.

She looked out of the café window. Through a veil of grease and steam she could see the station filling rapidly, the soldier's khaki blending with the muted tones of civilians. She noticed how many of the women wore dark colours – navy, chocolate, grey – as if they were in premature mourning. Where were the bright pastels of spring, the lupin blues and butter yellows? Where was white? The dark attire of the crowd and the grit-clad brown of the station walls fed the impression of a world drained of colour. Yet on the people's faces a bright cheer had settled like a fever. A determination not to relent, not to weaken.

At a table by the window, a sergeant from one of the local regiments sat with his wife and daughter. The little girl must have been about two. Her father held her on his knee and laughed as she batted his face with pink, seamless hands. His wife watched them, committing every gesture to memory. Elissa envied her such certainty of feeling. At the same time the prospect of being so completely involved in another's life – and death – terrified her. With love came the fear of separation, of loss.

Bored with the face-batting game, the little girl made a grab for the webbed strap on her father's rifle, propped against the wall.

"Now, now little one," he said, "that's not for you."

He cradled her in his left arm and moved the rifle away to a safe distance. The girl began to squall bitterly in frustration, reaching for the desired object. Her mother brought out a small, dirty-looking piece of patchwork, waving it at her daughter with cooing noises, but the girl was inconsolable. She began to scream and her face turned dark red with effort as she continued to reach for the elusive, forbidden thing. The man looked helplessly at his wife, who with a tired patience reached across the table for her daughter. She began to rock

83

the little girl, making soothing, singing sounds in her ear, all the while fixing her gaze on her husband. The clock shifted again. Eight fifteen.

Perhaps she should just do what he wanted. After all, they might never see each other again. Was she simply being heartless, insisting on honesty at such a time, denying him a shred of comfort to carry away? She knew the routine. Anyone would do – he just needed the idea of someone to come back to. Is that what disturbed her, the fear that she may not be special after all? Perhaps he had chosen her simply because she happened to be there, and available.

"I'll have to go in a minute," he said.

"I know." She did not know what else to say. "Write to me. Please."

He leaned back and exhaled a curl of smoke, which joined the general pall below the café ceiling. "I was writing a letter to you when you came in. I'll post it when I get to London."

Her eyes moved down, back to the clock. Twenty past eight. The sergeant and his family were leaving, the little girl quiet now, dozing on her mother's shoulder. The sergeant opened the café door and the noise of the station intruded, a raucous booming of many voices straining for cheer.

"I'd better not leave it any longer," said Daniel, fishing out a few pennies for the bill.

She watched as he calmly shrugged on his coat. Her tea sat untouched. If only things could remain in indefinite suspension while she recovered her bearings. This could be solved, she was sure, if only she had time.

"Are you coming?" he said.

She followed him to the door and he stood aside for her to pass.

"It's this way." He inclined his head towards a nearby platform.

As they made their way through the rising tumult she was terrified that they would become separated in the crowd. She turned around to make sure he was behind her and took hold of his hand. She could not look at him. Instead, she allowed her gaze to wander at random among the surge of people. Through the thin cotton of her glove she felt the warmth of his hand. She held on tight and they began to walk up the platform together. It was still there – the same feeling, the same heat – she could not ignore it.

The train was already full. Through the windows she could see a few men already withdrawn into newspapers, no loved ones to see them off. Or perhaps they were wise enough to say their goodbyes at home. But the majority leaned out of the windows, holding hands with wives or mothers, ruffling the hair of children, giving one last admonishment to be good and take care of mummy. He led her to the far end of the platform and released her hand.

"I'll say goodbye here then."

Elissa longed to repent. All around her, men were kissing their wives or mothers or sweethearts one last time. The women were all bright and strained, full of laughter, eyes shining. Whispered endearments, no tears. It was wretched. Her abandoned hand gripped the front edge of his coat. Down the platform, the conductors began to call out and the train doors slammed in a staccato rhythm. She gripped harder.

Quickly, he leaned down and kissed her on the cheek and then whispered in her ear. "I'm sorry, Elissa, truly sorry. For all the things I said. I hope one day you'll forgive me."

Before she had chance to reply he walked away and she was

left clutching the air. He disappeared almost immediately, the crowd folding in on itself in his wake. She craned above the swarming heads trying to see him, watching until the last possible moment. The crowd on the platform began to split in half. It was like a dance, formal and stately; men to the left on the train, women to the right on the platform. There was a sinister order to it that chilled her. She did not want to be part of it. She did not want to be involved. In the café, the clock struck the half hour. Eight thirty.

A whistle blew and the hubbub of goodbyes reached a climax. The final door slammed. The train, with an arthritic spasm, lurched forward a few feet, stopped, and then with a shriek of metal against metal, moved again. A few women walked and then ran alongside the train, still holding onto hands, shouting final goodbyes. Most stood, like Elissa, rooted in disbelief that after all the waiting this could actually be happening. The train gathered speed as it cleared the station platform and soon it had disappeared altogether, absorbed into the rim of white light beyond the arched roof. A cloud of steam circled above them then descended like a sooty benediction, dispersing at the women's feet to coat the surface of the platform with a layer of particulate dust.

Some of the women turned to go immediately, heads down, disconsolate. The ones that remained milled slowly, rudderless now that the job was done. Elissa found a grimy station bench tucked back between two pillars and made sure she was concealed behind one of them when she sat down. Then she took a handkerchief from her skirt pocket, hid her face in it and cried.

Chapter 9: March 1918

I t had been dry for days now and the earth was beginning to crumble and crack in the trench walls. The sun had burned off the early morning mist, carving deep shadows in front of the sandbagged parapet. It was unusually quiet and Daniel could hear the low hum of flies and the scratchy sound of a rat crossing the duckboards. He could even make out the desultory buzz of a distant aeroplane. Overhead floated an observation balloon, a silver caterpillar against a flat, pale sky. An occasional breeze brought with it the harsh, sulphurous stink of urine and in the background, never completely absent, the sweet, clinging odour of decay.

After an unexpectedly scenic journey south, first by rail and then by motor lorry, Daniel had found the remnants of C Company in a quiet sector near Péronne. He had travelled the rolling farmland of the Ancre valley, passing white turreted chateaux and blooming fields alive with spring. It was only when he embarked on the final leg of his journey that the landscape took on the ravaged face that inhabited his dreams. But the battered desolation he traversed had already been left behind by the war. Abandoned carts, guns, and tanks grew brown with rust and the churned ground had dried out. In places it blossomed with sprays of white and yellow spring flowers. Wrecked villages showed softened edges of green; grass and weeds had quickly captured what the clashing armies had for so long failed to hold.

He had joined his old section as they'd been preparing to go up into the support trenches. Frannie was still there and Fred Charnley, newly promoted to sergeant, but on the whole there were few faces he knew.

"Left most of them in bloody Wipers," was all Frannie would say when asked. "You were well clear of it believe me."

He supposed he should be grateful. Those that had spent the last six months in the salient proclaimed that this was a picnic, what with the good weather, the dry ground and Jerry keeping himself to himself.

He found a perch on a box of Mill's bombs and examined the letter that had arrived that morning. He thought it might be from Elissa. All around him, men were reading, lying stretched out or curled up on the fire step. Some had parcels, which they opened carefully, scrying the contents for meaning. Each item would be inspected, assessed, stored for later use or earmarked for sharing.

He examined the letter. He could not ever remember seeing her handwriting. In a way, he was more afraid of it being from her than not. Now he was at a safe distance she would probably dismiss him without compunction. She had every right. The profuse, embarrassing apologies of his own letter might only make her more determined. She had no doubt concluded that he was deranged.

He turned over the envelope, feeling its thickness through the envelope. At least three sheets. Not a short letter then. Was that good, or did it mean that she was letting him down gently?

A noisy group had gathered around Denny Wade, who'd been sent a Simnel cake by his mother. He was slicing it into tiny squares with a penknife. Cakes were always shared around – it was an unwritten rule. This was his best chance, while they were all preoccupied. He slit open the top of the envelope carefully with his index finger and pulled out the folded sheets. He held them up to his nose. Could one tell by the feel of a letter, its smell, what it contained?

Of course not. He was prevaricating. He put on his glasses and unfolded the letter. The neat, rounded swirls of ink resolved themselves into words.

Dear Daniel, it began. Dear. Not dearest.

I'm so glad you wrote to me. I can't say how relieved I was to hear from you and know that you are safe...

Well, that was good. He skipped to the last page.

Please take care of yourself and come back. I keep imagining the time when you come back. I miss you very much. I miss everything about you.

And then she signed her name. It was encouraging, definitely encouraging. He read the line again about her missing him. Then he turned back to the first page and read the letter through properly.

For the hundredth time he replayed those last few moments with her in the wood, before he had opened his mouth and spoiled everything. Was it so bad, what he'd said? It certainly hadn't been what he'd planned. He had rehearsed a calm, dignified declaration. He had intended to use such words as "affection" and "respect." He had imagined her responding with surprise, but not with fear, and certainly not with anger. He had imagined that they would touch only briefly. But she

89

had kissed him and held onto him in a way that he found hard to either dismiss or forget. And she had shown no sign of wanting to stop – until he'd told her that he loved her.

He'd stayed there for a long time after she'd gone, staring at the space that she had left. It was right. He knew it was right, so why couldn't she see it? Sometimes he felt a great certainty of things in these brief, heightened moments, and he never understood why other people didn't feel the same way.

A shadow fell across him and he quickly folded the letter away. Frannie was standing over him, holding a crumbling square of Simnel cake and chewing with an expression that wandered between surprise and disgust. He nodded towards the letter.

"Good news?"

"You could say that."

Frannie sat down next to him. "Well you're taking long enough over it. Want some cake?"

"No thank-you."

"Suit yourself." Frannie stuffed the rest of the cake into his mouth, munching noisily. "Waste not, want not." He began picking his teeth with the nail of his little finger. "From your mother is it?"

"No."

"My wife sent me some mint cake today. Ha! She knows I hate the stuff."

"How is she?"

"Fine, just fine. Who's it from then?"

"What?"

Frannie looked skywards. "The letter!"

"Oh. A friend."

"A friend, eh?" Frannie smirked and leaned back, crossing

his arms.

"A very *old* friend. From my student days."

But Frannie had stopped listening. He was peering upwards, examining the sky with intense suspicion.

"What is it? Did you hear something?"

"No." Frannie sniffed the air like a bloodhound. "That's just it. I can't hear anything and it's giving me the bloody heebies."

"Such a lovely morning," said Jo, flinging herself down in the grass. "It feels like summer already."

They'd followed the path from Elissa's house, down the slope and along the stream to a clearing, a flattened half-circle of grass surrounded by trees.

"Be careful, it might be damp."

"Oh do stop fussing Elissa, it's fine." Jo patted the ground next to her. "See for yourself."

Elissa tucked her coat under her legs and sat down. Jo was right – the ground was dry, though she could feel the underlying coldness of the soil.

The high, narrow sides of the valley funneled the sound of rushing water, creating a kind of multiple echo. There was a vortex of hissing and roaring, and it was both maddening and seductive. Jo lay back, hands behind her head.

"That noise is very soothing. It makes me want to go to sleep," she said.

"I know what you mean," said Elissa. "I used to come here with my sister before I was married. We'd bring along a picnic, and afterwards we'd always fall asleep. Every time. We used to joke that the place was enchanted and that one day we would wake up to find a hundred years had passed, and everyone we knew was dead."

"Perhaps if we fall asleep, when we wake up the war will be over."

"That would be nice."

Jo sat up and scrunched her toes into the grass. "Yes, except that I wouldn't want everyone to be dead."

The word hung between them. Elissa thought of Daniel, wondered what he was doing and if he was in danger. The more she tried to put him out of her mind, the more he insisted his way back in. She'd never worried like this about Harry.

Jo unlaced her boots, rolled off her stockings and buried her feet in the grass with a sigh of satisfaction.

"You're in a lively mood this morning," said Elissa.

"I know. Must be the season. Mad as a March hare and all that."

"You're not like this –"

"At the hospital? Of course not. I have to play the part don't I? Nurse Kenyon. You know the game, Elissa. I've seen you play it."

Elissa laughed. "Yes but I thought that was just me." She began to unbutton her own boots. The thought of the air and the green moisture of the grass against her feet was too tempting to resist.

"No, we all do it. Comes with the job. The patients – they expect you to be a certain way, so you play along." Jo stretched her arms above her head. "I don't feel like it today though. I think I'll just be me. A silly, overgrown schoolgirl."

Elissa kicked off her boots and wriggled her toes. "I wouldn't say you were that."

"I would." Jo let her arms fall. Her face crumpled suddenly. "Sometimes I think I have no more sense than a child, and a stupid one at that."

"Jo – what do you mean?"

"I'm such a fool." Jo gave a short, barking laugh. "I've been very bad Elissa. Very foolish. I thought that if I didn't tell anyone, then somehow it wouldn't be real and it would all go away. But it doesn't work like that, does it?"

"What is it? What's happened?"

Jo sat up and tugged at the grass, tearing off great clutches of it until her hands were wet and stained.

"Promise not to tell anyone?"

"Of course."

Jo wiped the grass loose of her hands. "It was nearly a year ago. Last spring. Do you remember? I took some days off to visit my brother."

"I think so."

"Well, I didn't visit my brother. It was a lie."

"That's not so bad. We all – "

"No, you don't understand. I was here all along you see, but I had someone with me. A man. That's why I lied. I met him at the hospital. I never should have…but I did. I was so tired of doing the right thing. He kept after me, you see. I was a little mad when I came back from France. Nothing mattered and I…oh it's so embarrassing."

"It's all right Jo."

"It's not all right. I slept with him." She glanced at Elissa. "Now I've shocked you."

"No. I understand."

"You don't. He was married. He was married and I slept with him. And not just once either."

"Oh, Jo."

"Now you think I'm terrible. And you're right, I am."

Elissa stared at her stockinged feet, lying limp and shapeless

93

on the grass. They felt hot and ugly in the scratchy stockings. "Did you know all along he was married?"

"No. He told me when it was…well, when it was too late. I tried to end it, but I couldn't. Still can't. I'm a feeble, selfish woman."

Elissa pressed the soles of her feet into the grass. "You mustn't think that. You made a mistake and you were deceived."

"I know I should be angry with him, but I can't manage it. He might die at any time. I'll probably never see him again anyway."

"You're not still in touch with him?"

"He sends me letters. Telling me that he's staying alive and coming back just for me. I told him not to, swore to myself I would give him up, but I didn't have the heart to put him off. And then I started to write back. Now I don't know what to do."

Elissa rubbed her feet back and forth on the cold ground but she could not seem to dissipate the heat. "What about his wife?"

"He says she doesn't care what he does. She hates him."

"Does he have any children?"

"Yes. Two."

"Oh, Jo."

"Stop saying that! I know it's wrong, but I don't know what else to do."

"Will you see him if he comes back?"

Jo pulled at the grass again, as if she were tearing out her hair. "I promised myself I wouldn't. But honestly, I don't know."

"Do you love him?"

"I've done my best to forget him, but I can't. Is that love?"

A question Elissa felt singularly ill-equipped to answer. She could feel the cold coming up from the ground now. She looked at Jo's hands, streaked with green juice and broken blades of grass, and tried to think of something reassuring to say.

A sheet of dirty brown canvas stretched like a membrane across the entrance to the dugout. The walls were sided with concrete and on rainy days they sweated, coating the steps with damp and making a difficult descent treacherous. But luckily today had been dry and the night was clear, if a little cold.

In his bunk Daniel had a sense of being insulated, though not exactly protected, from the bombardment above. A few candles burned, guttering occasionally in the dugout's obscure weather-system of breezes. Most of the time, fresh air was hard to come by – the dugout was a labyrinth of corridors, tiny rooms and niches – and as he inhaled, Daniel knew he was absorbing the breath and sweat of earlier occupants, then discharging it back into the air and adding to the general rankness and moisture. He was in a room near the entrance and although the noise of the barrage was louder here, at least he could detect a trickle of clean air from the world above.

He had managed a couple of hours sleep before midnight, but when the bombardment intensified he'd given up. The depth and thickness of the walls muffled the sound of the barrage, but only slightly. Each impact sent out a wave of vibration that rippled through the ground and as the next shell hit before the effects of the last one had dispersed, the effect was cumulative. The ripples overlapped and pushed against each other, and these contrary tides shook him and made his ears hurt. At times he thought the pressure would make him pop like an over-inflated balloon.

He lay on his back and concentrated on not panicking. The hard shell of unconcern that had grown around him like a protective callus was failing, and he didn't know what to do. He had lost the facility of indifference. And it was not just his own fear that preyed on him either, but the fear of all the other men who shifted and slept with him in this cramped darkness, all the fear together like a toxic cloud. Added to that was the ghostly fear of all those who had come before, the dead and gone, their final terror reanimated by those who had taken their place. He thought he would choke on it.

He tried to distract himself by searching for rhythms in the chaos. He was convinced that if he could find a pattern then it might mean that things were in some way predictable. He might know when the next shell would fall and the next, and the knowledge would somehow make him safer. He reached into his pocket and touched Elissa's letter. His talisman. He traced the ragged edge of the envelope where he'd torn it open.

I keep imagining the time when you come back.

A thin stream of dust fell onto his sleeve. He brushed it away and the particles danced in the air, making him cough. On the bunk below Frannie slept peacefully, while a few feet away Fred Charnley turned over on his bunk. The wooden frame creaked as he moved and the creaking reminded Daniel of something. There it was – a pattern. It reminded him of a tune, something he'd heard before. He began to whistle, tapping imaginary piano keys with his fingers.

Frannie knocked on the base of his bunk. "Put a sock in it Dan, old pal."

Daniel leaned over the edge of his bunk. Frannie lay on his back, one arm behind his head, tunic spread over him like a blanket.

"Are you really saying," said Daniel, "that you can sleep through all this racket, but my whistling disturbs you?"

"Yes." Frannie closed his eyes. "So shut your cakehole."

Daniel lay back down. It didn't matter – the tune was inside him now. He moved his fingers over the imaginary piano, playing it through, searching his memory. He knew it from somewhere. Years ago.

When the memory came, it was in the form of a frozen image like a photograph. He saw himself standing at the top of a broad flight of steps outside a concert hall. He remembered the night, and the occasion. It was just before the war, when he'd still been a student. A concert that he'd gone to with Rob. Robert Cole, his best friend, who'd known someone in the orchestra and got free tickets.

He remembered the concert – it was the piece they'd all been talking about that year – and he remembered how he had gripped the arms of his seat, first ambushed, then cornered by the music. Because it was all wrong. There was no unfolding, no development, just fragments of sound, cut up and stuck together in a dazzling, relentless collage. It was strange and unhinged. It was brilliant and he'd hated it. *The Rite of Spring.*

A vulgar noise they had called it in the papers. There had been a riot at the premiere in Paris, they said, the aesthetes and the *beau monde* screaming and scratching at each other. They said the uproar was so loud it had drowned out the music. Having heard the music, he found that hard to believe.

Afterwards, he and Rob had stood at the top of a steep flight of steps outside the hall, transfixed and babbling, excited, not listening to each other. Finally, when they realised that everyone else had gone home, they descended into a thick fog, the huge gas globes that lit the steps floating in the murk like miniature suns. They had walked the streets most of the night, arguing, oblivious to the cold and dark and the sooty air. Daniel remembered how his mind, his body, his whole being had resounded from the shock of the music. It had frightened him and the fear made him angry. What was worse, Rob had instinctively understood it. The music stirred him to life. While Daniel tried to make Rob understand how terrible it was, how wrong, Rob strove equally to make him see the truth, the rightness and the wonder.

He clenched and unclenched his hands. His palms were sweating and there were red gouges where his nails had dug into the skin. Rob had been right and he had been a scared, ignorant child.

And that's what he'd heard, lying here in the suffocating darkness. The opening notes of *The Rite of Spring*. Only a snippet of folk tune really, the bassoon straining at the top of its register. Simple, but then again not simple at all.

Now Rob was nearly three years dead, blown to pieces by a stray shell from his own lines two days into the battle of Loos. He'd been in France only three weeks. Daniel had received one long, jaunty letter, full of anecdotes and blustery humour and pluck. Then had come short note from Rob's sister with the news and an invitation to the memorial service. After the service, a stout woman in black had come up to him, pierced him with a dead stare and handed him a white feather.

The Rite of Spring. A simple, brutal tale of sacrifice to appease the gods and turn the season back towards life.

The trickle of dust from the dugout roof became a shower

as the barrage intensified. Daniel sat up, hugging his knees as a particularly loud crack broke over his head. He could no longer be indifferent to his fate. More than anything in the world he wanted to live. When he'd joined the army the day after Rob's memorial, he had vowed to leave music behind for good. But Elissa had brought him back that day when he'd played for her, when she'd listened with such complete and rapt attention.

Below, a dark form leapt like a jack in the box into the narrow space between the bunks.

"Stop it! Make it stop. Please make it…make it STOP."

It was Denny Wade, his eyes gutted by panic, his mouth stretched wide. He had crooked teeth, curved and yellow like claws. He was barely seventeen, but his face was made ancient by the demon that rode him. Daniel swung his legs over the bunk to jump down, but Frannie got there first. He grabbed Denny by the back of his neck like an errant cat and pushed him up against the wall.

"That's enough now, old pal," he said.

Denny struggled and flung about but Frannie held him fast, fixing him with his eyes. The two men seemed caught in a strange, frozen embrace.

"Enough," said Frannie again.

He had to be subdued or he might infect them all.

Chapter 10

E lissa put the kettle on to boil. It was strangely satisfying to be eating the first meal of the day when most people were returning from work. One of the many incongruities she enjoyed about working nights.

While she waited for the water to heat up, she lit the gas lamps in the hall. It was a gloomy, stormy evening and the low cloud had brought premature darkness Rain hit the window panes in gusts, driven by the wind. It howled and sang about the house like a mad thing and the trees at the bottom of the garden creaked as if they too were aching with wet and cold.

She had slept badly. Her eyes were hot, and she could not stop thinking about what Jo had told her. When she'd invited her friend to stay she had looked forward to having female company, imagining an intimate exchange of confidences. She had got more than she'd bargained for. The idea of Jo forming such a rash attachment, throwing caution to the wind so completely, frightened Elissa. How could she be so careless?

But then she supposed it was easy to be level-headed on behalf of others. After all, she had believed herself desperately in love with Harry before she'd married him – no-one could have persuaded her otherwise. Perhaps that's why she felt such dread in her heart for Jo. She saw her own blindness, her own mistakes reflected.

But it wasn't just concern for her friend's welfare that had kept her awake all those hours. She had to be honest. Beneath the fear, she had to admit that she envied Jo. *What was it like,* she'd wanted to ask.

She spooned tea from the caddy into the pot and reached for a stub of bread from the crock. She could probably get four slices out of it if she cut thinly. There was a creaking on the stairs and Jo appeared in the doorway, still in her dressing gown, her hair falling past her shoulders in a long, untidy plait.

"Goodness Elissa you're all dressed and ready. You make me feel like a slugabed."

Elissa poured boiling water into the teapot. "I woke early that's all. I didn't sleep very well."

Without being asked, Jo found cups, saucers and plates in the kitchen cupboards and began to lay the table. "It wasn't anything I said was it?"

Elissa busied herself in the pantry fetching butter and marmalade. "Of course not. It often happens when I switch to nights."

As they settled to their modest breakfast, she watched Jo spread marmalade thickly on her bread and bite into it with relish, making appreciative noises. They had shared many moments like this in the year and a bit they'd been together at Garrett Hill. Late night cups of cocoa and stolen biscuits, morning tea in the hospital gardens, snatched lunches of paste sandwiches in the drab little staff room off the kitchens. Their friendship was built on this string of short, snatched moments of nourishment.

It was only in the last month that confidences had emerged,

and it had mostly been on Jo's side. She'd told Elissa about her time in France, first at a field hospital, then six months at a railway station only a mile from the front. She had been shelled and air-raided and had treated men raw from battle, bloody and half torn apart. She had seen the true face of war.

"I couldn't wait to get away," she admitted. "Garrett Hill is a rest cure in comparison. I'm ashamed to confess it, but I would've gone mad if I'd stayed any longer. I feel like a convalescent myself, never mind the patients."

Elissa nibbled at a corner of bread. Now Jo had paid her the compliment of trusting her with an even deeper secret and she had not responded in kind.

"Jo," she said. "About what you told me, yesterday –"

"Oh Elissa, is that what's bothering you? I knew there was something. I really didn't mean to burden you. Please forget that I ever –"

"No, you misunderstand. I'm glad you told me. I'm glad you felt you could trust me. It's just that it made me think. About my own situation. It's not the same but…"

"Is this anything to do with that corporal?" said Jo, cutting to the quick of the matter as ever. "The one that used to wait for you outside the hospital? What was his name? Easton?"

"Earnshaw. Yes. It's to do with him."

Jo rotated her cup between her fingers. "Do I take it that I'm not the only woman here with a secret?"

"You could say that. I've been a terrible coward Jo. We had the most dreadful row before he left."

And it all came tumbling out. Jo listened silently, fixing her with that bright, blackbird gaze as she described the whole sorry mess of that day down by the stream. At the end of it Jo took a long gulp of tea and refilled both their cups.

"I don't think you're a coward at all," she said. "I wish I'd been as circumspect. It was all very well at the time, but now...I'm left with this terrible feeling, a yawning gap that I don't know how to fill."

"But that's just how I feel," said Elissa. "I thought I was doing the right thing, so why do I feel so miserable and guilty? I could have told him I loved him and at least sent him away with something."

"*Do* you love him?" said Jo.

"I...think I might."

"Did you know that before he left?"

"I wasn't sure."

"So you were honest, as you said. I don't see how that is cowardice. It's quite brave actually."

Her friend's eyes were soft with fellow feeling. It was such a relief to be understood.

"Then why couldn't I make him see?"

Jo prodded a finger at the crumbs on her plate and licked them up.

"Whatever his qualities," she said, "he's still a man. Everything is black and white and straight ahead to them, no twists and turns."

"What shall I do?"

"Have you written to him?"

Elissa nodded.

"Well then. If he's got half the sense you say he'll write back to tell you how grateful he is that you've forgiven him."

Mist had descended during the night and hung close to the ground in billowing clumps. It exuded an earthy smell that reminded Daniel of the deep cold of a cave. Fingers of it extended along the trench system, creating strange distortions in distance and sound. He heard voices that seemed to come from close by, but when he turned around there was no-one there and he realised the voices were projected echoes of men hundreds of yards away in another trench.

He peered into the haze and could make out only vague, lumpy shadows. He was completely unprepared when Fred Charnley stumbled into him, his face a half-moon of confusion.

"Where is everyone?"

"Damned if I know. I only turned my back for a minute and they all disappeared."

"Have you seen Mr Edmonds?"

"He was here about ten minutes ago. Said he was just going back to the dugout for something."

"Bugger. Suppose I'd better try to find him then."

Fred moved away down the support trench and in a second was re-absorbed into the fog. Daniel stayed where he was, waiting unless anyone else came along. But the only thing that seemed to be approaching was the sound of rifle fire and shouting from the front line. The back of his neck prickled. Something was wrong, he could sense it. He edged his way forward towards the communication trench. It was only twenty yards away, just around the next traverse, but the distance seemed to have stretched out in the murk. He held onto the trench wall as he moved. If he kept going he was bound to run into someone. The earth was tacky from the wet fog and smeared onto his hands as he shuffled forward. The wall seemed to bend before him in the mist, probably the beginning of the traverse. But it seemed to make no sense – the bend went on and on and the shape of it was all wrong.

He took two more steps and suddenly he was plunged into the middle of a heaving crowd. He had found the communication trench all right, but it was full of men moving back from the line. The wrong direction, surely. He tried to push his way against the flow but the mass of bodies pressed him back. Where had they all come from? He didn't recognise any of the faces. A private from the East Lancashires brushed past him, and he grabbed the man's arm.

"What's going on?"

"Let go!" He was young, only a boy really. His eyes were empty and terrified.

"In a minute," said Daniel. "First tell me what's happening."

"I have to go. They're everywhere!"

"Who?"

But the boy had wriggled out of his grasp. Daniel felt the general panic infect him. He had to get out of this crowd.

He pushed his way a few feet up towards the line and found the other support trench on his left. The mist enveloped him again, but at least he'd managed to get clear of the melee. The mist had dampened the sound of rifle fire, reducing it to the pop and snap of children's firecrackers, but there was no denying it was coming closer. He heard the metallic whine of a bullet passing close by his ear and crouched instinctively. Not that close, he told himself. Not that close.

He heard shouting above his head and decided to risk a look over the parapet. He climbed up onto the fire step and raised himself slowly, just high enough so that his eyes were level with the top of the trench. He prayed that the mist would conceal him from snipers. Just for a moment the fog lifted like a curtain and he could see clear across no man's land.

So much space.

He ducked down quickly, flattening himself against the trench wall. He had seen, crystal clear and only fifty yards away, a line of figures running through the mist towards him. He couldn't tell if they were his own side retreating or the enemy. To be on the safe side he pulled the rifle strap from his shoulder. The figures he'd glimpsed had come and gone, in and out of the mist like ghosts. He was almost sure they were the enemy. But how had they got through the wire? He jumped down onto the duckboards and edged back towards the communication trench.

The shouting was much louder now and he looked up, and about fifty yards away he saw a man standing on the roof of their dugout. A German officer. He had something in his left hand that looked like opera glasses. The man lifted the glasses to his eyes and Daniel raised his rifle. The man was turning towards him now, both hands on the glasses, then stopped, facing him square on, the glasses flattening against his head. Daniel hugged the rifle into his shoulder, ratcheted the bolt, and took aim.

Gripping the barrel with one hand, he squeezed the trigger with the other. His stomach twisted like a snake. He closed his eyes as he fired. He heard nothing, apart from the crack of the rifle. He felt nothing, apart from the spasm of its rebound against his shoulder. He crouched down and counted to thirty, the rifle discharge ringing tinnily in his ears. His heart thudded like a train.

Now there were footsteps approaching behind him. He straightened, leaning into the side of the trench wall to keep his balance, ratcheted the bolt of his rifle and raised it again. A dark shape approached through the gloom.

"Don't shoot me, for fuck's sake."

The mist thinned. He lowered the rifle in relief. "Frannie."

"Getting windy are we?"

"A bit."

"Just like every other bugger down here."

"What happened?

"Edmonds decided to make a run for it. Orders, he said. Full bloody retreat. Left me to mop up the stragglers."

"I don't think there's anyone left in the front line."

"It's a proper mess, all right. Come on, let's go. I'm in no mood to make friends with a big hairy Prussian."

The hole was about fifty feet across and deep enough to give cover while still being dry at the base This meant it was recent, most probably created during the bombardment that had pounded them in the dugout – two days ago by Daniel's reckoning.

He listened to Frannie's breathing, monitoring the regular rise and fall of his friend's shoulders for signs of wakefulness. Neither of them had overcoats and they were huddled together for warmth. Daniel had his leather jerkin, but Frannie wore only a thin pullover under his tunic. At the beginning he'd insisted that he did not feel the cold, but that only lasted until an hour or two after sunset on the first night.

It had quickly become clear that they could not get back to the line, even if they knew where it was. They'd been hopelessly disoriented by the fog and had stumbled into the hole by accident. Since then, surrounded by the enemy, they'd had no choice but to stay put. Even Frannie, dogged optimist that he was, could see no way out. But this last night had been quiet, and Daniel hoped that the coming morning might offer some new possibility of escape.

A thin edge of grey leached along the horizon. It had been clear for most of the night and he had watched the progress of Orion and Cassiopeia across the sky between brief, troubled snatches of sleep. Orion had always been his favourite constellation. As a child, he remembered looking out of his bedroom window, searching for that familiar broken "X." He knew that the constellations rose and set just like the sun and the moon, and he would wake himself up at different times of the night just to see if Orion had moved. But he never managed to stay awake long enough to see it set.

This past night, lying on his back on the cold ground staring at the sky, hardly blinking, he had finally achieved his childhood dream. He had looked on in a strange, almost tender mood as Orion disappeared into the black, starless region at the sky's rim.

He was not afraid any more. The solution was simple; lack of sleep, cold, hunger and thirst had worked where reason and self-control had failed. Being reduced to a cluster of bodily needs drowned out all other concerns. He felt light, as if his physical deprivations had loosened his burdens. At times, he felt something approaching happiness. Staring at the night sky, he had the feeling it might swallow him. He would not have minded if it had, for he knew that the coming dawn would reveal the twisted, humped shape of Denny Wade.

Denny had not proved to be very entertaining company these last days. He'd just lain there, face down, silent, arms stretched above his head as if in supplication. Above his waist there were no visible marks, though the material of his pack had been shredded as if he'd been clawed by a huge cat. However, past the joint of hip and leg there was nothing left of Denny but a few bloody shreds and obscene, glinting shards of white where the bone had been exposed. It was a remarkably clean cut, as if he had been pared like a pork chop on a butcher's block. All night Daniel had been sure that he could hear Denny's blood leaking into the ground and yesterday morning he'd noticed a thick pool of red around the raw, shiny split, but it had soon soaked away into the chalk leaving nothing but a brownish stain to draw the flies.

Frannie refused to look and urged Daniel to do the same. But when darkness fell, Denny seemed to take on a different kind of life from the one that had been wrested from him in the day. Part of the reason Daniel had not slept was that every time he started to doze he could hear Denny whispering. Denny was trying to tell him something. The trouble was, though the tone was urgent he could never make out the words.

As the sun rose higher and began to heat the ground, an odour crept forth, a clinging, sweet smell that grew intimate with his skin no matter how hard he tried to ignore it. A yellow stain of light spread across the battered ground, down into the hole, and slanted across Frannie's face. He twitched and flapped at his cheek as if he were swatting a fly.

"Two slices of bacon and a fried egg, please," he said. "And don't stint on the toast."

"Would you like some piping hot coffee with that?"

Frannie opened his eyes and rubbed at the grit on his face. "Yes, although I'll settle for a bit of petrol-tainted water."

"We had the last of the water last night."

Frannie blinked twice, and in that uncanny way of his was fully awake. "Well, we can't stay here much longer then, can we?"

"No."

Daniel could almost hear his friend's mind working, considering options. "Guns aren't so loud this morning," he said. "But no more mist, which means no cover."

"Perhaps we'd better wait until dark, hope things stay quiet," said Daniel.

"Maybe," said Frannie. "But that will make another day without water. What do you think Denny?"

Frannie cocked his head and pretending to listen.

"Denny thinks we're a couple of fucking cowards. He doesn't see why we should lie around here saving our skins while he's providing dinner for rats."

"He has a point."

"No he doesn't." Frannie reached for his rifle. "He was always full of shit, just like his stinking cake. I'm going for a look-see." He pulled his helmet low over his eyes and turned on his stomach, inching his way towards the edge of the shell-hole. He lifted his head slowly above the rim and was motionless for a few seconds.

"Can you see anything?" said Daniel

Frannie ducked suddenly and scrabbled back down, setting off a miniature avalanche of stones and grit. His eyes were wide, his face streaked with mud.

"The place is crawling. Fix bayonets, old pal."

Daniel retrieved his rifle from where he'd wedged it in the dry ground. His hands were shaking. He could hear voices approaching now, calls and replies. He could tell they weren't English. Then, so loud it must have been only a few feet away, came a high shriek of pain followed by a harsh laugh. The voices were shouting, to and fro across their heads, and Daniel could not stop shaking. He had faced endless bombardments, occasional sniper shots and, once or twice, the fury of a machine gun battery. But he had never seen his enemy close to. The thought of killing someone while looking into their face froze his marrow. The notion of dying in the same manner was the only thing that kept him from fleeing in panic. He tightened his hands around the stock of his rifle.

Frannie had flipped over onto his stomach and nudged Daniel to do the same. "Play dead until they're on top of us," he whispered. "With any luck they'll pass us over. If not, spike 'em, but keep it quiet."

Daniel turned over, concealing his rifle beneath him, curving one arm over his head. Now, between them, they could watch both sides of the hole. From behind came a loud shout and the sound of boots slithering down towards them.

"Here we bloody go," whispered Frannie. "There's four of them. Watch yourself."

There was the sickening sound of metal ripping into flesh and the harsh laugh rang out again. Frannie's face contorted. Daniel could not see what was happening but he knew they were sticking bayonets into Denny as if he were a pincushion. He forced the bile down his throat. In a moment it might be him, carved up like so much dead meat. The last shreds of his self-control snapped like perished sinew. He could not bear it. He wanted to live. He was desperate to live. He scrambled to his feet, his boots struggling for purchase in the treacherous earth.

"No!" hissed Frannie.

But it was too late, they had seen him. He took two lurching steps forward, rifle at the ready. Two of them were scrawny-looking specimens, one wearing thick glasses, the other barely old enough to show more than a wisp of moustache. But the other two were broad and fearsome. The broadest of all looked on Daniel with a gap-toothed grin, clearly happy at the prospect of fresh meat. He swung round his rifle, bayonet dripping blood and said something to the other three. The grin became a scratchy cackle. The one with the glasses looked down, his shoulders drooping. Daniel's hands still gripped his rifle, but his legs were about to give way. The gap-toothed man had bright blue eyes alight with a cold fire. Daniel had seen that look before. Not often, but enough to know what it meant. This was a man who enjoyed killing.

Gap-tooth shouted something to his comrades. Daniel was pinned by the man's predatory gaze and the dead, dark barrel of his rifle. The bayonet's tip dripped dark red and glittered in the rising sun. Gap-tooth closed one burning eye and took aim.

Chapter 11: April 1917

In Jo's mind, everything was encapsulated in that first day. As she dredged through the memories in the months that followed, that first encounter took on a clarity and purity it surely never possessed in real life. She was supposed to forget – she had promised herself she would – but instead she gorged on remembering, lived on it as if it were vital sustenance. She knew it would do no good, but she was lonely and couldn't help it.

It was a Friday, an afternoon in April. A blustery, uncertain day, a day like any other at Garrett Hill with its endless routines and occasional, all-too-brief moments of levity. There were floors to be swept and scrubbed, spare beds to be wiped down, sheets to be changed, dirty linen to take to the laundry, meals to be served then cleared, patients to be encouraged, cosseted or cajoled. And once a day, between lunch and tea, a short, blissful escape into the grounds for a cigarette.

On that particular day it was nearly four by the time she slipped out through the kitchen garden, a long rectangle bounded by a high brick wall. It had been a rose garden before the war – a rather poor one according to Mr Lavery – but was now divided into strips and plots. There were still a few climbers along the wall and they provided relief from the rows of cabbages, carrots, runner beans and potatoes.

Today, Mr Lavery was in the greenhouse and as she passed Jo caught the tangy scent of tomatoes through the open door. The plants almost reached the roof and they drooped, heavy with their load of fruit blushing from green to red.

"Afternoon Miss Kenyon," he called.

Jo waved a greeting, but did not stop. Garrett Hill's only gardener was inclined to wax loquacious on the subject of his tomatoes, having little other audience apart from the reluctant patients, and she was longing for a smoke.

Beyond the greenhouse a narrow arch was set in the wall, and beyond the arch was a bench, her sanctuary. Here she would sit and smoke and watch the cares of her day rise and evaporate. On a good day, when she had time, she would enjoy the view down into Calderby, but today she only had a few minutes and the weather was on the turn. It had been hot and close all day, and now storm clouds were gathering. They had a dense, crowded-in look as if they were pushing up against each other, jostling for position, and she felt disconnected and light-headed as she often did at the approach of a storm. There was a faint rumble in the distance and she smoked her cigarette quickly, ducking back under the arch at the first heavy, splashy drops of rain.

Five minutes later she was back on the ward. Sister Barnes was with a patient, bed curtains closed, and Elissa was wheeling round a tea trolley for visitors. A few of the other convalescents were playing cards. One read a paperback, and one or two had visitors and talked in hushed tones as if they were in a library.

She noticed him immediately; he was visiting his brother

114

who had lost an arm – an amputation, just above the elbow. The bed was half-way down the ward on the window side and he was sitting on a chair, turned away from her. He overflowed the chair in all directions – legs, arms, head and shoulders – creating the impression that he might burst out at any moment. She noticed how completely he listened to his brother. He was utterly still, his head tilted slightly up, and he did not even nod in acknowledgement. No-one listened like that, especially not a man.

She approached the pair silently, not wanting to break the spell. The brother smiled when he saw her. What was his name – Arthur? She felt guilty that she could not remember.

"Hello, Miss Kenyon," he said. "Where've you been hiding then?"

What did she say ? She could not recall, because at that moment, she looked at the man in the chair, and he was smiling, regarding her with the same unwavering attention that he had given his brother. She did not allow herself to return the look for very long, but in that short space she saw that he had fine, fair hair on the backs of his hands, his eyes were an unquantifiable shade of blue-grey, his boots looked in need of repair, the hair on his head was thick and reddish, springing up in rebellion against the harsh army crop. She noticed that he was a sergeant in the local regiment and his uniform was worn but well-pressed and clean. His nails were not clean.

"Meet my brother, Frannie," said Arthur Dwyer.

"Hello there," she said. "Nice to meet you."

"Nice to meet you too, miss," he said, unfolding himself from the chair and offering his hand. She knew exactly how it would feel. She knew that his hand would be warm and dry, the skin on his palms a little rough in places, the fingers thick and bony.

"Well," she said. "I hope you enjoy your visit."

She walked away before he had chance to reply, precisely because she did not want to, because she wanted to stay there and talk and look, and forget about everything else. She felt him watching her as she retreated, the heat of his eyes directed at her back. She marched straight to the sister's office and closed the door behind her.

She looked around, a little stunned. On the desk was a pile of papers – lists, patient's records, correspondence. Behind it a narrow bookcase held medical manuals, files and reference works. There was a locked cupboard containing medication. She examined her hands, red and chapped from endless soaking in soap and hot water. A working woman's hands. These hands had staunched and bound and washed and scrubbed and wiped and bandaged. She was not a naïve girl and she was not inclined to sudden romantic attractions. No, this was simply the sum of her fatigue and her loneliness. She thought of Sidney, her brother, dead for eight months, the gap he had left still new and raw.

She had a thousand and one things to do. There were the rest of the beds to be made up and three dressings to be done before the shift changed over. And Sister Barnes had asked her to begin an inventory of the linen cupboards.

There was a gentle knock on the door. "Sorry to disturb you."

She gave her best professional smile. "What can I do for you?"

"I have to be going now," he said. "But before I do, I wanted to ask you something."

116

She stilled her hands and made a point of looking him straight in the eye. Usually it either cowed or angered a man when she did this, but he simply looked back and smiled. He was leaning on the door-frame, arms crossed, and looked set to stay.

"I was wondering what time your shift ended."

"Why was that?"

"Because I wanted to wait for you. And I wanted to know how long it would be. I've only got four days and I've had one of them already."

"No time to waste then."

"I knew you'd understand."

She couldn't help laughing. If he had been all insolence she would have dismissed him. But one side of his mouth kept twitching into a smile, as if he were continually trying not to laugh at himself.

"Two hours," she said.

Later, crunching along the gravel drive towards the entrance, she tried to think of more ways to delay her departure She had spent the last two hours regretting her rashness and decided that if she procrastinated long enough he would give up and go. She'd talked at length with Hester Barnes, asked about her sick mother and her cats, then dropped in on Mr Lavery to collect the bag of tomatoes he'd promised her and listened to a long disquisition on root vegetables. She scanned the grounds, hoping and not hoping to see him. The once-manicured lawn was furrowed by the passage of motor ambulances, several of which still cluttered the smooth parabola of the drive.

Sure enough he was there, standing by one of the ambulances, sharing a cigarette with the driver. She was tempted to

117

ignore him and walk straight past just to see what he would do, but as she approached he ground out the stub of his cigarette and jogged across the gravel to intercept her.

"Hello again."

She kept walking as he fell in step beside her. She knew all the drivers were watching and she had to maintain at least a semblance of disinterest until they were out of sight. She wouldn't have put it past them to place bets on his progress.

"You see," he said. "I kept my promise."

"I wasn't aware that promises had been made."

"You didn't make any, that's true. But I did and here I am, and you're here too so we might as well walk down the hill together."

"I prefer to take the tram, Mr Dwyer."

"Let's do that then And why don't you call me Frannie?"

They passed through the hospital gates and turned the corner, and she sloughed off the weight of being Miss Kenyon for the day.

"Very well then," she sighed. "Frannie."

He grinned. "Can I call you Jo?"

"How do you know my name?"

"I have my spies."

"Do you?" She knew she should be indignant or offended, but he just made her want to laugh. "Well I wouldn't believe everything the drivers tell you."

"Then tell me what I've got wrong," he said. "I know that you're the youngest of the volunteers and the nicest. The nurses and the orderlies and the drivers all like you, but the doctors don't because you're younger than them and you've been in France. I also know that you live in Calderby, and you have a brother in the RAMC and your father was an artist who lost all his money and took up photography. Shall I go on?"

"No, that's quite enough. You certainly have a talent for finding things out."

"Oh I have lots of talents," he said.

"But not much in the way of modesty."

He gave her a sharp look, unsure whether she was joking. "No," he said, with abrupt seriousness. "Not much. But I'm sure you'll put me right there."

And just as abruptly, he broke into a loud, wheezing laugh that turned heads in the queue for the tram. She liked the way he laughed, the pure, sweet confidence of it. He had not fluffed himself up with humbug or pomposity, or hit back at her to put her in her place. That put him beyond the run of the mill in her estimation. She looked up at him and he looked back at her without guile or shame, and that was when she decided she would spend the night with him.

Not that she let on of course. She simply let him sit with her on the tram to Calderby and walk her across the canal bridge to the end of her street. And on the way she allowed him to talk her into an evening out at Godwin's, the old water mill, now a very respectable tea-room. She left him by the bridge, promising to meet him there in an hour.

She was ready in half that time, but made him wait an extra fifteen minutes just for the fun of it. She studied herself in the hall mirror, tilting her wide-brimmed straw hat so that it showed off her thick dark hair to its best advantage. She'd always thought her hair her best feature and she knew that it suited her when she wore it side-parted, dressed low across her forehead. She wore a white dress with a lilac and green print that she'd had since before the war. She liked the way the fine cotton fabric clung and draped in soft lines, so different from the starchiness of her uniform. Tonight she wanted to look as unlike a nurse as possible.

She glowered at her reflection. What was she thinking, dressing up like a simpering idiot? She should know better. She knew where this was leading, and it was not a romantic evening of hand-holding and sweet whispers. All he really wanted was to get up her skirt and she had already decided to accept those terms. She would have him, and that would be an end of it. No-one would be any the wiser. The risk was minimal; her curse had just finished. Of course there was always the risk of catching a disease, but that far she was not prepared to imagine.

Godwin's stayed open until ten on Fridays and Saturdays. Sometimes there was music of an edifying kind from a string quartet, but tonight there was only a gramophone playing sentimental songs and light operetta. The place was full of men in uniform, some with their families, some with their girls. All very polite and respectable.

As they were shown to a table, Jo noticed how many of the women, and a few of the men, looked up at Frannie as he passed. He was the sort to draw the eye. Not just his height, but a certain manner of ease that he possessed. He was not handsome in the conventional way, but there was something compelling about him and it seemed she was not the only one who thought so. She tried to work out what it was. Some combination of confidence, amiability and just the slightest hint of diffidence. He could probably get any woman he wanted if he tried, and she was likely one in a very long line. But then she wasn't supposed to be minding about that.

"Have you been here before?" she said, as they took their seats at a small corner table.

"No," he said. "It'd only just opened last time I was home, and my – and I never found a girl nice enough to take."

It was the first thing he'd said that struck her as false.

"Will you make an agreement with me Frannie?" she said.

He peeped at her from behind his menu in mock apprehension. "What's that then?"

"Can we be completely honest with each other? You said yourself, time is short. Let's not waste it with nonsense."

He gave a queer kind of smile, as if he were laughing at something secret that amused him. "Right you are then. Honest it is." He held her gaze, a provocation in his eyes. "You're an unusual woman Jo."

His eyes looked darker in the uncertain light, more definite a shade of blue. She could feel her face getting warm.

"Oh no I'm quite ordinary really. Hasn't a woman ever spoken to you like that before?"

"Honestly – No."

"Then you can't have met many nurses."

The loud, wheezing laugh issued forth, bringing curious looks from the surrounding tables. "I like it though," he said.

Now it was her turn to hide behind the menu. He had the strangest contradictory effect on her; she wanted to cringe and hide when he laughed, then the next minute when he looked at her intently, as if she were a feast and him a starving man, she wanted to throw sense and caution to the wind.

"What are you thinking about?" he said. "With that little smile on your face."

"Oh I'm just wondering what I'm doing here," she said. "I'm trying to decide if it was your subtle powers of persuasion or

121

just your barefaced cheek."

"Well faint heart never won fair maid," he said. "As the saying goes."

"You haven't won me yet."

"You are here though, aren't you? If it hadn't been for my barefaced cheek, you'd be at home on your tod and I'd be down the *Shepherd* with my pals, wasting my pay on watered beer."

The moon was up by the time they began the walk back, and it was still warm enough for a slow stroll. Though they were alone and in the dark he did not try to touch her. He had not touched her all evening. Along by the canal there were drifting swarms of midges and Jo felt them bite, burrowing into her neck where the flesh was exposed. Frannie was quiet now, although he'd been talkative enough at the mill, telling her about his army pals and his brothers.

They'd reached a stretch of thick woodland off to the left of the towpath. She knew this place – it had a certain notoriety. Is this what the evening had been leading to? She imagined him dragging her in among the shadows and could not decide whether the prospect was alarming or enticing. But he made a point of dropping behind her on the path, as if to reassure her that molestation was not on his mind.

When they reached the bridge and the steps that led up to the road, he said: "Why don't you go up alone? I'll wait here for a few minutes and have a ciggy."

"Are you trying to preserve my reputation?" she said.

He shrugged. "I'll only be a few minutes. Meet me along the road, then we can say a proper good night."

She was not sure what he meant by that, but went without demur. The canal bridge was quiet when she climbed the steps, but as she crossed into the high street there were plenty of people out walking. She didn't want to be seen waiting, so she ducked into the shadows of an alley. After what seemed like an age she saw him, walking behind a slow-moving group of men who were much the worse for drink. They hailed him and he returned the greeting. One of them fell in alongside him, stretching an arm around his shoulders. He bore it happily enough and gave the man a cigarette. They were closing in on her now and she stepped back, further into the dark. Despite herself, she felt a shiver of excitement and hopped from foot to foot. She had to admit it – a part of her liked this clandestine carrying-on.

He passed the mouth of the alley and noticed her lurking. He plunged into shadow as he approached and became just an outline in the dark. He could have been anyone. For all she knew, he was anyone. She knew him in only the slightest of ways. She backed away, wanting to run and wanting to draw him in at the same time. This was perfect. They could reach her house by the back way along this alley and no-one would see.

She said nothing, but turned her back and walked to the end of the alley, listening for his footsteps behind her. It was like a game – perhaps he would follow, perhaps he wouldn't. She took a left turn and then a sharp right, her best shoes scuffing the oily grit between the cobbles. It was even darker now, but she knew the way. She soon reached her gate. She unlatched it, left it open and crossed the paved yard to the back door. As she delved into her skirt pocket for keys she heard a creak behind her but did not look round. The latch clanged as the gate closed, then he was right behind her. She turned to look at him for the first time since the bridge.

"Now then, Jo," he said.

The moonlight spilled across the side of his head and down his arm. She could see his right hand, the fingers working against each other. The bones of his face looked severe in the grey light.

"Time to say goodnight."

She wanted him to kiss her, but there seemed to be a battle going on inside him. He clenched and unclenched his fists. Perhaps he would do the right thing after all and take his leave. She hoped not.

"Would you like to come in?"

He stopped clenching his hands. "Yes," he said. "I believe I would."

She made him tea in her tiny, curtained-off kitchen while he surveyed her sitting room, looking at the sketches and photographs on the walls. She saw her little sanctuary through his eyes; bare, cramped and meagre. She had one room with a corner kitchen and a cold-water tap, and up a narrow, winding stair in the eaves of the house, a slope-ceilinged bedroom. He probably would not be able to stand up in it. The thought of him in her bedroom reminded her of what he was doing here, and her stomach turned over. In the light, in the plain ordinariness of her room, the magic of their encounter had shrivelled and her courage with it. She could not look at him.

"It's very nice," he said, gesturing vaguely around the room. "You have it all to yourself?"

"All to myself." Her hand shook as she spooned tea into the pot. "The building belongs to my father. He bought it a few years ago to open as a photographic studio, but then the war came. He rents out the shop downstairs while I have the upstairs to myself for the duration."

He nodded. "Must be nice to have a place that's all yours."

The words that flowed so easily between them at the mill had dried up. What did she think she was doing, bringing a strange man in here? She had made a stupid mistake. What was worse, she had no idea how to get rid of him.

He cleared his throat. "I can go if you want. I know this must all be a bit –"

"No," she said, "it's all right. Stay." Stupid, stupid. As soon as he mentioned leaving she was desperate for him to stay. She must be cracked. The kettle whistled and she lifted it from the gas ring but did not pour the tea. It was a relief to turn her back on him. He crept closer, pushing open the curtain to expose her little kitchen. She kept her back turned.

"What do you want from me Jo?" he said. "Tell me." She heard the smile in his voice. "And be honest, mind."

"I'm not sure I can be."

"Shall I be honest for you then?"

"Yes. Please." She felt him approach and gripped the cold lip of the sink. She had reached her limit and sensed he wanted to push past it. The notion was terrifying and irresistible.

"Will you be shocked?"

"Quite possibly. It doesn't matter."

He placed a hand on either side of her waist, thumbs against her back, and bent to whisper in her ear. She gripped the sink harder.

"I want to stay with you. All night, if you'll let me. I know it's been only a short time, I can't help that. If you'd rather I go, I will. Just say the word."

She reached down to touch his hand, lacing her fingers in with his. He kissed back of her neck, sending an electric current down her spine.

"Do you want me then Jo?"

She twisted around, made herself look at him squarely. His eyes were dark now, dark blue, his skin flecked with pale gold hairs.

"Yes."

His eyes widened. He had been expecting rejection.

"Now what?" She'd hardly got the words out when he kissed her mouth. He lifted her so that her feet almost left the floor. She felt the softness of his mouth, his tongue, a bruising hint of hardness, as he brushed his teeth against her lower lip. She could feel his heat, even through the layers of clothes. She wrapped her arms around his neck, brushing the harsh, cropped stubble at the nape with her fingers. He released her briefly and ran his hands over her face, as if checking her for damage.

"I've been wanting to do that all day," he said.

She left the curtains open in the bedroom and did not light the lamps. He sat in the chair by her tiny fireplace, taking off his boots. She was right – he had to bend slightly to avoid the ceiling. She began to undress, concentrating on the buttons of her dress, the hooks of her girdle, the soft film of her best stockings. All the time, she was aware of him watching. He sat in the chair, bare-footed, his tunic half undone. She stripped down as far as her camisole and drawers.

"I want you to take off the rest," she said. She would show him she was not a naïve little scaredy-cat.

He patted his knee, unperturbed. "Come here, then."

She perched on his lap precariously, wrapped her arms around his neck to steady herself. He began running his hands over her breasts through the cotton of her camisole. then he undid the buttons at the front and pulled it open, the flesh of his hands on her flesh now, making her wriggle. She reached down and ran her hands over the buttons of his trousers then pushed her hand inside, struggling through the fabric of his clothes. He raised his hips and her fingers closed around flesh. She had seen plenty of naked men in her time as a nurse, but she had never touched a man like this. Even in her one brief, sweet experience of the sex act, she hadn't quite dared do anything like this. He put his mouth to her ear.

"Why don't you sit on me?"

"What do you mean? I – "

"So that I'm inside you."

She didn't realise you could do it that way. She raised herself so that he could pull off her drawers.

"Lovely. You're lovely." With a quick movement, he pulled her down. She gave a yelp of surprise. "I'm sorry, did I hurt you?"

"No," she said. "No." She wrapped her legs around him and he held her, not moving.

"Go on," he said. "Do whatever you want."

She heard a rumble outside in the distance. Thunder. She brought her legs up, and squatted over him, resting her arms on his shoulders. She remembered these fluttering feelings, she'd had those before. But this was more; there was a kind of greed in the way that her body drank in his. It had not been like that before. It had been nice, and this was not nice. He brushed the hair back from her face, examined her. She could not read his expression.

"Jo?"

"Yes?"

"I think I love you."

She laughed softly. "You hardly know me."

"I'm not just saying it to soften you up. I mean it."

She pressed against him, feeling the rough places and the smooth. Outside, the thunder was dying away and she could hear the sharp, metallic drum of rain. It was coming down hard now.

"How long have you got left?"

"Three days."

"Will you come back tomorrow night, meet me after my shift?"

"Yes, and the next night, and the night after that if you'll have me."

Chapter 12

In the morning Jo stopped off at the market in Calderby, catching the bakers early to get a loaf that might actually have some flour in it. All she could find in the way of vegetables were a few wrinkled potatoes, but she would dig up a couple of carrots from the kitchen garden at Garrett Hill, and then there were the tomatoes from Mr Lavery. She also managed to get some scrag end from the butchers, which would make a serviceable stew.

When she returned from her shift, string bag heavy with plunder, Frannie was waiting on the corner outside the tobacconist's shop. He had his pack and rifle with him and was talking to Mr Hanbury, who was just closing up for the evening. Mr Hanbury greeted her, as he always did, with a "how do" and a twitch of the cap, and Frannie winked at her behind his back. Every Saturday she bought a packet of cigarettes and a bag of mint imperials from this man, and every Saturday he would ask her how she was and call her a "fine lass," though he clearly did not approve of her smoking. What would he think if he knew? He was a chapel man, so he'd probably cut her dead or call her a harlot.

She turned the corner into the alley, leaving the yard gate unlatched just as she had done the night before. After a few minutes she heard Frannie scuffing along the cobbled alley

He squeezed through the gate with his kit bag and rifle slung. He looked all ready for the off. It came home to her then – they had no future. If he was lucky he might get another leave in a few months and she might see him again, but it would be a long wait. At best, he might survive the war, but then a long time would have passed – god only knows how long – and who knew how things would be?

"Can I have a kiss?" he said.

"Let's go in first."

It was awkward, embracing in the narrow hallway. Her string bag caught in his rifle butt and she pulled it free quickly. She had a deep abhorrence for the instruments of war, having witnessed the damage they could do to human flesh. She could not look upon a weapon of any kind without a deep, tight shudder.

He followed her up the stairs and made himself at home by the fire, taking off his boots and loosening his tunic.

"Good news," she said. "I've managed to get the next three days off."

"Can I stay?"

"That was the idea."

"How did you get time off at such short notice?."

"I lied."

"Oh Miss Kenyon! Won't you be for it if they find out?"

"They won't find out. I told them I was visiting Adam, my brother. I said that he'd got some last minute leave and I hadn't seen him in over a year. Well, at least that part of it is true. I do feel badly about it, but I don't care if it means that we can have this little time."

"I'm honoured."

"You should be."

She gave him her best pert smile, but the fizz of humour seemed to have drained from him.

"I'm sorry Jo."

"Why?"

"Because...I don't know. It's so little. I wish I could give you more."

"We'll make it enough," she said. She sat on the arm of his chair and traced the sharp line of his cheekbone with her finger. "We'll make it everything."

The stew she made was runny and a little tasteless, but he ate it without complaint. He lit a fire while she washed up, using the various odds and ends of wood she'd collected. Coal was in short supply, and she had taken to spending her days off hunting for scraps in the woods.

Chores done, she lit the gas lamps above the fire and joined him.

"I've a surprise for you," he said, rummaging in his kit bag, He pulled out a bottle of whisky like a rabbit from a hat. "Pudding."

"Are you trying to ply me with drink?" she said. "Anyone would think you had immoral designs on me."

"Anyone would be right."

He produced a small metal cup, poured a tot and offered it to her. She took a quick gulp.

"I can't afford the good stuff," he said. "So you'd best go easy."

"Now you tell me," she said, her eyes beginning to water.

She handed back the empty cup and he poured himself a larger measure and drank it straight back. He studied her for a moment, as if making up his mind about something.

"What is it?" she said.

"Nothing." He threw his arms around her, so quickly that she almost lost balance. He kissed her head, her neck, her shoulders, telling her that he was hers and that he loved her.

They stayed by the fire, sipping cup after cup of the awful whisky. Their bodies were already acquainted, but now she found herself telling him about her life. The truth unravelled from her, all of it, things she had never admitted to anyone.

She told him about her scruffy, bohemian childhood, her father and mother constantly short of money, always making do. She described their ramshackle house on the coast near Whitby, the long summers of her childhood playing among the rock pools with her brothers. How different her brothers were; Adam, curious, always smiling at the world, and Sidney, determined, taut as a bowstring. How she loved them both. How Sidney had died.

Before the war, Sidney had dreamed of becoming a doctor. He'd spent two years at night school studying biology and anatomy while working as a hospital clerk and saving money for medical school. In 1914, he'd abandoned his plans and joined the RAMC to become an ambulance driver. She knew from his letters that he'd haunted the field hospitals, watching the doctors like a hawk. He was still determined to learn medicine and for him the war was an opportunity to be in a different kind of front line. He had relished it, had seen it as his apprenticeship. The last time she'd seen him, he was full of his bright, new future in the bright, new world of medicine the war was making. He had been killed by a stray shell on the road to Amiens, driving an ambulance full of casualties.

Adam, on the other hand, had never dreamed of anything in particular, but in 1915 he too had joined the RAMC as a hospital orderly. When Jo asked him why, he merely shrugged and told her that he was not really fit for soldiering but if he had to wear a uniform he'd rather be put to work saving lives than taking them.

All this she told Frannie, and more. When he discovered that she'd spent time near the front line, a veil seemed to lift from him. He told her about his childhood in Calderby, how he had run wild on the streets with his three brothers, but at home had been ruled with a rod of iron by his father. He told her about his formative years as a petty criminal, stealing from the coal barges along the Calderby Canal, and how at fifteen years old his uncle had got him a job at Clough's Mill and forced him onto the straight and narrow. He described how he'd worked his way up, sweating through two years as a piecer before becoming a weaver. At the end of his time, he'd been in charge of half the looms in the shed, he told her proudly.

When he was eight years old he had fallen into the canal. It was only the presence of mind of his two younger brothers that saved him. They fished him out and he went home stinking and coated with slime. His mother cried and his father took a strap to him. Jo could see him in her minds eye, small and wide-eyed, wet and smeared with green, determined to be brave. He made a joke of it, but she could tell that it had frightened him badly. He told her how he still dreamed sometimes of the thick, dirty water closing over his head.

As the night deepened and the fire burned down, it became easier to say all the other things that they had not found words for. They spoke of the dead, conjuring them up, then surrendering them back to the dark. Sleep must have claimed her at some point, because she woke from a dream to find him crouched beside her, rebuilding the fire. She was curled up on the rug, a cushion beneath her head, his overcoat covering her.

"What time is it?" she said.

"I don't know. Late."

"Would you mind getting me a glass of water?"

While he was at the sink she sat up, wriggling her toes. It was only then she realised he'd taken off her boots. She could heard him rattling the cupboards and it was some time before he returned, flourishing a tray with a heavy jug she used for cooling milk alongside a little teacup. He ran two fingers over the sole of her right foot as he sat down beside her.

"That tickles."

"It was meant to." He filled the cup and handed it to her. "I couldn't find any glasses."

"It's all right." She swallowed the contents of the cup in one gulp and replaced it on the tray.

"It's just like you and me," he said. "I'm the jug, heavy and thick and clumsy, and you're the fine, delicate little cup."

She laughed at this description of herself. Her hair was coming unpinned, strands of it falling across her face. She felt anything but fine and delicate. She lay back on the rug, pulling his coat over her. He curled up next to her, his eyes catching glints from the firelight.

"Can we go to bed soon?" he said.

She let him undress her. Still sleepy from her nap, she stood motionless as he undid her collar and the back of her nurse's uniform. She did not offer to help. She submitted like a child while he did everything; pulling the sleeves down over her arms, rolling the dress over her waist until it fell to the floor. She laughed helplessly as he fumbled with the hooks of her corset and the clasps that held her heavy stockings. She even let him unpin her hair, although he managed to pull it into a complete tangle. When she was naked, he stood back and looked her over, admiring his handiwork. She did not feel embarrassed or ashamed. She felt free. The cool air on her body was like a caress and she wanted to laugh and laugh.

"What are you smiling at?" he said.

"It feels nice."

"It looks nice too, from where I'm standing."

She reached for the buttons of his tunic. "My turn now."

She tried to stop time, pretend that it did not exist. She turned her clock to the wall and decided to make a lifetime out of three days. She would stretch every moment, plumb each second to the depths. Early on the second morning, he went out to buy a loaf of bread and some cigarettes, but otherwise her meagre rooms became their whole world. They talked for hours, late into the night, and slept half the day. She tried not to sleep for too long. She didn't want to waste precious hours, but sleeping with him calmed her, his heaviness an anchor while she drifted and dreamed.

On their final night, neither of them slept. She begged him to rest, mindful of the long journey he had to make and the dangers that awaited him at the end of it, but he took no notice. All he wanted to do was watch and listen while she talked and she had the impression he was storing away every detail of her in his memory. She concocted wild schemes in which they would run away, or hide in her flat, but she kept them to herself. She knew that he would consider it an insult if she suggested them. The war pressed on her with a crushing inevitability. He was going to die and she was never going to see him again.

At sunrise on the final morning they sat at her small table under the window, eating breakfast from the last of her supplies. She was dizzy and dislocated from lack of sleep and her appetite had deserted her. She watched him mopping up the juice from fried tomatoes with a slice of bread and tried to fix every detail of form and feature in her mind.

"That was good," he said, wiping his mouth. "A good, solid breakfast."

"Frannie," she said. "We haven't long. We have to leave for the station soon."

His smile faded. He looked down at the plate. "I know," he said. "And there's still something I have to tell you."

She could not imagine what could be bothering him now, after everything they'd talked about. "What is it?"

He prodded the floor with the tip of his boot. "Jo, I wish I could make everything different. You remember when we promised to be honest with each other?"

"Yes of course."

"Well I'm trying to keep that promise. Please remember that. I should have said this right at the start, but I couldn't. I was too scared."

"I can't imagine why."

"Because you don't know."

She leaned forward, reaching for his hand. "Then why don't you tell me?"

"Oh hell."

"It'll be all right, you'll – "

"I'm married."

The room tilted.

"I have a wife. And a son and a daughter too. I'm sorry Jo."

It had never occurred to her. The one thing that she had never imagined. She held on to the edge of the table to steady herself.

"So all that time… all the things you said."

"They were true. I meant them. I love you. That's why I'm telling you now."

She stood up, pushing her chair back from the table. "But you have no right to say that you love me. You had no right to make me…"

But he hadn't made her do anything. She had decided the matter all by herself. She had taken a strange man into her house, into her bed, and this was her reward.

"So let's see," she said. "When we spoke that first night about being honest, you might have told me then, but you didn't. You didn't, because you knew that I wouldn't have let you stay."

"That's not –"

"Don't bother to deny it. It's obvious. And now you're about to leave and you've had what you wanted, and you've had an attack of conscience, so you thought you'd get it off your chest."

"It's not like that."

"Of course it's like that! Do you think I'm completely stupid?"

"I didn't have to tell you at all, did I? I could have just kept silent and gone off, pleased as punch. But I didn't. I told

137

you the truth because I didn't want to deceive you any longer. Because I love you, whatever you think. It's true, at first I did want to just... but that changed. Everything changed." He ran out of steam and stared at his empty plate, as if it might provide an answer.

"So where does your wife think you've been all this time?" .

"She doesn't care where I am. She hates me."

"I'm not surprised, if this is how you carry on."

"You must believe me, I've never done anything like this before...not like this. Kate and I, we haven't got on for a long time. Since my youngest was born. Even before that, if truth be told." He looked so downcast that she almost felt sorry for him. "I don't think she ever loved me."

She steeled herself against him; he had lied, he might be lying now. "Do you think that excuses what you've done?"

He reached for her hand and grasped it tight in his. She went limp, not fighting him. "I'll leave her for you, Jo. If you'll have me, I'll leave her. I'll separate from her."

"And what about your children?" she said.

His grip loosened and she pulled her hand away. He really had no idea what he was saying. "If you left her, you may not be allowed to see the children. Have you thought of that?"

"She couldn't stop me. She hasn't the right."

"How do you know? Are you sure?"

"I wouldn't let it happen."

She stared at him in exasperation. He was prepared to throw away everything to take up with her and he hadn't thought about it at all. He just saw what was in front of him. It tore her heart that he was prepared to give up his family for her sake, but how could she believe him? He might have said this many times to many women, only to go crawling back to his unfortunate wife. And his children – how could she break up a family like that, on a whim?

"Please leave me alone now Frannie."

"You want me to go?" She couldn't stand it, the raw edge to his voice.

"No. Just … leave me alone for a few minutes. I need to think. It's too much for me to take in all at once."

He wavered, reluctant to leave her side. "You're still coming with me to the station aren't you?"

She wanted to take him in her arms and forgive everything. Forget everything. He would make it very easy to forget.

"Why don't you wait downstairs?" she said. "Take your things. I'll meet you outside in a few minutes."

She stood at the landing window and watched him pacing up and down the narrow yard, smoking. In a little over an hour he would be gone. She might never see him again. It was so tempting to let it all go, the deceit and the betrayal, and be swept up in the feeling of the moment. The war gave her a perfect excuse to ignore the usual notions of morality. She could tell herself that she'd only just found him, and now she was about to lose him again – and it wasn't fair. A quiet, niggling voice reminded her that she had already lost him. He had lied. He was married. He would never truly be hers, war or no war. Better to end it now.

They arrived at the station with only ten minutes to spare. He would not let her see him onto the train, so they found a quiet spot under the arches. She kissed him and clung and tried to imprint every part of him into her mind; the way his hair sprung up off his forehead, the faint sprinkling of freckles

139

across his nose and cheeks, the little, half-moon scars on his hands, a legacy of his time in the mills. She pleaded silently to God, to whoever might be listening, that he be spared.

"I'll write to you," he said. "I'm not much good at letters, but I'll send you something every week, I promise. And I'll be back in a few months. We'll be together again, I promise."

"Yes, Frannie." She couldn't bring herself to reject him, not now. She hated herself for her weakness.

"I must go," he said. "If I stay any longer I won't get on the damn train at all."

"All right then, go now, quickly. Please"

"Yes that's best. Make it quick. No goodbyes." He took a step back, away from her and raised his hand in a little wave. She watched him for as long as she could, weaving his way through the crowd, but all too soon she lost him. His uniform merged with all the other uniforms and try as she might she could not find him again.

Chapter 13: April - November 1918

E lissa's father rearranged the napkin on his lap and wiped a spot of gravy from his fingers. "Meat and potato pie is all very well, Elissa, but I do miss my Sunday roast. Though I suppose it's not very patriotic of me to complain."

The family were having their traditional Sunday lunch in her conservatory, taking advantage of the bright spring weather.

"No," said Elissa, "and what's more it's pointless. Janet tried her best but there was only just enough mutton for the pie. And I know how much you dislike pork."

Her father's face lit with mischief. "Ah, so there was *pork*, was there."

Elissa played the game. "Don't tell me you would have preferred it."

"Of course not. This is very nice. Really."

They exchanged a secret smile.

"You're lucky to be getting meat at all, daddy," said Amy. "And you should be grateful that you're able to sit here and enjoy it in peace. There are a lot of people going hungry while you're complaining about your pie."

Her father's smile faded. "Yes, Amy, I know."

"And many others who have given their lives so that you can

sit here and eat your lunch in comfort."

Her mother sighed. "Yes, *thank you* Amy. Can't we get through a simple family meal without a lecture?"

"How are you getting along with terrorising the fourth form?" said Elissa, trying to change the subject. "Any budding Tennysons in your class?"

"Hardly. Though one boy wrote a rather touching poem about his brother. Do you remember Michael Denning, Elissa? He was killed last year. He's been awarded the Military Cross."

Amy snorted. "I'm sure that'll be a great consolation to his mother."

Her mother clattered down her fork. "Amy, how would you know what would or would not console a mother?"

Amy pushed her plate away, as if it were responsible for her dark mood. "At least you had the chance to become one."

Elissa winced. Her mother's face reddened. "I beg your pardon."

"Ruth –"

"No, Edward, I'm tired of minding what I say. And I'm tired of being snapped at every time I do say something. You don't have the monopoly on suffering you know, Amy."

"Oh, I'm terribly sorry, mother. Shall I pull myself together? Shall I paste a smile on my face and pretend that everything is all jolly and fine?"

"That isn't what I meant."

"Yes it is. You're tired of me being miserable. You've made that perfectly clear." Amy flung her napkin down on the table. "Well I'm terribly sorry for being an inconvenience." She stalked off into the sitting room and slammed the door.

Elissa suppressed an urge to laugh. When they were small, Amy was always throwing down her napkin at mealtimes when she hadn't been able to get her own way. It seemed she hadn't grown out of the habit.

"I'll talk to her, mummy," she said. "But first let's leave her to cool down while we finish our lunch. If it stays fine I'll take her for a walk."

Her mother began to pick at the remains of her pie. "Thank you Elissa. I must admit, I hardly know what to say to her these days. Nothing seems to bring her any comfort."

"I'll see what I can do to cheer her up."

"Poor Elissa," said her father. "Amy makes all this bother, and you sit quietly and say nothing."

"Oh there's no need to worry about me father, I'm fine."

"Are you? It's only been a few months after all."

Elissa had to remind herself then. She was a widow. Sometimes she forgot altogether, and when she was reminded there would always be a brief struggle in her mind and a little flush of guilt as she attempted to re-accommodate the memory of Harry. It had been so easy to fill her thoughts with someone else.

"My work at the hospital keeps me busy. It helps."

"Yes I suppose it must do."

It wasn't difficult to lie to her father. She knew exactly what to say; decent, worthwhile work was the cure for all ills. But she knew that he had some sort of bit between his teeth and was waiting for an opportunity to let loose an opinion. His bright blue eyes, so like Amy's, honed in on her like a hawk.

"How is Janet these days?"

"She's quite well thank-you."

"And she can manage, can she, in her reduced circumstances?"

"Her circumstances are not reduced, father. I still pay her

the same wage."

"But she has to find her own lodgings, now that she's not living in?"

Elissa knew where this was leading. It was not the first time she'd had this discussion with her father, but she knew she would have to go through it all over again.

"She's living with her daughter in Calderby," she said. "She wanted to go. I didn't force it on her."

"And this arrangement suits you, does it?"

"Perfectly. It's silly to have someone here all the time. I'm at the hospital most of the day. And Janet only began living in because Harry insisted." And now he was no longer here to insist she was going to do as she pleased.

"Ah," said her father, with weighty significance.

"He obviously had your welfare in mind," said her mother.

"And what exactly does Janet have to do with my welfare?"

"You know perfectly well." Her father leaned forward, planting his elbows on the table. "Don't pretend to be naïve Elissa. It looks odd, you living alone like this."

"I don't care how it looks."

"Well you *should* –"

"We're just concerned," interrupted her mother. "We're not criticising the way you run your household."

"I know, mummy. I could understand it if I was here all the time, but I'm not. It's absurd to carry on in the old way. In this one small part of my life, I can do as I please. I'm not harming anyone by it."

"I suppose not, dear. You must do what you think best."

Her father's bird-of-prey gaze modulated into a smile. "Good heavens Ruth, look out, or she'll turn you into a suffragette!"

"Yes daddy," said Elissa, "and I'd watch my step if I were you, because you'll be next."

She left her parents to their coffee and joined Amy at the bottom of the garden.

"Are you the official delegation come to cheer me up?"

"I wouldn't presume," said Elissa. "Though I thought you might like to go for a walk. I brought your coat."

"A walk sounds bearable. What about going up past the stepping stones? There's that rock where we used to sit, do you remember?"

"It's a bit far," said Elissa. "And it's looking a bit like rain." Why did she have to pick that particular spot? Amy always had an unerring instinct for probing her tender places, even if she didn't know what they were.

"I'd still like to go," Amy insisted. "We haven't been up there for simply ages. Must be years."

Luckily the rain came to Elissa's rescue, and before they'd had a chance to get more than a few yards down the path, a hard, sudden downpour drove them back to the house at a run. Sheltering beneath the porch, Amy's face was flushed and shining, and a smile flickered at the corners of her mouth. Once, they might have laughed together over this, giggled for hours insensibly. They had not done that for a long time.

"Elissa, I'm sorry," said Amy. "I didn't intend to spoil your lunch."

"You didn't."

"It's just that mummy and daddy never seem to understand. They think I can forget, just like that."

Amy plunged her hands deep into her coat pockets. Her pale hair was plastered to her cheeks beneath her drooping

145

hat. The smile was gone and her blue eyes were bright with tears. "It never gets any better, never. They tell me all that nonsense about time being the best healer, but it's not true. Every day is so *long*. I just want it to end so I can sleep. So I can not be awake, and not remember."

With her hair in elf-locks across her face, she looked about twelve years old. Elissa's irritation vanished and she brushed Amy's hair back, drying her face with the fabric of her gloves. "My poor, dear Amy."

"I can't stand it, Elissa. I can't. It's making me mean and old before my time. I know how badly I'm behaving but I can't help it. I'm making everyone hate me. Even you."

Elissa put her arms around her sister. "I don't hate you," she said, "but I do miss the old Amy. I used to be able to talk to you about anything. Now when I tell you something, I never know how you're going to react."

Amy sniffed. "You mean about Harry, don't you?"

"Not only that." Elissa was glad that, wrapped in her arms, her sister could not see her face.

"I know I wasn't much help to you when he died. But it just seemed so unfair."

"I suppose it must have."

"You don't know what it's like to love someone, Elissa. I mean *really* love someone. You told me yourself that you didn't love Harry."

There it was again. That blind, unerring ability to find her weak spot. "That's true."

"So you can't possibly understand."

Elissa knew that Amy did not mean to be cruel, but she had a killer's instinct for tender feelings. "I suppose not."

"John was everything to me and he was taken away from

me and I can't seem to get past that. It's like a great rock and I keep coming up against it, hurling myself at it. What am I going to do?"

"I don't know my darling, I really don't. But whatever you may think, I do understand."

Elissa was tempted to say more. She wanted to say: *you're not the only one.* She was tempted to remind Amy that she hadn't even been sure she wanted to marry the man. She remembered endless conversations after John Farrar had enlisted and proposed in the same week, when Amy had rehearsed her doubts at length. Elissa had listened patiently and advised and been ignored. But all this was lost in the myth that Amy had created since her fiancé's death two summers ago. In death he seemed to have acquired a power over her that he'd entirely lacked in life. But as usual when dealing with Amy, Elissa kept her real thoughts to herself.

"I'm sorry," said Amy again. "I know I'm being a bore."

Before Elissa could reply, her mother appeared at the door to the conservatory.

"Elissa," she said. "Someone's here to see you. We invited her to wait, I hope you don't mind. She said it was important."

"Who is it?"

"A Mrs Earnshaw."

"Did she say what it was about?

"She seemed a little upset. I didn't want to pry."

"I'll be in directly," said Elissa. Her mother disappeared into the house and she was overcome by a sudden dizziness. She could think of only one reason why Hannah Earnshaw might call on a Sunday uninvited. And why she might be upset. She steadied herself against the wall. When she saw Hannah's face, she would know. She would know without being told

"Are you all right?" said Amy. "You've gone quite pale. Who is this Earnshaw woman?" She seemed put out that her private audience with her sister had been truncated.

"She's the mother of a friend of mine. I'll explain later."

Hannah was sitting with her back to the sitting room door, nursing a cup of coffee. Her father, in his favourite armchair by the fire, looked up with relief. Nursing an upset stranger was far outside his realm of comfort.

"I'm sorry to keep you waiting, Mrs Earnshaw," said Elissa.

Hannah turned to greet her. Her mouth was tightly compressed. "Don't worry, dear. Your parents have looked after me very well. I'm sorry for interrupting your Sunday, but I thought you'd like to know."

Know what, Elissa wanted to scream.

"Hello," said Amy, who had followed her in from the kitchen. She looked from Hannah to Elissa curiously.

"Mrs Earnshaw, this is my sister Amy," she said.

"Nice to meet you," said Amy.

Please go, please go, she begged silently. She shot a beseeching glance at her mother.

"It's late," said her mother, "time we were off. Amy get your coat."

"But I've just –" said Amy.

"There's a train in about fifteen minutes if we hurry."

"You mustn't let me spoil your afternoon," said Hannah.

"Nonsense," said her father, glad to be relieved of the responsibility. "We were about to go anyway. It was very nice to meet you, Mrs Earnshaw."

In a flurry of coats and hats, Elissa bustled them into the hall.

"Not bad news I hope?" whispered her mother.

"I'm not sure to be honest. Don't worry, mummy, I'll let you know if it's anything important."

She forced herself to stand at the door and wave until they were out of sight down the hill. Returning to the sitting room, she made every step slow and deliberate. Her hands were shaking. Hannah was sitting, staring into the fire, her cold coffee abandoned on the table.

"Hannah? Please tell me, what is it?"

Hannah stood, raising her shoulders as if preparing for a blow. "I've had a letter from the War Office."

"Oh no." She wanted to block her ears.

"No." Hannah grasped her hands tight within her own. "You mustn't, Elissa. It's not what you think. Please listen. Daniel is missing. Only missing. The letter said he might have been taken prisoner. As soon as I read it, I knew that's what must have happened. I know he's not dead. I'm sure of it, in my heart." Hannah's looked full of righteous conviction, as if she was about to preach a sermon. "You must believe me."

But Elissa didn't believe her, for she knew what Hannah did not. She knew what "missing" really meant. She knew that it was a mere politeness, a code. What it really meant was that they had not yet found a body, or that there was no body left to be found. John Farrer, Amy's fiancé, had been missing for three months before he'd been finally given up for dead, and she had seen how the word "missing" had tormented her sister with false hope. There was no "missing." He was dead, and that was that.

Jo tucked the newspaper under her arm and huddled in the lee of the arch. She sucked deep on her cigarette before grinding out the dampened stub beneath her feet. The wind brought swirls of fine rain against her face and the light was fading. She had to be back on the ward in five minutes, so there was no point in delaying further.

She flicked through the paper to the pages where the long columns of dead, injured and missing marched across the paper. Her practised fingers quickly found the right column, the right section. She had never meant to make this a habit, but it had insinuated itself in her daily routine. A brief, painful exercise in self-torture.

The letters she'd never wanted had come every week and she'd read them, at first with reluctance, then increasingly with longing and relish. She had never meant to answer the letters – had sworn not to – but it seemed churlish to ignore them and a conversation had begun against all her best intentions. The letters were a secret, forbidden vice and she had not realised how necessary they were until they'd stopped.

There were only two possible reasons for this; either he had decided to give her up, or he had been killed. She prayed for the former, however painful it was to contemplate. It would be better for them both if he simply tired of her. The other possibility she could not bear to consider, but still there was the compulsion to know. Not knowing whether he lived or died was the worst.

So every day she bought a newspaper from Mr Hanbury on the corner, and folded it into her coat pocket where it lay like unexploded ordnance until her afternoon break. Every day she would scan the casualty lists for Frannie's name. Rigid dread would turn to relief when it did not appear, but the relief was always temporary. His name might be there tomorrow, or the next day. And in the absence of a letter there was no other option but to keep on looking.

This time, as her index finger scanned the columns, spots of rain smudged the ink and blurred the names. Of its own accord her finger stopped. There it was. It could not be, but it was.

Dwyer, Francis William, Sgt.

Her finger moved on to the next word.

Missing.

Nothing else. Nothing to help her. He was in limbo and so was she.

The paper fell to the ground in a sodden heap. She leant her head against the rough brick of the arch and put her hands against her head as if to squeeze the knowledge out. Knowing it might happen had not lessened the shock. The world darkened and her mind fled to a safe distance as she covered her mouth to hide the sound of her crying.

Chapter 14

Elissa shut herself in the linen store to read the note from Hannah. It was the only place where she'd been able to find any privacy. Among the pressed sheets and towels, she learned that Hannah was to receive a visitor, a friend of Daniel's home on leave. And this friend had a story to tell.

After five months, Elissa could only imagine what kind of story that might be. She knew what Hannah thought. Hannah believed, with a devotion that bordered on zealotry, that Daniel was alive and a prisoner. But there had been no news from the Red Cross or his regiment, and her second letter to him, impassioned, confessing all, had come back weeks ago, stained, creased and unopened.

The fact that no body had been found was proof enough for Hannah, but Elissa knew this probably meant he had been annihilated. She could not bear the thought of Hannah's face, listening to this man, brimful of hope as he spoke his half-truths and misbegotten words of comfort in the belief that he was doing some good.

But she went all the same, despite the headache that had been plaguing her all afternoon. The rose bush outside 82 Weir Street was still in bloom, even in September, sporting loud yellow flowers well past their prime. There was something cabbagey and dirty about them, and she wanted to pinch them off and scatter the petals on the ground. The scent of sweetness turning to rot made her nauseous. She rubbed her forehead, surprised to find it wet with perspiration.

Hannah appeared at the door before she had the chance to knock.

"I heard the gate," she said, all breezy and optimistic. "Thank you so much for coming."

Hannah's eyes shone, but she was less neat and polished than usual. There was a button missing on her blouse and a stray thread dangled, echoing an errant lock of hair that had come free from her bun.

"Thank you for asking me," said Elissa, the pleasantry sticking in her throat. But then she couldn't very well say, *actually, I didn't want to come at all.*

"We're in the back," said Hannah, leading her along the narrow hall. "I thought it would be more comfortable."

The door to the front parlour was firmly shut. Elissa imagined the piano sitting in there, locked up, the pile of music mute and dusty.

"Have you had your dinner? I can make you a sandwich."

"Please don't put yourself out. I'm really not hungry."

She followed Hannah into the small, cluttered sitting-room. She'd never been invited in here before. The young man by the fireplace stood hurriedly and a few drops of tea from his cup dripped onto his trousers.

"Elissa, this is Sergeant Fred Charnley."

The man straightened up. Elissa thought he was going to stand to attention.

"Fred, this is Elissa Church, a friend of the family."

"I'm very pleased to meet you Sergeant Charnley."

He looked at her queerly as he shook her hand. "Mrs… Church?"

He had large hands, fleshy and callused. His skin was browned by exposure to the elements but there was a softness around the edges of his face and his shorn hair stood up like fine, brown fur. He looked only part-hardened. She liked him immediately and knew that he would undoubtedly lie to Hannah.

"Fred has some news for us, don't you dear?" Hannah had discovered her escaped lock of hair and twisted it tightly around the back of her head.

"Yes I do, Mrs Earnshaw." Though this was directed at Hannah, Elissa noticed that he hadn't taken his eyes off her.

"Sit down, both of you, please."

Elissa took the seat on the far side of the fire as Hannah poured tea. The coal was banked high and glowed bright orange. It was unbearably hot – why was Hannah wasting fuel on such a warm day? She noticed that Fred Charnley was still looking at her quizzically.

"Is there something the matter Mr Charnley?"

"Oh no. It's just – I was thinking – I might have known your husband, Mrs Church."

"It's altogether probable if you were Daniel's friend. He served with my husband too. That's how we came to know each other."

"So – Lieutenant Church *was* your husband?"

"That's right."

To her surprise he began to blush, a slow creeping pinkness across the face. She wondered what Harry could possibly have said to him. They could not have been friends, after all.

"I suppose you must have been Daniel's superior officer?"

"Oh no!" He laughed and his face creased appealingly, eyes almost disappearing into folds of flesh. "I was a lance-corporal up until he was injured last year. We were short after that, and I got promoted. It was just luck."

"You're very modest, Mr Charnley. I'm sure it was more than that."

He shrugged, still blushing. He seemed so much younger than Daniel. She wondered what kind of friendship they'd had.

"Now then, Fred," said Hannah, clearly not interested in the merits of his rank, "why don't you tell Mrs Church what you were just telling me?"

Elissa's heart sank. She didn't want to hear his well-intentioned lies. "You don't have to go through it all again for me, not if you don't want to."

He frowned, clearly puzzled by her lack of enthusiasm. He had the most transparent face – one could read him like a book. So different from Daniel.

"It's no trouble Mrs Church, really. There's not much to tell. I only wanted to say..." He hesitated.

"Yes?"

"I do think he's alive. Yes, I do think so."

"You see?" said Hannah. She gripped Elissa's hand tightly. Elissa knew now why she had been invited. Her scepticism was to be vanquished by this evidence of Fred's, and any remaining doubt in Hannah's mind would likewise be erased.

"Go on, Mr Charnley," said Hannah. "Tell us the story again."

Fred leaned back in his chair and stared into the fire as he spoke. "It was early in the morning when I last saw him. That day was very foggy, and there was an attack. We were

155

expecting it, but it was much worse than we thought. We were in a right bl – a right old mess. It went on all day, and all the next day. It must have been…oh, the third day when I thought I – when I saw him. He was with a whole group of other men who'd given – who the Germans had captured. They were being led away, I don't know where. I was lucky to escape. I found an old funk hole and hid and then managed to find my way back. It took a long time. Days. They pushed us a long way back."

Elissa waited for him to continue but he sat, staring into the flames.

"So he was alive when you saw him, definitely alive?" said Hannah.

Fred dragged his attention back to the room. "Yes, Mrs Earnshaw, most definitely."

"And a prisoner?"

"As far as I could see."

"You see, Elissa, he's alive!" Hannah's expression was triumphant and her eyes glowed.

"I'm sure he'll be back, Mrs Earnshaw," he said. "Yes. I'm sure."

"Thank you Fred, you're a very dear boy. I can't tell you what it means." Hannah turned her head away. "I'm sorry," she said, pulling a handkerchief from her skirt pocket. "Sorry to be such a silly old fool."

Fred looked at Elissa helplessly.

"Hannah, it's perfectly all right. There's no need to apologise." Elissa's words felt flat and inadequate. Hannah was not an easy woman to comfort. Words of reassurance would run off her like water. They sat for a few moments in awkward silence as she wept.

"Perhaps we should go," Elissa said. "Leave you in peace."

Fred stood up, all too eager to be out of the presence of weeping. Hannah mopped her tears, palpably relieved.

"You mustn't go yet," she said. "You've only just come."

But she argued no further as Elissa rose from her chair, ignoring a fresh wave of dizziness, and Fred Charnley took a last, regretful mouthful of cake.

It was a relief to be out of the fug of heat and into the fresh air.

"Mr Charnley," said Elissa. "Would you mind terribly walking me to the station? It's only about a mile and I could do with the company."

"I'd be happy to."

He seemed such an obliging sort of character. He had the kind of open face that would appear innocent no matter how old he was. She had an urge to hold onto his arm as they walked. Partly she wanted to cling to someone for comfort, but she also felt protective of him. He had the kind of boyish looks that invited mothering. Yet this seeming innocent had experienced terrible things beyond her imagining. He had seen more of the dark truth of life than she was ever likely to know.

"Might I ask you a personal question?" she said.

There was just the slightest break in his step. "Of course."

"I'd like to know how much of what you said to Hannah back there was actually true?"

"Oh it's all true Mrs Church."

"Please be honest with me Mr Charnley. I understand that you wanted to comfort Hannah, but I want to know what really happened. Not what you imagine I'd like to hear."

157

He reached under his cap and scratched his head. His eyes shifted towards her then quickly away.

"You didn't really see him, did you?"

He stopped, stared at the ground for a moment, scuffing the pavement with his toe. He looked like a child who had been caught stealing barley sugar.

"Not exactly, no."

"I thought not."

He reached out, gripped her arm hard. "But I do think he's alive. Him and Frannie. They didn't turn up with the others and we didn't find their – I didn't lie to Mrs Earnshaw. I wouldn't do that. It's truly what I believe."

He didn't know. Just like Hannah, he had convinced himself because Daniel was his friend and it suited him to think that he was alive. Who was she to take away his hope?

"I believe you Fred," she told him. "Do you mind if I call you that?"

"Of course not."

"And you must call me Elissa."

"Oh no –"

"Yes, you must."

She stopped, overcome once more by a bout of dizziness.

"Are you quite well, Mrs Church?"

She took a deep breath and found a smile. "Elissa."

"Sorry."

"I'm fine. Just a little tired. Perhaps you wouldn't mind…?" Before he had the chance to reply, she took his arm. Her skin tingled with the warmth of the contact. They walked on in silence.

"May I ask *you* a personal question?" he said.

"Yes you may, though I can't guarantee I'll answer it."

"Well…I was wondering how you came to meet Dan. Did you know him before –?"

"I didn't meet him until after my husband was killed, if that's what you mean. It was similar to how you and I met just now. He was admitted to Garrett Hill. I work there as a volunteer and I discovered that he'd seen Harry killed. I wanted to know about it, you see. Just like –"

"Just like now."

Now it was her turn to blush. It wasn't the same at all. "Was Daniel a good friend to you, Fred?"

"Yes he was. Him and Frannie. It was the three of us, we went about together. They looked after me. Prisoners now, both of them. Nothing I could do about it. Anyway, perhaps they're best off out of it."

"Yes. You may be right about that."

The evening was not particularly cold, but a deep chill had penetrated her bones by the time they reached the station. Her teeth chattered with cold. "Which way are you going?" she said.

"Back to Raistrick. I'm staying with my sister."

"Perhaps you and your sister would like to come to my house for a visit?"

"That's very kind of you Mrs Church, but I don't think there's time."

"Please call me Elissa."

"Sorry. My leave ends the day after tomorrow and I've hardly seen Lucy – that's my sister. I said I'd spend the day with her. But thank you for asking."

"That's quite all right. It's a shame you're going so soon though."

Now she would have to say a final goodbye to him at the station and the idea of that was suddenly intolerable. They walked along the deserted platform.

"Will you write to me Fred? Let me know how you're getting on?"

She hadn't meant to say it. She scarcely knew him, but for some reason she couldn't stand not knowing what would happen to him.

"Well, if you like. I mean, I'm not that good at...are you sure?"

"Quite sure. But if you'd rather not I don't mind."

"Oh no, I'd be...I wouldn't know what to say that's all."

Perhaps she should not have asked. She had made him nervous. "Just tell me how you are, what you're doing. Everyday things."

"Yes I can do that. I'll find something to say."

"You don't have to censor things, you know. There's enough people to do that."

"Yes. You've been very nice to me, Mrs Church." He pushed his cap back and scratched at his hair. "I'm sorry I can't get used to calling you –"

"Then don't."

"It's daft isn't it? I'm just a daft-headed fool. That's what you must think."

"Oh no, Fred. I don't think that at all."

She didn't know what possessed her then. Perhaps it was a simple, basic need for human contact. Perhaps it was the place, the circumstances that reminded her. She was so cold. She wanted the warmth of another body. She just wanted to hold onto him, that was all. She stepped in close and slid her arms around his neck.

At first he stiffened and she thought she'd gone too far. But then she felt his arms wrap tight around her back. She wanted to stay like that. It felt safe.

She was quite unprepared for what happened next, but when it did happen it seemed entirely natural. He detached himself from her slightly and she could feel the softness of his cheek brushing against hers. She hadn't imagined that he would kiss her, but he did, and he tightened his hold on her more. She equally hadn't imagined that she would enjoy it, but every part of her seemed sensitised. Fever ran through her like an electric current. It was not the same, of course, not that desperate compulsion, but she could not pretend that it was unwelcome. So she just allowed him to kiss her and warm her. She could feel his heart beating. She felt him, she drank him in as he clutched her, sensing the flush of blood under his skin.

He whispered in her ear. "Elissa."

"Yes?"

"Would you come with me, down by the canal? It's dark there. And private."

At first she did not understand what he meant.

"I'm going so soon. The day after tomorrow. I might never see you again."

Then it was all too obvious. It was something she'd heard, in variation, many times; shouted from buses and trams, whispered by patients, insinuated by their visitors. She ought to be upset, outraged, but she just felt sad.

"I'm sorry Fred. I've made a mistake." She disentangled herself as gently as she could.

"I didn't mean –"

"I know what you meant."

He grasped her hand. "Please, don't be offended. It's just

161

that…you don't know. I love you. I know we've just met but I know you. I saw your –"

"There's no need for you to say those things."

"I mean it. Honestly. I saw your picture. I'm sorry, but your husband had it. He showed it to me and I knew…"

It came home to her then what she had done. He had developed an attachment to her before she'd ever met him. A schoolboy crush perhaps, and nothing to do with her as a woman, but who was she to criticise? She had used him to mop up her sadness, to fill a hole without any regard or care. She had fed on his obvious liking for her, an affection that she had neither questioned nor considered.

"Can I still write to you?" he said.

"Of course." She let her hand rest in his.

He glanced towards the tunnel and the oncoming train and wrapped her hand tight. "Can I see you again, next time?"

"Yes," she lied. She couldn't bring herself to be honest, not any more. "Next time."

By the time she got home her limbs had turned to lead and she staggered through the unlit hall into the sitting room, seized by an uncontrollable bout of shivering. Janet had banked up the fire for the evening, but she was still cold. Not bothering to remove her coat, she sank down into her favourite chair and rested her feet on the hearth. There was a crocheted blanket draped over the chair back and she pulled it down over her. The book she'd just started – *Sons and Lovers* – fell off the arm of the chair onto the floor. She loosened the stiff collar of her nurse's uniform, ripping it in her impatience.

Even with her coat on and the blanket around her she could not get warm. She leaned forward and reached for the poker, rooting ineffectually at the coals until a streak of flame licked up the chimney. Wiping her face with the back of her hand, she found it soaked with perspiration At the same time she felt a trickle of sweat run down the centre of her back.

She curled up in the chair, pulled the blanket up around her neck and fell into a burning, fitful sleep, thick with confused dreams. At times she thought that someone was sitting in the chair opposite her. She would keep trying to talk, but her mouth was dry and sticky and nothing came out. First it was Daniel, then it was Fred Charnley. They were both angry and disappointed with her, and no matter how hard she tried to explain she could not get through to them. She had a terrible sense that she had let them down.

Time blurred. Once, she drifted towards wakefulness, burning hot and drenched in sweat, to find that the fire had gone out. She threw off the blanket and tried to stand up and was struck with an attack of the shivers that make her teeth chatter. She began to cough, and a thick liquid filled her throat. She had seen this before. Four months ago at Garrett Hill this fever had cut through the men like a scythe, and some of the nurses too. One day she'd even seen a woman collapse in the street. The three-day flu they called it. Some recovered, some died. But over the summer it had subsided, and everyone thought the danger had passed.

The room seemed to have grown lighter. She was shivering again, and had a terrible thirst. Someone was shaking her.

"Mrs Church?"

She opened her eyes to see Janet looking down at her, brow creased with worry. What on earth was Janet doing here in the middle of the night? She tried to say that she was fine and just wanted to be left alone, but she could barely croak.

163

Another blanket was put over her and icy cold water was put to her lips. She gulped it down, which set off another fit of shivering.

At some point she must have got to bed, she wasn't sure how. She heard different voices around her. There was her sister Amy, her mother, then Janet again. Then a male voice she did not recognise until her mother addressed him as Doctor Brand. She hadn't been to him since she was a girl.

She itched and struggled, seared by a flaming heat, and when she tried to escape it by throwing off the covers, an icy draft made her shake so badly she thought she would come apart. She was locked in a tortured ecstasy. Her dreams were not dreams but the hauntings of angry spectres, all of whom wanted something, but would not tell her what. She lost track of day and night. Once she woke to find the gas lamp at her bedside lit. A warm, damp cloth mopped her face gently and a voice said:

"You must get well Elissa."

It was Jo. Her face was close, her dark eyes soft and kind. "Don't go away from me, my dear. Where would I be without my friend?"

Elissa was not accustomed to gentle words from women. Her sister was not inclined to it, neither was her mother. It struck her hard, right in the heart, and hot tears streaked down her face. She fumbled at the covers, her hands trapped beneath the sheets, and she panicked because was like being trapped in a winding sheet. Then Jo was gone, and she was left to struggle on alone.

CHAPTER 14

Chapter 15

Elissa's face was grey and frozen in the frail light of early morning. Jo sat on the edge of her bed, struggling to stay awake, drained by a night shift of fevers and emergencies. For days now they'd been fighting a desperate rear-guard action against the Spanish Flu, and she had known, all through the night, that Elissa would be engaged in her own battle. This was the fourth morning she had visited on her way home from Garrett Hill, so she knew that the news would be decisive, one way or another. This disease was a hasty abductor, felling its quarry within a day, killing or curing within three. She laid her warm palm over her friend's cold, clammy hands.

Elissa's eyes flickered open. Rimmed with red and dulled with fatigue, the false light of fever had departed. Jo sighed with relief, and a wave of exhaustion rolled over her. She hadn't realised how frightened she'd been.

"Jo."

"Yes, I'm here. Would you like some water?"

She poured out a glass from the jug by the bed. Elissa pulled herself upright, painfully slowly, so that she could take the glass. She downed the water in quick, ragged gulps while Jo tucked pillows behind her back.

"Were you here before? Or did I dream it?"

"I've been a few times."

Elissa tugged at her knotted hair. "How long has it been?"

"About four days. Janet found you downstairs on the floor on Saturday morning."

"I don't remember anything. I fell asleep on the chair, I think." Her face creased with misery. "That was the day I went to see Mrs Earnshaw."

Jo traced the stitching on Elissa's quilt. She wasn't sure if she should ask. She was even less sure if she wanted to know.

Elissa shuddered, and Jo pulled up the quilt to cover her shoulders.

"You're very good at this," she said, bunching the quilt under her chin. "Anyone would think you were a nurse."

Jo managed a watery smile.

"Hannah Earnshaw thinks her son is a prisoner," said Elissa. "She had one of Daniel's friends there, home on leave. He spun her some tale."

"You didn't believe him then?"

Elissa shook her head. "He admitted to me afterwards that he didn't really know one way or another. But we both know what 'missing' means, don't we?"

Jo wanted to argue with her. Although she would never tell a soul, she had not given up hope. She knew it was silly and pointless, but she was determined to keep the idea of Frannie alive branded in her mind, until she knew unequivocally that he was dead. She did not think she could carry on each day without this hope, however vain. But she did not know how to explain this to Elissa, who seemed equally fixed onto the idea of her corporal's death.

"It's over two years now since Sidney died," she said.

167

"Your brother?"

"It was very different, though. We knew within a few days. We had a telegram and a letter from his CO, and we knew exactly how he went. A shell destroyed his ambulance as he was delivering casualties to a field hospital. We even know where he's buried. Nothing about it was uncertain." She traced the intricate flowered pattern on the quilt. "But it didn't make things any easier. The pain of certainty and the torture of uncertainty are different, but one is no better than the other."

Elissa sighed, then coughed. Jo refilled the glass with water and passed it to her and noticed there were tears in her eyes.

"I'm sorry Elissa, I didn't mean to upset you."

"You didn't. But you have made me think." She smiled crookedly, without humour. "It was the same with Harry. I knew within days that he was dead, though not exactly how. I suppose certainty is more comforting if you don't actually love the person in question." She pulled up the quilt to disguise a sob.

"Oh Elissa you mustn't keep punishing yourself over that."

But Jo knew it was no good telling someone not to do something if they didn't know how to stop. So she let her friend cry in silence and stroked her hair and let fall a few tears of her own.

After a while, Elissa's sank back onto the pillows and drifted into sleep. Jo sat with her for a while, empty of thought and feeling, and let herself hover on the brink of a doze. She blinked awake when Elissa turned over and curled into a ball.

As she stood up to go, the letter that had lain forgotten in her coat pocket fell out onto the floor. She picked it up and propped it on the bedside table.

"What's that?" Elissa was watching her, wide awake suddenly.

"I'm sorry, I thought you were asleep. I found this on the hall table so I brought it up for you, then forgot about it."

Elissa reached over for the envelope and glanced at the handwriting.

"No stamp," she said.

"I think it was hand-delivered this morning."

Elissa looked closer at the writing then sat up as if she'd been stung, tearing open the envelope.

"What is it?" said Jo. She could see a few scrawled lines, obviously written in a hurry. Elissa shrugged off the covers and swung her legs over the side of the bed.

"What are you doing?"

"I have to go out."

"You can't possibly."

"I have to. Mrs Earnshaw is sick."

"So are you, Elissa. You mustn't."

"Her brother wrote this. He says that she's asking for me." Elissa tottered to her feet, leaning on Jo's arm. "I have to go to her. She may be dying."

"Well then, I'm coming with you."

The Reverend William Ashworth and his family squatted like a colony of crows in Hannah's cramped front parlour. The Reverend stood by the fire, tall and thin, fingers hooked in the pockets of his waistcoat. His wife Eleanor sat in an armchair by the fire. Two of the three daughters, who all seemed like lesser versions of their mother, faced each other at the table. The third daughter was perched on the piano stool, swinging her legs back and forth. They were all dressed in black, which seemed a little premature to Elissa. She almost pitied the

169

mighty piano, swamped by this excess of relatives.

The only member of the Ashworth family to display any enthusiasm for the visitors was the youngest, Billy, who ran about the room in the usual way of four-year-olds. He had taken to Jo immediately, wrapping his arms around her legs, holding on with a fierce determination as he looked up at her. Elissa saw Daniel in that look; the same grey eyes, the same fixed, determined expression.

They were waiting for the doctor to finish with Hannah. Elissa fought the exhaustion that had enveloped her as soon as she'd stepped out of her front door. The train journey, the tram and the climb up Weir Street had nearly finished her.

"Do you think the doctor will be much longer, Reverend Ashworth?" she said.

"Are you in a hurry, Mrs Church?"

She closed her eyes. The man had such an insinuating manner. She could see Daniel in him too, could hear him in that tone of voice, but this was a Daniel without warmth, without heart.

"No," she said, "Of course not, it's just that…" She tailed off, rubbing her forehead. It was damp and hot again, and she was afraid the fever might return.

Jo came to her rescue. "Mrs Church is recovering from the influenza herself and she's still in a delicate state. This is the first time she's been out and I'm not sure how long she'll be able to stay. Also," she added with a tight smile, "we'd hate it if you or any of your family became infected because of us."

"I hardly think that's likely," said the Reverend, ignoring Jo and addressing his remarks to Elissa. "I don't think your presence will make much difference, Mrs Church, given that we've been here every day with Hannah."

Poor Hannah, she thought.

"But I'll take you up as soon as the doctor is finished, if that is what you'd prefer."

"Thank-you. You said that Hannah had asked for me by name?"

"Yes, several times. Although it took me a while to decipher who she meant. I wasn't aware that the two of you were acquainted."

Clearly an opening for an explanation. She smiled at him sweetly and didn't give one. Billy came over and leaned his elbows on her lap.

"I've got *lots* of solders," he said.

"Soldiers?" said Elissa. "Will you show me?"

"Not *here*," he said, scornfully. "At home."

"Of course, how silly of me. Another time then."

He nodded sagely. "Have you got any?"

"No, I haven't."

"Why?"

"I'm too old for toys, I'm afraid."

"Why?"

"Now then, Billy," said his mother.

He ignored her and continued to stare at Elissa. Yes, the same eyes. She wanted to take him in her arms and hug him tight.

There was a sound from the floor above, followed by footsteps on the stairs. Elissa did not bother to conceal her relief. The Ashworths were oppressing her to the point of suffocation. Even Jo, who was usually gregarious in company, had given up the ghost and stood wan and silent behind Elissa's chair. None of the daughters had offered up a seat, and their parents did not prompt them to do so. So much for Christian charity.

The doctor stuck his head around the door. "You can go up now," he said.

This was addressed to the Reverend, but Elissa took it as her cue and struggled to her feet. Jo stepped forward to help, but Elissa dissuaded her with a quick shake of the head. She made for the stairs, ignoring the protests of her body. The Reverend followed in her wake.

"Wait a moment, Mrs Church," he said. "I'll accompany you."

"Don't worry, I know my way."

She did not look back, and thankfully he pursued her no further. On the landing, she was confronted with three closed doors. Despite what she'd said to the Reverend, she had no idea which room was Hannah's. She guessed at the furthest door, which looked like it led to the back of the house. She knocked.

"Hannah?"

There was no reply. She inched open the door and knew immediately that it was Daniel's room. She couldn't resist going in to look. The room was small, and uncluttered to the point of monkishness. There was a narrow bed against the far wall and a small table beside it with no books. In the corner, a wardrobe. By the window, a desk. On the shelf above the desk were piles of music scores and manuscript, untouched. Nothing on the desk itself apart from a lamp.

Despite herself, she lingered. The only decoration was a sheet of paper pinned to the wall over the desk She crept closer. This was her one clue, the only personal mark he had left. It was a concert handbill, the date some three years previously, and it showed a woman dancing in some kind of traditional costume. She had long plaited hair and the plaits flew in an arc as she danced.

Elissa had heard of the orchestra, knew the concert hall – they were both well known – but she had never heard of the composer or the piece. Stravinsky. *The Rite of Spring.*

She heard the rhythmic creaking of footsteps behind her on the stairs; the Reverend was in pursuit after all. Her fingers itched to take the handbill as a trophy, but she did not dare. She slipped out of the room, pulling the door closed behind her as silently as she could.

"I didn't know whether to disturb her or not," she said, as the Reverend loomed on the landing. "There was no answer when I knocked."

"Hannah is not always aware of what is going on around her, even when she is awake," he said. "I thought you'd know that from your own experience with this terrible illness, Mrs Church." He knocked on Hannah's door. "There's no point in wavering now."

What a hateful man he was. Thankfully he didn't seem to notice that she'd left the door to Daniel's room ajar.

"Hannah?" he called.

He opened the door without waiting for an answer and she followed him into the darkened room. The curtains were pulled to even though it was the middle of the day, and a gas lamp sat on the dressing table at the far end of the room, turned down low. The atmosphere was thick and hot – the sickroom smell. Hannah lay propped up on pillows in the middle of the large bed, lost in it. The covers had a twisted, disordered look, as if she had been fighting them as she fought her illness. Her hair was threaded into greasy plait, wisps of it drooping free about her face.

Elissa approached the bed. The Reverend closed the door

and stood in front of it like a sentry.

Hannah's eyelids were flickering and her hand twitched slightly. Her skin had a pronounced bluish cast. She was wearing a worn, yellowing nightdress and the shawl wrapped around her shoulders had a long pulled thread that puckered the weave. Hannah usually took such care to be neat and it distressed Elissa that she should be left like this.

"Hannah, it's Elissa Church" she said. "You asked to see me." Nothing.

"I received a note this morning, from your brother. I would have come before, but I've been ill myself, you see. A terrible thing this flu, isn't it?"

Hannah's eyes opened and she turned her head in the Elissa's direction. She tried to speak.

"Would you like a glass of water?"

Hannah moved her head slightly. Elissa looked for what she had assumed would be there – a jug of water and a glass at the bedside. She looked up at the Reverend.

"Can we have some water for her?" she said.

"Of course," he said. "I'll ask my wife to fetch some." He left the room reluctantly – clearly such banalities as water were beneath his consideration.

When he had gone, Elissa drew up a chair to the side of the bed.

"Elissa," Hannah said, trying to smile.

"Don't talk if it hurts."

Hannah shook her head. "Doesn't matter. Glad you came."

"I'm sorry I couldn't come sooner."

She shook her head again. "No need to be sorry."

"Your brother has just gone to get some water."

There was a minor convulsion in Hannah's chest that might

have been a laugh. "Sent him packing," she said.

"He'll be back in a minute. How are you feeling?" A stupid question.

"No," Hannah said in a whisper, shaking her head. She reached out with her hand and Elissa moved to sit on the edge of the bed.

"What is it?" she said. "What can I do?"

She could hear the Reverend, mounting the stairs. She was certain that Hannah had something to say to her and was equally certain that it was not meant to be shared with the Reverend Ashworth.

"I think your water is on its way," she said.

The door clanged open and the Reverend struggled through it, clearly unused to negotiating such things with a tray. Clearly unused to carrying a tray at all. Elissa took the tray from him and he did not protest. She poured a glass of water for Hannah.

"Would you like me to hold the glass for you?" she said.

Hannah nodded and Elissa sat on the edge of the bed, bringing the glass to her lips to drink. She felt the Reverend watching her and allowed herself a certain smugness. At least he could not fault her nursing skills.

"Thank you," said Hannah, after drinking most of the glass. "And thank you, William," she continued in a clearer voice, "for so kindly bringing water for me. Perhaps you would give me a few minutes alone with Mrs Church."

"Of course, sister dear. Call me if there's anything you need."

"I'll be sure to."

He left the room, closing the door behind him with exaggerated quiet.

"He's getting tired of waiting for me to die," said Hannah as soon as he'd gone. "I can scarcely credit that man is my own blood."

"Hannah –"

"Oh don't pretend you haven't noticed. I know you're not a fool." Hannah tried to pull herself up into a sitting position.

"Let me help you," said Elissa, glad of a distraction. She leant over and tucked her arm under Hannah's, raising her and rearranging the pillows behind her for support. She was still weak, and the effort made her bones ache, but Hannah weighed almost nothing.

"Is there anything else you need?"

"You're a good girl," Hannah said. "But no, there's only one thing more I need from you, and that's to listen. I have something to say. And something to ask."

"Hannah you don't have to –"

"Oh no," said Hannah. "It's not what you think. I know that you love him. You don't need to tell me that."

Elissa's throat contracted. "That's not –"

"Don't pretend you don't understand me. I could tell, you know. From the start."

She laughed again, and wheezed. Elissa refilled the glass and brought it up for her to drink. A trickle escaped as she drank and it ran down her chin onto her night-gown. Elissa wiped it up with her sleeve. She did not dare look Hannah in the eye.

"Clear as day," Hannah said.

Elissa could feel the heat rising in her face. There was no point in denying it now. *But he's dead.*

"He's alive," said Hannah.

Elissa wished that she was better at hiding her feelings. She could not bring herself to say that she knew Daniel was dead.

She could not use the truth as a bludgeon to obliterate what must be this woman's last comfort.

Hannah reached for her hand. "I know you don't believe me, but it's true. I *know* it."

"I can't be quite so certain as you, that's all."

"Don't lie to me, Elissa. Just hear me out." Her grip tightened. "I want you to promise me something. It's a lot to ask, I know, but there's no-one else, you see. No-one." She closed her eyes and coughed, struggling for breath.

"Hannah?"

"I'm all right. You see when he comes back, and he will come back, I may not be here –"

"No."

"Please don't interrupt me Elissa, or I'll never get this out."

"Sorry."

"He has no-one else, you see. Never mind them downstairs, they'll not help him. They've never wanted to know him these last fifteen years, or me." She gripped Elissa's hand again. "So there's only you. You must promise to take care of him when he comes back and finds me gone. Do what you can for him, that's all I ask."

Elissa swallowed. Her head reeled. The flu had sucked her dry and she had no stomach to fight Hannah even if she wanted to. A few months ago it would have been too much to ask, but no longer.

"Yes Hannah," she said, "I promise."

Hannah's eyes closed and she took a few rough, shuddering breaths. After a while she seemed to settle and her grip on Elissa's hand slackened. Elissa watched her as she struggled. She could see, almost tangibly, the life draining away.

She might have promised anything. It didn't matter, that

was the worst of it, because there was no chance she'd ever have to keep her word.

Chapter 16

Elissa was not sure what had drawn her to the churchyard on this of all days. Janet had shown her the newspaper early that morning – until then she had not quite believed the Armistice would actually happen. They had embraced silently, then she'd sent Janet home. Left alone in the house she could not settle, so she had braced herself against the cold with a woollen scarf and gloves and gone out to walk. She had no destination in mind, but from habit she found herself walking to the station and taking the train into Calderby.

The town was alive with celebration She felt the fevered brightness in the people all around her and plunged through it like a lead weight on a cord. There were others like her, here and there, who did not share the general mood. She spotted them easily; they were usually women alone, and she saw how they looked away and down when anyone caught their eye. They swallowed their grief, not wanting to contaminate the merriment. And there were those too who joined in the celebrations liked masked ghouls, faces wrapped in cloths or handkerchiefs against the influenza.

In the outlying streets there were houses closed in on themselves, curtains drawn against the celebrations. She passed several on Weir Street, including number 82, though it was not shut up because it's occupant was grieving. She knew the house had already been let, though it showed no sign of its new tenants. The Ashworths had not wasted any time.

She marched on, eyes front, taking the turning into Church Road, pushing herself against the steepness of the climb. She did not slacken her pace until she reached the railings that bounded the churchyard. By then she was gasping – breathlessness still plagued her almost a month after the flu.

There was a wooden bench at the side of the church, placed to give a grandstand view down towards Calderby. The graves canted steeply downhill, pinned at intervals by small, twisted yew trees. The trees leaned at a crazy angle, as if they all strained to stay upright in a constant wind.

Hannah's grave had originally been in a quiet spot near the boundary wall, but several fresh mounds had sprung up in the two weeks since Elissa had been here for the funeral. The new graves looked raw, like open wounds. The flowers left by the bereaved had been scattered by the previous night's bad weather, but some broken stalks still clung to their pots, the remains of flowers curled and brown. They looked all wrong to Elissa and she wanted to clear them away, sweep the place clean. The trees were better; they fitted the season's mood, their branches dark against the sky like veins.

The tree that sheltered Hannah's grave was perhaps the oldest in the churchyard. It was less racked than the others, having found shelter in a shallow dip. A headstone had been added since last she came. The Reverend Ashworth was nothing if not efficient.

She had not been there at the end. After her visit she had returned to her bed and slept through the night and most of the next day. She had awoken to discover that Hannah had died, left to spend her last moments on earth at the mercy of the Ashworths. All the frustrations of her illness concentrated into this one failure – it was final thing she could have done for Daniel.

Everything of him was gone now. Family, home; all trace of his life had been wiped away. At least Hannah had a grave. What would he have? At best a name somewhere, on a list or a memorial. Just one name among hundreds. Nothing to mark him out, only what she held in her memories of him, and these were transient, subject to the whims of time and inevitable fading. What was worse, she could not share these memories with anyone. She carried them alone, sealed inside. That was the cruellest thing – there was no-one left to tell.

She thought of Fred Charnley, killed less than two weeks after they'd met. She had found out a few days ago, quite by chance, reading the casualty lists in search of Daniel's name, hoping and not hoping that he would be among the confirmed dead.

She thought that here she might find peace, but the grave-yard made her angry and wretched. A thready mist of rain shrouded the side of the hill, and the church glowered at her through the damp, its red brick stained black from the weather and the years. She felt a vague, dull hatred for its ugliness, the way it seemed to frown on her with flinty disapproval. She didn't belong here. In spite of her sorrow, she was not yet ready to be walled up along with the dead. Not like so many of the women she'd seen, frozen in heart and in spirit.

The streets had quietened by the time she returned to Ludden-ridge. The endless pealing of the bells had stopped, though she could hear singing from behind the doors of a public house. Restlessness plagued her, and she could not face her empty house so she decided to make one final pilgrimage.

She picked her way slowly, concentrating hard, choosing every placement of her feet. The path was particularly bad after a night of rain and wind, and dead leaves formed a thin coating over the dark, churned undertow of mud. The mud clung to her boots and the hem of her skirt, but she didn't care.

At the bottom of the slope, she was struck by the sound of the water. The night's rain had swelled the stream and it roared in fullness like an animal. The naked trees did not absorb the sound as they did in the summer, so it struck bare rock and bare wood and was magnified. The water was opaque, churning leaf scraps and twigs, hurling on in a headlong rush. There was no clarity to it, no peace, even here.

She walked as far as the stepping stones where once she had run away from Daniel, skipping her escape from a man she would now give anything to have back. She kept going, following the path, against the flow.

It was easy to find the path up onto the rock. The brambles had retreated like everything else, brittle skeletons of themselves that broke easily under her feet. The rock was slimy with moss. Undeterred by the cold, it flourished obscenely, the only green thing amidst the black and grey. It was too wet to sit, but she sat anyway.

She could not tell if the moisture in the air was rising from the stream or falling from the sky, or a mixture of both, a dance of indeterminate mizzle. Her clothes were heavy and she felt the damp begin to penetrate the back of her neck. But she was glad that she had come and that it was different, this place that had lived so long and so intensely in her memory. It would have been worse somehow if nothing had changed.

She was not going to be misty-eyed and romantic. Brutal honesty was called for in these brutal times. She could see all the difficulties of a future with Daniel Earnshaw. He had not been an easy person, and a life with him would not have been easy. She did not like to be provoked and pushed and goaded. She had feared that sensation of walking a tightrope, but she had to admit it had been thrilling. There would have been no peace with him, but there would have been love. That, she could not deny. This is what she had lost – someone who had offered her love without reserve or condition. He had listened to her that day on the rock, and he had not judged her or moralised, or even advised. He had not wanted anything from her but what she was.

She had his letter in her pocket. His one letter, begun in the station café last spring. She took it out and rested it on her knees. In the fading light, the words blurred. The mist made the paper soft, like fabric, and the ink began to smudge and bleed. It didn't matter. She knew it by heart.

The last thing I wished was to cause you offence or hurt, but in truth, I cannot take back what I said.

It was the only thing she had left of him. Perhaps she should destroy it, rip it to shreds and scatter the pieces into the stream. That would be the final act of severance. Perhaps then she would finally be able to give him up.

She held the letter to the light, stretching it apart with both hands. It would not take much. She need only pull her hands apart a little more. The moisture in the air and the fragility of the paper would do the rest. She held it up a little higher and the last, grey remnants of daylight penetrated the thin skin of paper, setting in relief the dark, spiked scrawl of his script. A stray sentence caught her eye:

I love you, and that will never change, and if that is unpalatable or hateful to you, then so be it. I cannot be sorry.

She lowered her hands. What was she thinking? She placed the letter on her lap, blotting it carefully with her sleeve. She could not dispose of him so quickly and coldly. Just because he was gone did not mean that she could erase him from her life.

When she thought of the future she could see nothing. It was clouded and opaque, like the water. All joy and pleasure seemed to be in the past, and in the future she could see only mist and darkness. She could only fumble her way on, without mind or purpose. As the light faded she remained on the rock, clutching her letter, thinking of nothing but the roar of water and the mist of rain.

Chapter 17: December 1918

Elissa cracked open the diary, bending back the spine and flattening her hand along the first page to make it lie down. She had bought it because she liked the smell of the cover, acid and tart, and the less obvious but equally beguiling odour of new paper. It had thin, silky, ruled pages, edged with a kind of powdery red dye that came off on her hand.

She had never been one for keeping a diary, unlike Amy who had scribbled relentlessly into exercise books throughout their childhood. But after Armistice Day, up on the rock, she had been seized by a peculiar urge to record her thoughts. Not for the consumption of others, or even herself, but simply to get them out of her mind. They had become a load, building up at the edge of her awareness, demanding form and articulation. She knew that if she didn't get them out of her they would weigh her down until she was paralysed. She saw it as an exercise in drainage.

Only a few lines came at first, but soon her thoughts began to flow and her hand sped across page after page until it ached. She looked at the clock to find more than an hour had passed and she was filled with a strange, almost forgotten sense of contentment. She put down her pencil and examined the worn, pitted surface of the desk, set in relief by the lamplight. Out in the dark, rain hurled to and fro, driven by gusts of wind against the glass in a hissing, metal rhythm. She closed her eyes, enjoying it. Peace might be possible. Even happiness might be possible – in moments like these she could just about believe it. Then another, harder sound broke in on her thoughts, a harsh, knocking counterpoint to the fine pulsing of rain. Someone was at the door.

It must be a hawker or a tinker, though what they were doing out on a night like this she could not imagine. The knocking came once more, sharp now, insistent.

"Go away," she muttered, but the knocking continued. Whoever it was, they weren't going to give up. Away from her desk and the circle of lamplight she felt the night's chill, though a fire burned high in the grate. She gathered her cardigan around her as she opened the door into the hall. She turned up the gaslight and peered at the a dark form outlined against the door.

"Who is it?"

The reply was lost in the violence of the weather. The front door creaked and vibrated as she drew back the bolts. She opened the door a few inches and a gust of wind shouldered its way past her into the hall, wrenching the door out of her clutches and bringing a shower of water against her face. A drop hit her eye and she blinked. In the blur, she could not quite make out the figure standing quietly on the porch, hunched against the weather. His face was shadowed, the street lamp hitting the back of his head like a halo, the light fragmenting, split by the raindrops hurtling slantwise across her vision.

"Elissa?"

But she knew the voice. Would know it anywhere.

She opened her mouth to speak. A knot lodged in her throat, and all that came out was a hiss of breath, an exhalation that was not quite a gasp.

"Elissa. It's me."

Her hand, of its own volition, came up to her mouth.

"Can I come in?"

He stepped into the light. She stared. She couldn't help it. She was afraid to take her eyes from him in case he vanished like a ghost. She was not entirely sure he wasn't a ghost.

"Daniel." She stood aside to let him in. His army overcoat hung off him and his face was pale and shiny. He was terribly thin. "I'm so sorry. It's just such a –"

"Didn't you get my letter?"

"No. I thought you were..."

Dead. She couldn't say it. Couldn't stop staring. The rain had soaked through his coat. It trickled off the brim of his cap onto his face and thin silver tracks ran down his coat, dripping onto the floor. She was hypnotised by the hard, dead sound of water hitting the tiles. He took off his cap and pushed damp hair back off his face. It stuck up in clumps. He was in need of a shave, but somewhere recently he'd got a haircut. The sides of his head were shorn so close they looked raw.

"I wrote, from Boulogne."

"I didn't get it."

He had his kit bag with him – he must have only just arrived.

"There's something I must tell you," she said.

"If it's about my mother you needn't bother."

"You know?"

"Mrs Lord, our neighbour, kindly told me when I got to Weir Street and found no-one there. In fact, *nothing* there at all."

"Did she –" Elissa held onto the hall table. "Do you know about it, I mean how it happened?"

"The flu?"

"Yes." She wanted to go to him. She wanted to touch him, to know for certain that he was real.

"I was on my way up to farm," he said.

"Tonight? You can't possibly."

"It's the only home I have left."

"No, you must stay here."

She saw how he tried to conceal his relief. "I don't want to cause you any trouble."

"You won't." She reached out a hand to him. He flinched.

"I was just going to take your coat."

"Thank you," he said. "I will stay. Just for tonight."

"Good," she said. She felt herself steady, feet back on the ground. Tomorrow would look after itself. "Now, are you hungry? You look as though you haven't eaten in a month."

He ate the sandwiches she made him in great, wolfish bites. She asked if he'd like more, and the second batch disappeared as quickly as the first. She poured him tea, which he drank down in a few deep gulps. She sipped hers, watching him. What had given him this deep, terrifying hunger?

"Would you like something to drink?" she said. "Something stronger, I mean."

He nodded. "Thank you." He still regarded her warily, as if she were a wild animal that might turn on him and bite.

She searched the cupboard where the spirits were kept, but could find only sweet sherry. "I'm sorry, this is all I have."

"It'll do," he said.

188

She poured two small glasses and sat down at the kitchen table opposite him. This was for her as much as him – every time she looked at him she was overcome by vertigo. The sherry was sugary and thick on her tongue, but it warmed her stomach. Slowly, her limbs began to unlock.

"What happened to you?" she said. "Were you a prisoner-of-war?"

He nodded. "Not far from the front. In Belgium, at the end."

"Did they just let you go after the Armistice?"

He traced the rim of the glass with his finger. "No point in doing anything else. We had a long walk, but...I suppose it could have been worse. I was in hospital in Boulogne for a week. That's when I wrote."

"And then they let you come home? For good?"

"I have to report back in two weeks, but it's a formality. I don't think they'll want me back, do you? A used-up, half-starved infantryman." He poured another drink and refilled her glass without asking.

"Hannah always believed you were alive," she said. "She never doubted it. She was convinced you were a prisoner."

He shrugged.

"Don't you believe me?"

"Of course I do. I'm not surprised, that's all. She has – had – a way of knowing things, my mother. Intuition I suppose you'd call it. She was always that way."

"How can you be so calm about it?"

"What do you mean?"

"I didn't believe her!" She pushed away from the table. Her sherry spilled and spread in a muddy brown stain. "I didn't believe her. I thought you were dead."

"As you can see, I'm not."

189

"Don't be flippant. I thought you were *dead*. I was convinced of it. Don't you understand?"

"What do you want me to say? I can't help what you thought, Elissa." He struggled to his feet. "Perhaps it was a mistake, coming here."

"No!" Without thinking, she moved in front of the kitchen door to block his way. "You can't go."

He didn't move. His hands hung limply at his sides. He looked so pale and fragile.

"I thought you were dead." She didn't seem able to say anything else.

"I was afraid that you'd hate me," he said.

She took a step towards him. She reached out, gripped the front of his tunic. A button cut into her palm. "What possible reason could I have to hate you?"

"I don't know. I made such an unholy mess of everything. All the stupid things I said. I'm sorry, Elissa."

"You mustn't be. You're here, that's all that matters."

He reached for her then and she wrapped him tight against her, clung to him and cried and would not let him go. She clung and clung, afraid that if she let him go he would disappear. Her tears formed a wet patch on his shoulder.

"I've missed you so much," he said. "I was so afraid you wouldn't forgive me."

"Don't be silly," she said between sobs. "There's nothing to forgive."

She led him to the sitting room, where her diary still lay open on the desk in the light of the lamp. They huddled together on her broad armchair by the fire and watched the flames. They did not talk; there was no hurry, now that the most important thing had been said. There would be other times to say the other things.

His uniform smelled of camphor and though his hands were clean his nails were ragged and etched with grime. She still didn't want to let go of him. She was afraid that if she did he would vanish like a will o' the wisp. Slowly, moment by moment, in tiny adjustments, she accustomed herself to the fact of him. The fact that he was alive after all and here, in her house. The fact that she had been wrong, that she had made the logical choice, reached the rational conclusion, and she had been wrong. She had pitied Hannah, and beneath the pity there had been a grain of contempt for what she had seen as stubborn self-delusion.

She had a way of knowing things, my mother.

That, Elissa had never considered. She had never thought that there might be more to it than a mother's blind love for her son. She did not really want to consider it now.

Soon, fatigue began to overtake him. His eyes closed and she could see him struggling to stay awake. She squeezed his hand.

"There's hot water if you'd like a bath."

He looked as if he'd never heard the word before. "I don't want to be any trouble."

"You won't be. I have a boiler, you know. Come on, it'll make you feel better. I'll make up the bed in the spare room."

He followed her up the stairs, silent and obedient as a dog. While he bathed, she lit the fire in the spare room. She listened out for sounds of him moving about in the bathroom, just to make sure he was still there and alive. She had schooled herself for so long to think of him dead that she could not relinquish the idea in an instant. When he was out of sight it was as if he were floating between life and death. She feared that, as easily as he had returned, he might be taken. She couldn't help it. She found herself monitoring each sound; the gurgle of water from the bath, the sound of his bare feet on the tiles, the sound of the sink tap being turned on, then off.

She made up the bed, folding in the corners of the sheets as she'd done countless times at Garrett Hill. Smoothing down the bedspread over two thick blankets, she looked up to find him standing in the doorway, half-dressed in a grubby undershirt and ill-fitting khaki trousers. He probably had no other clothes.

"I can't quite believe I'm here," he said.

"Neither can I." She took his hand in hers. "I want you to stay with me. In my room. I don't want to be away from you, not tonight."

"Then you won't be."

When she returned from the bathroom he was already in her bed, trousers folded neatly on the armchair. She sat at the dressing table to brush out her hair. In the mirror she could see him, propped up on one elbow, watching her silently. Here they were, like a married couple, but they were almost strangers. Still there was a sense of familiarity, as if they'd done this a hundred times before. She could even imagine him saying in a husbandly kind of way: "Hurry up and come to bed Elissa."

She shrugged off her dressing gown and slipped into bed quickly, turning down the lamp. It wasn't so awkward in the dark. He reached for her immediately and she buried her head in the hollow of his shoulder. She could smell her soap on him. It was unthinkable, but here he was. It was as if he had died and some capricious spirit had unearthed him, spat him up out of the ground and sent him home. There was a strangeness in him, an otherworldliness that did indeed make him seem like a dead man revived. She had seen it in his eyes when she'd sat with him in the kitchen – a hollowness, a dark echo of the things he had seen. And he was so thin! She could feel the sharp ridges of his ribs, the edge of his pelvic bone against her arm. It shocked her to think of what he must have endured.

Had he been broken beyond repair? She would not believe it. He was no ghost. She could feel the blood pumping through the vein in his neck. He was alive, had been alive all this time. His heart had beat and the blood had flowed through his veins all these long months she had thought him gone.

Chapter 18

In the last few months Daniel had awoken in many strange places; on a cold stable floor, in a cart jolting along the road to Valenciennes, in a hospital bed, on a train and now here, in a proper bed. Not his bed.

After months of sleeping on hard ground and in stony, littered huts even a chicken coop for a while it felt like ecstasy. He could lie here forever, or simply die in his sleep, and consider himself lucky. And last night there had been a bath, a hot bath! He fancied he could still smell the traces of soap on his skin. It was Elissa's smell, the soap, and he'd lathered himself with it like a mad man.

She was lying next to him – incredible! – sound asleep, head turned away, one hand clutching the edge of the sheet. He leaned over her to look at the clock on the bedside table. It was just after five. He had slept for nearly eight hours and he felt like he could sleep for another eight. Or even eight days.

The fire had dwindled to a heap of dirty red embers. He dragged himself out of bed to revive it, shivering in the early-morning chill. Unable to find tongs or bellows, he threw on more coal with his fingers and kicked the grate to agitate the flames. As the fire responded, he wiped his hands on the front of his undershirt, then cursed himself. There were streaks of coal dust like tiger stripes along his ribs. He was not used to being clean or caring about being clean. He had forgotten how to live like a human being.

The bed called him like a siren. The warmth, the blankets, the softness, and her. How many years was it since he'd shared a bed with a woman? Not since before the war. He brushed off the dirt as best he could and slid back under the covers. Elissa did not open her eyes but folded an arm around his neck as he pressed against her. It felt so natural lying with her like this, so easy to forget that they scarcely knew each other. Was it wrong of him to throw himself on her mercy, to curl up and take shelter in her? He wanted to speak to her, tell her everything he was thinking, but he could not bear to wake her.

He could not feel his mother's death, not yet. There was simply a numbness when he thought of her. She had always been there, enduring and permanent as rock, and he had taken it for granted that she would be here when he returned, and as far into the future as he could think. He had assumed that, in this upside-down world of war, he would be the one to die first.

When she had not come to meet him at the station he'd been surprised but not worried – perhaps she hadn't been able to leave the shop or hadn't received his letter. When he found the shop shuttered and locked he was still not particularly alarmed. But when he went to Weir Street and found it dark, apprehension wormed its way through his gut. The house had not just looked empty, but abandoned.

He'd knocked at Mrs Lord's, their neighbour. Her face had been a picture. She'd looked like she'd seen a ghost – it was almost funny. He wasn't very polite to her either, firing questions: Where was his mother? Why was the house empty? Why was no-one at the shop?

She made him come inside, sat him down at her kitchen table and told him as gently as she could. Dead of the flu a month since. The shop closed down, the house let, its contents sold. All his things – clothes, music, piano. Worst of all, the piano. Uncle William had done a grand job; his mother's life and his own, neatly disposed of.

Gertrude Lord had felt sorry for him. She'd invited him to stay, wanting to make him tea and feed him, but he didn't linger. Her narrow house, so like his own, closed in on him like a coffin. He climbed the hill to the church, found his mother's grave, and sat for a long time on a bench, staring at nothing, unable to think or move.

The fading light had roused him. He needed a place to sleep. He knew that Frannie would take him in at a pinch, but he did not want to press his welcome on an overcrowded household. So he decided to go to the farm. It would at least be a roof over his head, if not much more. But when he'd got off the train at Luddenridge it was raining hard and he'd changed his mind. Desperation had made him bold.

It was light when he woke again, and Elissa had disappeared. Now that she had gone he would have to get up, leave this bed, this room, and everything would have to be ordinary again. He would have to go. He considered feigning illness, anything to be able to stay longer.

The room was full of her. He reached for her pillow and pulled it under his nose, breathing in her scent. The fire was blazing, but he tucked the eiderdown around him for extra warmth. Such heat, such luxury. The eiderdown was deep green with a pattern of vine-like plants, sprouting pink and indigo blooms. He liked the twisting pattern of the greenery, the way it knotted together in a form surely unknown to nature. Fancifully, he imagined that this knotting, this weaving together was more than just a pattern, but something that held him in place and protected him.

He heard her coming up the stairs. She opened the door quietly, holding a cup of tea. He was surprised to see her in her nurse's uniform.

"Good morning," he said. How should he behave? He was in her bed – uncharted territory in every way.

"Oh you're awake." She handed him the tea.

"I suppose I should be getting up," he said.

"No, you must stay in bed today. You need your rest. Nurse's orders."

"Am I your patient again then?"

"For now."

"Then yes, nurse, I'll obey."

"I have to go soon. I'm on duty at Garrett Hill."

He'd assumed that she would be finished with all that. She sat down on the edge of the bed. He took her hand.

"Elissa –"

"I wish I didn't have to leave you alone."

"But you must. I understand that."

"It's only for a few more days. They're closing down Garrett Hill at the end of the year. All the patients who can't go home are going somewhere more permanent."

"Poor bastards." He rubbed his forehead. "Sorry. I've not been used to minding my language of late."

She kissed him lightly on the cheek. "I've heard much worse."

"But not from me."

She looked just the same as he remembered; the soft brown eyes, the curves of her face. But there was something else, something different. The restraint he'd always felt from her, that sense of withholding and concealment, had gone. She had always been kind, but a new gentleness bloomed in her. It made him fear for her vulnerability because she had no guile, but he was awed by her too, her ability to flower in a wasteland.

"Promise me that you'll be here when I get back," she said.

"That's an easy promise to keep."

"Good. Then tonight we'll talk." She rewarded him with a brief, feather-light kiss on the mouth. "I've missed you."

"I've missed you too. I won't go off, Elissa, honestly. In fact I was just thinking that I could stay here forever." He thought that might be too much, but she did not even seem surprised.

"There's something you should know," she said. "Janet will be here soon. She comes every morning to clean. I've left her a note, telling her that you're here, and I've asked her not to do upstairs today so that you can sleep. But...I led her to think you were staying in the spare room."

"Very sensible."

She smoothed an imaginary stray hair. "Aren't I the hypocrite?"

"No, Elissa. You're simply being careful. You can't expect people to understand."

Although he was not sure that they understood either, not yet.

"There's one thing more," she said. "In the front parlour there's something that belongs to you. I want you to know that it's still yours. I want there to be something left for you.

They took everything else."

"Dear Uncle William."

"Quite."

"What is it?"

"You'll have to find out for yourself. It's a surprise."

The third time he awoke it was to the sound of a shell crashing close by, too close for comfort. He curled up by instinct, covering his head. Then, with the sheets twisted around him, the eiderdown tickling his nose, he realised where he was. Far beyond the reach of high explosives. It must have been the front door slamming shut. The mysterious Janet had come and gone while he slept.

He waited for his heart to settle. He was panting like a dog and the pillow beneath him was damp with sweat. He could see bright daylight through the crack in the curtain, and the griping in his stomach informed him that it must be at least midday.

He got up and pulled on his trousers, shivering. The fire had gone out, and the room was chilly. He crept onto the landing and stood for a minute, listening to the deep quiet of the house. He was alone, he could tell. He retrieved his kit bag from the spare bedroom and dragged it into the bathroom.

There was a scummy tide mark around the bath where he had luxuriated the previous night. He found a cloth beneath the sink and scrubbed at the greasy line. He managed to get the worst off, though the cloth ended up grey and nasty-looking. He hid it behind the sink.

After washing and shaving, he pulled a moth-eaten woollen cardigan from his kit bag. It smelled musty, but it was the only warm thing he had apart from his tunic. He would need to buy some new clothes. In fact, he would need to buy everything. Surprisingly, the absence of his possessions troubled him little. He would have liked to have something of his mother's, but no doubt he could prevail upon Uncle William to do the decent thing there.

Ablutions complete, he padded down the stairs, feeling like an interloper. He expected someone to appear at any moment, out of the hall closet perhaps, and order him off the property. He had a sense, digging his bare feet into the soft stair runner, that this all must be a dream and soon he would wake in a dark, dusty corner of the farm, water dripping onto his head from a leaky roof.

He followed his nose into the kitchen, where he could tell some sort of cooked meal awaited. Sure enough, there was a covered plate of meat pie and potatoes on top of the range. He started to shovel up the food with his fingers, then remembered where he was and picked up the knife and fork that had been left out on the kitchen table. Eating quickly was a hard habit to break. He wondered how deeply entrenched these habits had become. He couldn't imagine eating with moderation ever again.

He sucked the meat juice from his fingers, but managed to restrain himself from licking the last traces of gravy from the plate. Then he drank down two glassfuls of water from the tap, refilled the glass a third time and went back out into the hall. The grandfather clock at the bottom of the stairs informed him that it was ten past one. He must have slept for fifteen hours.

He felt strange and heavy, and realised that this was the consequence of a full stomach. He looked around at the black and white tiling of the hall floor, the pale green patterned wallpaper, the roman numerals on the grandfather clock. Everything had a sharpness that was fresh cut. He was here, really here. The constant background noise of fatigue and hunger had faded, and the battle to keep awake, keep moving, keep living was no longer a battle. The loudest thing, standing here in the hall, was the quiet. The wood-on-metal ticking of the clock divided up the silence but did not break it.

He considered the door to the front parlour, the room that held Elissa's mystery. It was standing slightly open, as if daring him to go in. He knew that it must be something from Weir Street, some souvenir she'd kept. It touched him that she'd wanted to keep something of him. Hope rose, in spite of everything. Dare he think it, that they had a future together?

He pushed open the door tentatively. On one side of the room was a deep, overstuffed armchair. Further back, against the wall, was an old-fashioned settle all heavy curls of dark wood and thick, scratchy-looking upholstery. Just to the right of the window was an upright piano. The fire had been lit, and in the alcoves on either side were tall cabinets with glass doors full of books. He looked around the room twice more before he realised what it was. The piano. His piano.

What could she possibly have wanted with it? She didn't play, and it seemed an unwieldy thing to keep for a souvenir. If he didn't know better, if she hadn't convinced him of her certainty that he was dead, he would have thought that she'd been saving it for him.

It's yours. Still yours.

He wondered what Uncle William had made her pay for it. Far more than it was worth probably. And she could afford such a grand gesture; she could afford to buy something that she didn't need and would never use. He always forgot that about her – she had money, she was comfortably off. Unlike him, who, quite literally, had nothing.

That had been his first impression of her; a woman far above him socially and not even worth contemplating. Closer acquaintance had made him forget, but it did not make it any less true – at least in the eyes of the world. Did she realise what she'd done, giving him this thing? Didn't she know that it would remind him of the gap between them, just when he did not want to be reminded?

He thought of her letter, tucked away at the bottom of his kit bag. All through his time as a prisoner he'd kept it. All those months it had been hidden, deep in the lining of his leather jerkin, and like him it had survived, crumpled, dirty and much the worse for wear. He had kept faith with her, and she had believed him dead.

He sat down on the stool and laid his hands on the closed lid of the piano, feeling the smoothness of the wood. How cold it was! The music stand had been folded up inside the top, and he stared at the leaf-pattern inlay on the front vertical. The wood warmed under his hands. He should try it, at least to see if it was in tune.

She found him slumped in the armchair in the front parlour, half-hidden at the edge of the firelight. The piano lid was closed.

"You've seen it then," she said, "your surprise?"

"I can't accept it, Elissa."

She had been expecting resistance, but not such bald, unequivocal rejection. "Why not? It's yours. It was taken from you unfairly."

"That may be so, but it's too generous a gift. You must let

me pay you for it."

"Absolutely not. And how can a gift be too generous?"

"You know very well. It's humiliating."

"So it's your pride that's the problem?"

He leaned forward in his chair. She knew that expression of old; harsh and uncompromising. "And is that a thing of mockery to you, that I might have some pride? That I might not want to accept your charity?"

She sat down on the settle, loosening her coat. He seemed a long way off.

"Don't let's quarrel," she said. "I wanted to give you something. I didn't intend to embarrass you. I did it because…"

"Yes?" he said.

She looked at the floor. "Because I wanted to show you that I loved you."

The irony of this did not escape her, the way the tables had been turned. Now she was the one offering her heart, begging for love, and she liked it not one bit.

"I have nothing to give you," he said. "How can I make you happy?"

"You don't have to *give* me anything to make me happy."

"You at least deserve to know exactly what kind of prospect I am." He was all in shadow, apart from the red glint of fire reflected in his eyes. "Half the time I can't sleep because I have nightmares. I can't bear crowds of people. Noise frightens me. Everything bloody frightens me. Sometimes I have to get away from everyone, everything. Even you."

"You need time, that's all.."

"Perhaps. But how long? How long can I continue to take from you, take all your love, tenderness and concern, and give nothing back?"

"But that's not how it is."

"How do you know? You haven't –"

"Listen to me," she said. "You think you've given me nothing. It isn't true. All this – it will pass. I know your heart is good, and the rest of you will be whole given time. I believe that, I really do. You were dead and you came back. Don't you realise what that means? Don't you understand? I won't lose you again. I won't."

The force of her conviction had lifted her to her feet. For the moment, she felt invincible.

"I believe you," he said.

She began to cry with relief. Quietly, he came to her. She felt him shaking. He had been frightened. He'd been trying to give her a way out, not realising that was the last thing she wanted.

"I love you Elissa," he said. "I never stopped. But I don't want to make you unhappy."

"You won't."

"I'm afraid that I will."

"Only if you leave me."

In the aftermath of confession, they became practical. They sat at the kitchen table and ate the remains of the meat pie and talked of the future. They allowed themselves to speak plainly.

I have no money, he said, and no prospects of any, and I won't take yours.

I don't want you to, she said, but you needn't worry about keeping me.

Marriage. They both said it. Neither could remember who

mentioned it first. They both agreed.

I don't want a church wedding, she said.

Let's keep it quiet, they agreed – and as soon as possible.

They made their plans. It was easy. For him, it was very easy. He had nothing, after all, apart from the clothes he wore and the piano.

And me, she said. Now you have me.

Chapter 19

Four days later, Daniel was strong enough to venture out. A meeting with his mother's solicitor in Calderby and a visit to Bowden's department store for clothes left him exhausted but optimistic. His financial situation was better than he'd anticipated thanks to his mother's considerable, hard won savings.

He returned to Elissa's house – he couldn't think of it as his yet – clutching several large paper parcels and a copy of his mother's will. Outside Luddenridge station, he posted a letter the solicitor had helped him write to Uncle William, explaining his inconvenient resurrection and requesting the money from the sale of her effects.

It was Elissa's last day at Garrett Hill and she wasn't due home until six, so he helped himself to a lunch of bread and jam. He sat down in the front parlour to rest for a few minutes and fell asleep for two hours. When he awoke it was almost three. Though there was only an hour of daylight left, he decided there was still time for a walk. The farm called him.

Climbing out of Luddenridge onto the Raistrick road, he found himself falling into the old marching habit, watching his feet. One foot forward, then the next. Nothing else. It had kept him going through all the endless months of moving from town to town, village to village, camp to camp.

At least he had a reasonable pair of boots now, even if they were a dead man's boots. After eight months of captivity his own had been held together by twine, the soles like Swiss cheese. He had a dead man's uniform too, and another dead man's greatcoat. They'd been given to him at the hospital in Boulogne. The remains of his own uniform had been disposed of sniffily by the nurses when he'd arrived – dirt was the only thing holding them together.

He knew he was wearing a dead man's clothes because of the musty smell and the wear and shine at cuffs and collar. No doubt they thought he wasn't worth a new uniform, the war being over. The coat was two sizes too big but at least it wasn't verminous.

He began to find his rhythm as the road curled around a large, wrinkled outcrop of rock marking the half-way point to the farm. How many miles had he covered these last months? He remembered his first walk as a captive, full of confusion, racked with hunger and fatigue.

The big, ugly Boche, his gap-toothed nemesis, who he'd been certain was about to kill him – so certain that he'd momentarily lost control of his bladder – had instead given him a big, friendly smile then struck him hard on the head with the butt of his rifle. He had awoken with a blinding headache to find Frannie dragging him onto his feet. He staggered and prepared himself for another blow, but gap-tooth and his friends had disappeared. Instead, he and Frannie were stripped of their rifles, webbing and kit-bags by a nervous-looking private who did not look old enough to shave.

They had been pointed towards a road and simply left to walk. They soon understood why; there was nowhere to run.

The Germans had advanced so far that the front line was miles behind them. On the road they found a long straggle of prisoners trudging in the same direction. They passed a clump of ramshackle tents at the roadside that turned out to be a dressing station and asked for water. A German medical officer ignored their pleas and pointed to a stretcher. He babbled at them, indicating the road and the direction they were going. It was not difficult to understand what he wanted.

What was the first town they'd walked to? Cambrai? They'd moved so many times over those long, hungry months that it was hard to keep track. He remembered the weight of the stretcher though, and its occupant, a large, sausage-shaped man with a red face. He was not badly injured, and when they stopped for a rest after an hour or two he took out a tin of pork and proceeded to eat it in front of them. They'd had nothing in two days.

"I've had enough of this," Frannie had said.

"No, don't."

He tried to hold his friend back, but Frannie was not in search of confrontation. He shuffled over to the edge of the road and began waving at each passing wagon, pointing to the stretcher. Eventually, a civilian driver with a half-empty cart took pity on them. They loaded up the stretcher case, who had by this time finished his pork, and hauled themselves into the back of the wagon. The stretcher case threw his tin away onto the road. It fell at the feet of a passing prisoner, who grabbed it and scraped out the scant remains of jelly with his fingers. Daniel turned away.

"Thanks pal," Frannie called to the driver and then rolled over onto his back. The driver spat, whistled to his horses, and with a twitch of the reins they lurched away.

Frannie was asleep in seconds, but Daniel was too paralysed with exhaustion to rest. The man on the stretcher and the driver kept up a half-hearted conversation in German until the stretcher case dozed off, snoring in great wet snuffles. At some point, Daniel must have slept too, for the next thing he remembered was entering the town.

The noise awoke him; the sound of many men concentrated in a confined space, voices amplified by the refracting surfaces of stone and brick. He sat up in the cart and looked out onto a scene both familiar and alien. The rubble, the dust, the half-fallen houses, the crowded streets – all these he knew. The columns of soldiers marching, knots of them gathered in groups, loitering, eating, urinating – all recognisable, all part of his life these last three years. Only the details were different; the insignia of rank, the shape of helmets, of weapons, the grey uniforms. The clash of voices, if one did not listen too closely, sounded familiar too. It was only individual voices piercing the general hubbub that were recognisably foreign.

By the time they reached the town square the light was failing. The driver took charge of the stretcher case and shooed them in the direction of a German officer on horseback. The officer looked at them as if they were horse manure soiling his boots and told them in perfect, if heavily accented, English to walk to the town cemetery. They would be held there for the night and "dispersed" in the morning. He pointed the way with a riding crop and looked as if he might like to beat them with it. They walked away quickly, following his directions along a narrow, cobbled side street.

"Do you know what this place reminds me of?" said Frannie.

"Can't say that I do."

"That town near Wipers, where we used to go. What was it

called? You know, just before you got your Blighty."

"Poperinghe."

"That's it. They all have such daft names don't they, these Frenchie towns."

"That was Belgium."

Frannie scratched at his ribs through his tunic. They had been deloused before they'd gone up to the support trenches – was it only four days ago? Now they were both scratching like monkeys.

"Don't you think it looks the same though?" said Frannie. "Those funny cobbles."

"All these towns have started to look the same to me."

They passed a group of German soldiers on their left, camped out with a fire going in the shattered remains of a house.

"I'm going to ask for some water," said Frannie.

Before Daniel could stop him he was off, picking his way across the broken bricks and plaster dust while the Germans watched, their conversation dying away as he approached. Daniel hesitated, cursing his own cowardice, then ran to catch up with his friend. He just hoped they were more amenable than the officer in the square.

Frannie stopped a few feet away and held out his hands to mime drinking. "Kamerad, please," he said pointing to himself and Daniel. "Water."

One of the Germans beckoned them over. These men didn't look in a much better state than they did. They were dirty and unshaven, and their uniforms were caked in mud. They too looked in need of a good meal.

The one that had beckoned them took the billy can from the fire and filled a tin cup. He handed it to Frannie, who gulped down half the cup and handed it on to Daniel to finish off. He chewed on the dregs, feeling the heat of the liquid lick at his stomach. Coffee. It was hot enough to burn his throat and tasted like roasted acorns, but he didn't care.

"Thank you, my friend," said Frannie. "Thank you."

The German nodded but did not speak. He had large, round brown eyes that seemed to float in the sunken hollows of his eye sockets.

"Come on," muttered Frannie. "Best not push our luck."

They nodded to the Germans and made their way back to the cobbled street. Daniel looked over his shoulder at the men, grim-faced in the light of their camp fire. They had resumed their conversation, the foreigners already forgotten.

It took only a few minutes to reach the cemetery, attached to a ruined church at the edge of town. The older, stone-marked graves nestled close by the church, but on all sides they were outnumbered by new wooden crosses, some crude and ramshackle, others white and neatly painted with dedications.

Daniel spotted the other prisoners immediately, sitting disconsolate amongst the graves furthest away from the church, guarded by four very young and very bored-looking Germans with rifles. He and Frannie presented themselves to one of the guards, who pointed with his rifle to the clump of prisoners. They made their way over, hardly bothering to speak to the others, who in turn hardly bothered to look up at them. Daniel lay down on the damp grass, resting his head against the hump of one of the graves, reflected on how quickly he'd lost all curiosity about life, then fell asleep.

When he awoke, the sun was bright in his eyes and Frannie had gone. He was unexpectedly panic-stricken; Frannie was the only familiar face left in his world. He looked at the grave

211

where he'd laid his head – a plain wooden cross, unpainted except for name and dates in gothic script:

Dieter Heinrich Hauptmann, 1897-1916

Poor bastard. Only nineteen. Still, he wasn't the only one and he wasn't the youngest, not by a long chalk.

It sunk in then that he was a prisoner. No longer a soldier. So many dead, yet he was still alive. He did not deserve it. He should be under the ground like Dieter Heinrich here, feeding the worms.

He almost missed the turning to the farm, so deep was he in remembering. Since reaching Boulogne he'd avoided thinking about his time as a prisoner. Finding his mother dead, finding Elissa, all that had kept his attention on the present, even if his dreams stubbornly harked back. He did not want the past to swallow him up, but forgetting was not so easy – one could not simply close one's mind to it like closing and locking a door.

The track to the farm had grown over with disuse, and his boots sank through layers of wet grass and weeds. The house too was showing signs of neglect. Another winter had done its damage, and the place was beginning to buckle under the weight of being untended for so long. The roof had lost tiles, and he didn't doubt that there would be leaks in the upstairs bedrooms. A tide of lichen was climbing the walls, almost to the window-sills. The shutters looked warped by wind and wet. The garden – well, it was a garden no more. Last summer's wild growth had died back, leaving storm-racked skeletons of all those climbing, strangling weeds that his grandmother had worked so hard to quell.

He circled the house once, then again. He stood at the front door, willing himself to go in, and noticed the rain barrel to the left of the front door, full to the brim, and coated with a thick, brown layer of scum.

Farm – that was a joke. In truth, it had not been a working farm for years. That had ended long before his grandparents died. Sheep farming had been a thin living at the best of times, especially when there was better money to be made in the mills of Calderby. He remembered his grandfather coming home from work, covered in fine trails of cotton dust from the looms. He would wash here, in this very barrel, the water left mired by a spider's web of wet cotton. Later, he would sit by the fire smoking his pipe, and Daniel would perch on gran's knee while she sang him a lullaby. He half-expected to see them there still. He imagined the smoke from the kitchen chimney and the squawking fuss of hens in the yard.

But his grandparents were long dead, and now his mother too. And this house – this house was going with them. It was sliding into ruin and he did not know if he could stop it. He was not sure he wanted to. He thought of his mother, working, striving all those years to make a better life. She'd been driven hard by this place; she had been so desperate to escape, so afraid that she would be dragged back to a life that was bleak, grey and unyielding. He had never really understood that before. He'd always come here to be happy, to be loved and cherished by his grandparents. He had not seen the harshness. The rock was close to the surface here, the soil thin and insubstantial. This was a place to visit, to admire in all its drama and grandeur. Not a place to live.

For so long he'd thought that this was where he belonged. He'd always dreamed of reawakening the house and making it a home, but he had no heart for it now. Elissa was his home,

213

not old bricks and mortar and a dead past.

He made his way across the wrecked garden and hitched himself up onto the stone wall. Perhaps he should just let the whole place go. He imagined opening up all the doors and windows, letting the air blow through. He pictured the wind eroding the walls, loosening the house's hold upon the ground until it was a shell and in time a few mossy stones half buried on the moor.

Chapter 20

Elissa paced the kitchen. She had done everything she could think of to occupy herself. She had changed out of her uniform, heated the stew that Janet had left, written her diary. Now it was dark and he had still not returned. Is this how it would be, fear waiting to ambush her every time he was gone, or was this just a temporary madness? She hoped to god it was. She could not live in a state of perpetual threat that *he would be taken from her*. But however she tried to explain it away or bully herself out of it, the fear remained. She reasoned with herself; he had been here – the brown paper parcels in the hall reassured her of that – and it was not so very late. It just seemed so because of the dark.

She stepped out onto the back porch, hoping that the cold, fresh air might clear her head of dark imaginings. The light from the kitchen extended in a semi-circle, petering out half-way across the lawn. There was no moon and the end of the garden was thick, black dark. She heard a sharp snap like a breaking twig, then the rhythmic rasp of footsteps on the path. A shadow solidified out of the night and her fear dropped away like a shredded veil.

"Where have you *been?*" she said.

He stepped up onto the porch, wrapped her in the rough dampness of his coat and kissed her on face and hair and mouth. There was something different about him. He had more substance, as if he had acquired weight and density in the course of the day. She felt, in a way she hadn't since that day last spring, the electric charge of his presence.

"I'm sorry I'm late," he said. "I took a walk up to the farm and lost track of the time."

"Well I hope you've managed to acquire an appetite on your walk."

"Lead me to the table. I could eat a horse."

As they ate dinner and he told her about his day – the visit to the solicitor that had been more productive than expected, the walk to the farm, the state the farm was in – she could not shake off a certain nervousness. At first she thought it was an after-effect of the fear, but as the evening wore on she began to realise that it was more. He was getting better. His skin had a healthy pinkness from his afternoon in the open air, and the benefits of the last days of sleep and good food were beginning to tell. He was not an invalid anymore. If he continued to share her bed, he might want to do more than sleep, and she would not mind if he did. How could she let him know?

After dinner he wanted to play the piano for her. She followed him into the front parlour and lit the fire while he leafed through the pile of music and selected a thin, tattered book of manuscript.

"I haven't played this in years."

She pulled her chair up to the fire in anticipation. He adjusted the height of the piano stool, adjusted it again, then fiddled with the music on the stand. He laid his hands on the keys, lifted them again, hesitating. She watched him and said nothing, remembering the first time he'd played for her, almost a year ago. It seemed to be necessary, this procrastination. She knew that for him, playing was like launching himself out into space with no prospect of a safe landing, or any landing at all. She knew that when he looked down at his hands on the keys, he saw an abyss.

When he began to play, it was not what she'd expected. The melody was pretty, but there was a subtle undercurrent of melancholy and she found it oppressive, like a dark mood that would not lift. She would never admit it to him, but she was glad when it ended. He sat silent, flexing his fingers. The darkness of the music had seeped into him and he was somewhere else, far away. She didn't know what to say.

"That was pretty abysmal," he said at last.

"It sounded perfectly fine to me," she said. "But sad. What was it?"

"Chopin," he said, closing the piano lid. "The C Minor nocturne. It's always been a favourite of mine but I never could play it worth a damn."

He came to sit at her feet by the fire, leaning his head on her knee. She brushed her fingertips through his hair.

"Why on earth did you give up?" she said. "You never did tell me, not really."

He sighed and shifted his weight. "It's difficult to explain."

"If you'd rather not –"

"No it's all right. You should know." He fidgeted again, pulling away from her and turning around so that she could see his face. "It's just – I feel ashamed of it now. It seems so petty."

"I can't imagine you being petty."

He curled his arms around his knees. "Oh I was," he said. "Believe me. You wouldn't have liked me then, Elissa." He looked like a little boy. Like his nephew, Billy.

"Why?"

"I had a very great opinion of myself. I thought I was going to set the world alight with my divine musical gift. A few months at the academy cured me of that."

"What happened?"

"It turned out that my so-called gift was actually quite humdrum. There were a lot of other men who were as talented as me, and a few who were a damn sight more talented than I'll ever be. I saw real genius there, Elissa, and it made me realise how far I was from having it."

Although he was turned towards her, he could not meet her eye. The memory still burned him, she could tell. "Is that why you left?"

"Not immediately. There was a particular friend of mine, Robert. We used to share a practice room. He was brilliant, simply brilliant. I've never heard playing like it, before or since." He smiled at the thought, drumming his fingers, as if they contained the memory of his friend's playing. "He was a good friend to me too. He talked me out of leaving that first year. But then *he* left. As soon as the war started, he volunteered. I tried to persuade him not to, in much the same spirit as he'd persuaded me to stay, but he wouldn't listen. A year later, he was sent to the front and within three days he'd got himself killed. Stupidly, pointlessly. That's when I left."

"I don't understand."

"I left because I enlisted."

"Why?"

"I had to. It was unfair that he'd been so brilliant and he was

218

dead, and here I was plodding along, mediocre and alive. I suppose in some perverse way I was trying to atone."

"Did you think you were offering yourself in his place as a kind of sacrifice?"

He gave her a searching look. "It sounds insane, doesn't it?"

"No," she said. "I can see why you did it. We've all done insane things, haven't we, these last few years?"

He gave her a small, secret smile. "Yes. But some of them I don't regret."

She hoped that he might embrace her then, kiss her like he had earlier, but instead after a short interval he said:

"I'm a little tired. I think I might go up take a bath if you don't mind."

She made sure she was tucked up in bed by the time he came out of the bathroom. He creaked along the landing and she waited for the tentative knock at her bedroom door.

"Elissa? Can I come in?"

"Of course."

He pushed open the door and hovered on the threshold. He was wearing a dark-blue dressing-gown and pale striped pyjamas.

"Those look nice," she said. "Are they new?"

"Yes, but I didn't come for your opinion on my night-clothes."

"Then why did you?"

He took a couple of hesitant steps into the room. "Is it all right if I stay with you?"

"Yes, of course."

He took off the dressing gown, flung it over the end of the bed, and slipped under the covers. He did not gather her up into his arms as he usually did but lay on his back, staring at the ceiling.

"What's the matter?" she said, knowing full well.

He turned over to face her. "The thing is, Elissa –" He cleared his throat. "I want to –"

"Yes," she said.

He blinked. "I'll understand, if you'd rather wait."

"I don't want to wait."

"It's just that, if you do, I think I should start sleeping in the other room."

"I said I don't want to wait."

"Yes you did say that, didn't you."

Still he hesitated. She wondered about him. Surely he must have been with a woman before? If he hadn't, it would be the blind leading the blind. She slid across the cold sheets until she could feel the warmth of his body. "Are *you* sure that you don't want to wait?"

He moved his hands over the thin cotton of her night-gown, travelling from her hip bone upwards to the folds beneath her breasts. "Oh yes," he said. "I'm sure."

Possessed by a sudden boldness, she pulled her night-gown up over her head and threw it on the floor. He did nothing, just looked. She wriggled her toes and blushed, feeling exposed. When he finally reached for her she slid her hands beneath his pyjamas, feeling the smooth skin of his back, nicked by small scars from the shrapnel that had felled him over a year ago. His ribs still protruded and the edges of his shoulder blades were sharp beneath his skin. His breathing quickened and he leaned away from her to strip off his pyjamas with neat efficiency. She wanted to survey him like he had done with her, but didn't quite dare. Not that the male anatomy was such a mystery to her. Not after three years of marriage and four years working in hospitals (the latter being more informative in many respects). She was still a little shy of him, that was all.

Clothes disposed of, he seemed in no particular hurry. He began kissing her neck, her breasts, her stomach, making her helpless with a kind of liquid frustration. When she couldn't stand it any more she pulled him close and wrapped her legs around him. He raised himself on his elbows so that he could look at her. She looked back at him and begged him to delay no longer. He kept whispering to her as he made love to her, endearments and obscenities all mixed up together. It surprised her, shocked her a little, but she liked it. She liked all of it. She strained and twisted against him and he pressed his cheek against hers and made a low, guttural sound – that, she knew. At least that much was familiar. She felt his weight sink onto her as he relaxed and she stroked his hair. It had been so lovely. She just wished it had lasted longer.

"Sorry," he muttered into her breast. "Sorry. I couldn't stop." He kissed her neck. "It'll get better, I promise. It's been a long time."

She was not sure what he meant and he saw it.

"You didn't – you know," he said. "Finish."

She still did not know what he meant, then dimly she realised. "Oh, that doesn't matter." She felt ashamed of her ignorance and angry with him for knowing more about it than her. He smiled at her, eyebrows raised, looking horribly smug. Then he turned on his side towards her, pulled back the covers and began tracing her skin lightly with his fingers, dipping down around the curve of her hips and between her legs. She looked away, outraged, and wondered how he knew to do these things, touch her like this. There must have been others, that was clear. It seemed more intimate, strangely, to have his fingers there than having him inside her. She could not prevent the response of her body, her movements against his fingers, the inarticulate sounds she made.

It took a long time. She tensed, relaxed, struggled. She wanted him to stop. She never wanted him to stop. At the end, she grabbed his hair and pulled it as he kissed her gently. She thought she might kill him. She had not bargained for this; she had imagined herself apart, enjoying his enjoyment but essentially an observer. She hid her face in the hollow of his neck..

"Doesn't matter, eh?" he whispered.

"Stop it," she said, wanting to kill him all over again.

"Never," he said.

Chapter 21

Down at the far end of the high street, across the railway bridge at the lowest part of the town, lay an ugly conglomeration of cramped streets huddled around the canal. This was the dirty, machine-driven heart of Calderby, brown and intractable as the stones on the hillside. It contained mostly cotton mills, but there were a few of the old woollen mills too, and recently someone had opened a slipper factory.

Surrounding these engines of industry were narrow, dirty houses in narrow, dirty streets spreading out like a stain. Nothing had changed in the many years since Daniel had last walked these streets. That had been well before the war, when he'd visited one of his mother's more recalcitrant customers in an attempt to collect money long owed. It had not been a pretty experience. He had been threatened by the woman's older brother and sent off with a curse and a cuff about the head. At the time he had been mortified with embarrassment. Now he looked back on the episode with something like nostalgia. He almost welcomed the bitter smell of smoke and coal, and the fine, black dust that coated every surface.

He found Frannie's house in one of the better streets near the canal. The terrace was no less narrow or mean than the others, but it opened out onto the canal path, which afforded at least the illusion of escape, and there was some pride of place in the scrubbed doorsteps and meagre flower-pots decorating the window-sills.

Frannie answered the door himself, a dirty-faced little girl in his arms.

"You found it then?" he said.

"Of course."

"Well I expect you'd better come in."

He followed Frannie into the gloomy hall and was assailed by the competing smells of fried fish and carbolic soap. He almost fell over the solid, redheaded boy that darted past him.

"Jack!" The voice rang out like the crack of a rifle. "Come here!"

As if he was being wound in by an invisible thread, the boy hunched his shoulders and turned back towards the kitchen.

"What did I tell you about running about in the house?" A small, indescribably fierce woman appeared in the kitchen doorway.

"Sorry mum," said Jack.

When she saw Daniel, the woman forced her grimace into a smile. She had dark hair, pulled back tight in a bun, bright blue eyes and high cheekbones. She might have been beautiful, but her face was wrenched out of true by a narrow, bitter frown.

"I'm sorry about that, Mr Earnshaw," she said. "It is Mr Earnshaw, isn't it?"

"This is my wife Kate," said Frannie, reaching in his pocket for a handkerchief to wipe the trail of drool from his daughter's mouth. "And this is Evie," he said, holding his daughter's elbow and waving her hand.

"How do you do," said Kate Dwyer.

"It's very nice to meet you," he said. "And you too Evie." He smiled at the little girl, who promptly burst into tears. He clearly had not lost his Jonah's touch with children. Frannie carried her into the kitchen, making soothing noises into her ear. Kate Dwyer looked him up and down as if assessing his net worth.

"Well, you've better manners than my husband, I'll say that for you. Would you like some tea?"

"If it's no trouble."

"No trouble at all." She beckoned him through. "Jack, go and sit by the window." The boy, who had been watching the exchange between his mother and the strange adult with fascination, obeyed with a pout. He was about five and the image of his father.

Daniel was placed at a scrubbed table next to Frannie, while Kate Dwyer moved about the kitchen making tea. He watched his friend, dandling Evie on his knee. Frannie had gained weight and on the surface looked well, but somehow he was diminished. Daniel couldn't quite put his finger on it, but there was an absence in his eyes, as if his mind and spirit were somewhere else, far away.

Kate leaned over and said to him quietly: "Can't you shift yourself and get some cups for our guest?"

Frannie put down his daughter and went out of the room without answering her. An awkward silence ensued as Kate Dwyer stood with her back turned, watching the kettle on the range. It gave Daniel an inexplicable chill. Something was wrong here.

"And what will you do with yourself," Kate said to him, pouring water from the kettle into a pot, "now that the war's over?"

Daniel hesitated. This was the moment to tell them about the wedding – after all, it was why he'd come – but he wanted to give that moment to Frannie alone.

"Well," he said. "I was studying music before the war, Mrs Dwyer, and I intend to go back to it."

"Please call me Kate."

"And I'll be doing some teaching as well, Kate." He didn't want to make himself sound too much like the idle rich.

"Very nice," she said. "A nice plan."

Frannie reappeared with willow-patterned cups and saucers and Kate deliberately raised her voice.

"It's good to have something planned, isn't it Daniel? It's no good coming back from war, is it, and expecting things to be provided for you on a plate? A man needs to work, don't you think, or what good is he?"

Daniel looked over at Frannie, who remained silent, staring at the floor. This was not the Frannie he knew.

"Well," he said carefully. "I've been lucky in many ways. Apart from my mother –"

"I was sorry to hear about your mother," said Frannie, abruptly.

"Thank-you."

"Yes," said Kate. "A terrible business isn't it, this flu? Terrible. It's killed five people in our street." She laid the teapot on the table with a thud. "When you think about it war seems like child's play in comparison."

Daniel could not trust himself to reply.

"Now," she said. "How would you like your tea?"

Frannie stood up abruptly and disappeared from the kitchen without a word. Daniel hid his embarrassment by drinking his tea, which was strong and bitter. Frannie re-emerged a minute or two later in coat, scarf and cap, ready to go.

"Let's be having you then," he said to Daniel, and walked off towards the front door without looking back. Daniel was compelled to follow, abandoning Kate and his cup of tea with a shrug. He wasn't particularly sorry to go. Kate said goodbye to him civilly enough, though he could feel the heat of her fury.

The moment the front door closed behind them, Frannie pulled out his cigarettes and grinned. Just for a moment the old Frannie was back.

"*The Shepherd*," he said. "Yes, I think that's our best bet."

Squatting on a gloomy street corner surrounded by warehouses, *The Shepherd* public house was a beacon of light and warmth in a forlorn neighbourhood. The place was usually frequented by cotton weavers, but at this early hour it was nearly empty. The public bar comprised a few crude wooden benches and tables arranged in rows, with two lumpy upholstered chairs next to a soot-blackened stove. The stone-flagged floor was uneven and uncarpeted.

Daniel insisted on buying the first drinks. He ordered two bottles of pale ale, though he hated the stuff, and two large whiskies. That would save Frannie from having to part with his money too soon.

"I've something to celebrate," he said, by way of explanation.

Frannie drank back half the ale in one gulp. "Go on then," he said. "I'm all ears."

Daniel decided there was no point in mincing his words. "I'm getting married."

Frannie almost choked on his second mouthful. "You're – Well, you're a dark horse aren't you? Who's the lucky girl?"

"You don't know her."

"I know I don't bloody know her but who is she?"

"Her name's Elissa."

"Well, you're a lucky man. Congratulations." He held out his hand. Daniel tried to ignore the slight tremor as he gripped it in his own.

"Thank you."

Frannie shook his head. "Well well. How long's this been going on then?"

"I met her about a year ago while I was in hospital."

Frannie slapped the table and the ale bottles danced precariously close to the edge. "I knew it! I knew you had something brewing then. So she waited for you did she?"

"She did."

Frannie swallowed the rest of his ale. "Now then," he said reflectively. "You must have been building up to this for a while. You must have been thinking about her while we were prisoners. Why didn't you tell me? I thought we were pals."

"I didn't tell you because I wasn't sure how things stood. We'd known each other quite a short time and…well, I've only just asked her. It's all been very unexpected. You're the first person to know."

That mollified him, though not for long. "So why didn't you bring her along with you? I'd like to meet her, your intended."

He knew what Frannie was thinking, that he was ashamed to bring his fiancée down to Canal Bank.

"I would have," he said, "but she's gone to see her parents today. She's breaking the news to them too."

"Doing it all in one fell swoop, eh?"

"That's right. Anyway, you're invited to the wedding. You and Kate."

"Wild horses wouldn't keep me away, old pal. When's it to be?"

"Two weeks' time. After Christmas, at the registry office. I'd like you to be best man of course."

"Very kind of you to ask, old pal. Very kind. I'm honoured."

Daniel knew that this would please him. In fact he looked quite overcome, fixing his gaze on the sawdusty floor with brimming eyes. Daniel could not put his finger on it, but his friend was different, the old manner a cover now for something else. It was as if he were a shell, an automaton making the movements and saying the things that the real Frannie would say, but with no heart. He wondered how it had happened. Was it coming home, finding things the same, but unalterably different?

Frannie turned his attention to the whisky. "So how did you meet her?" he said.

"She was a volunteer at the convalescent hospital."

"Not Garrett Hill?"

"You know it?"

Frannie rubbed the back of his neck. "My brother was there for a while. Does she have a name, your intended?"

Here it was, the question that Daniel had been dreading. "Elissa Church."

He could see his friend's mind turning, remembering. "Church... bloody hell, no relation to –"

"Lieutenant Church. Yes. She's his widow."

Frannie stared at him. "Well, I'm speechless. Bloody speechless."

"Evidently not."

Frannie laughed – genuinely this time – and lifted his glass in a mocking toast. "Well you're full of surprises aren't you?

Mr bloody Church's bloody widow! How the hell did you manage that?"

"I didn't *manage* it. It just happened. She asked me about him one day, when I was in hospital, and we started to talk. She'd found out that I was there when he was killed."

"And so you mopped up her tears did you? You sneaky bastard."

Daniel sipped his light ale. "It wasn't like that."

"Oh no, I'm sure. Well, I hope you'll be very happy together."

"Thank you."

"There's nothing like marriage, you know."

"So I hear."

"It gives a man," Frannie spread his hand over the table top, "stability. That's it. Someone to take care of. Then there's children, as well." He stopped. His hand, which had been resting flat and still on the table, began to tremble. He stared into space, his eye fixed on something over Daniel's shoulder. Daniel could not help but turn round, but there was nothing out of the ordinary; the pub was still almost empty. He turned back to Frannie, who was rubbing his eyes. Initially pleased to be spared a homily on the delights of marriage, he watched his friend and did not know what to say.

Frannie gulped the rest of his whisky and said: "Do you remember George Fisher?"

"The thief? How could I forget?"

"I saw him the other day."

"Where?"

"Outside Clough Mill. Got a job there, the bastard. Said hello to me, cool as cucumber. Called me pal."

"What did you do?"

"I told him to sling his hook – well I was a bit less polite than that."

"Christ. Wouldn't you know he'd still be alive?"

Frannie played with his empty glass. "His sort always end up still alive."

"What did he do when you said – what you said?"

"I didn't stay long enough to find out. If I'd have stopped, I think I would have killed the little cunt." He leaned back from the table and clasped his hands together between his legs, as if restraining his murderous impulses.

He had, in fact, almost killed George Fisher once before.

It had been over rations. Everything had always been over rations. A quarter of a loaf a day – dark, heavy bread that tasted like it had been baked from coal – and a bowl of thin soup, little more than the water potatoes had been boiled in. That's what they lived on. That, and what they could steal. A paper twist of jam here, a tin of meat there, and occasionally bread, proper bread.

Once they'd unloaded a whole motor lorry full of bread, passing the loaves from one to another down the line. Still warm, the smell had driven them all mad. The guards had watched them closely, counting every loaf off the lorry and onto the cart they were loading.

It was an hour before Daniel had been able to palm a loaf when the guard's back was turned, and he'd hidden it quickly under his jerkin. Asking to be excused to go to the latrine, he ripped a hole in the lining and slid the loaf inside. But not before he'd torn off an end of crust to chew.

That night they'd had a veritable feast. Someone had got hold of a tin of pork, someone else a few cigarettes. It was Frannie's birthday that day, and they'd called it a party. That was early on, in the spring, when there was still spirit left in

231

them. Before the deaths from dysentery and the mysterious sickness that set men coughing bile and turned their faces blue before killing them. The sickness that at home they called the Spanish flu.

Stealing food from the enemy was one thing, a necessity. Stealing from each other, especially in those last days, was a different matter. Some – most – would gobble down their ration of bread as soon as they had it. Some would eke it out, a mouthful here, a nibble there, throughout the day. A few would hold onto it to savour in the evening when work was finished, and it was these rations that began to go missing. Not every day; sometimes only once or twice a week. But when it happened to Frannie three times in one week, he'd turned over the bedding of every man in the hut in a fit of fury. And there, hidden under Fisher's blanket, was a whole stash of bits and pieces; empty paper twists, empty tins, none of which he'd shared, and most incriminating of all, two heels of bread.

The others were ready to beat him on the spot, but Frannie had held them back. We'll do this properly, he said. He was calm now that the traitor was exposed, and he went off to report to the guards. He returned saying that they'd been told to sort it out themselves, which of course he had fully expected. He said that he would wait until the time was right and then made it clear that the subject was closed. He continued to say nothing – and do nothing – about it for several days. It completely unnerved Fisher, much more than a straightforward beating would have done.

He finally took his revenge a week later. One afternoon they were in the stable yard, having been assigned to care for fifty or so horses from the transport corps. Heavy brutes they were, though thin from overwork and underfeeding. Daniel knew how they felt. Still, it wasn't bad work, mucking out the stables, grooming the horses, cleaning their gear. Better than loading munitions anyway.

Often they were left to themselves in the afternoons. The guards would go off to smoke or play cards, or occasionally, if they thought they could get away with it, get roaring drunk.

This particular afternoon the guards were well out of sight and the prisoners took the opportunity to slacken. They were sitting on a heap of straw bundles, pretending to clean the horse's tack. Perhaps Fisher had started to relax, thinking that after all this time nothing would happen. He'd been sent to Coventry all week; no-one would go near him if they could avoid it. But now he edged up to them quietly, hoping that all was forgiven and forgotten and he could sneak back into the fold. Frannie pounced before his backside had hit the straw.

"Right then, Fisher," he said, rubbing his hands together. "Time to pay the piper."

Fisher thought that he was going to say something else, begin some lengthy confrontation, and the first blow took him completely undefended. He sprawled backwards onto the straw bales and the other men backed off to a safe distance. Fisher scrambled up and raised his hands to defend himself, but Frannie caught him on the side of the head with a jaw-grinding right hook. After that he did not even try to put up a fight, but curled up in a ball, whimpering. Daniel thought that Frannie would give up then in disgust, but he didn't. He kicked the prostrate Fisher in the back, the stomach, the head, taunting him all the while. In the end, he was too out of breath even to hurl insults. The only sound was his laboured breathing and the soft thud of boot against flesh and bone.

The other men had drawn round in a circle to watch. They reminded Daniel of a pack of wolves. He couldn't condemn them because he knew all too well how they felt. Each blow was taken by proxy for them. There was a satisfaction in it, in being able to blame someone, anyone, and crush them in righteousness. To drain this terrible, dark anger.

He would never forget the expression on his friend's face that day – a wildness that had a tinge of madness. He had not observed that in Frannie before or since, not until now. Just a flicker, but it was there in his eyes and in his manner. His nervous, angular manner.

"Ready for another drink then?" he said, ferreting in his pocket for change.

Daniel had not touched his whisky and drunk only half the light ale. "Just a small one," he said.

"You'll get what you're bloody well given, and that'll be a double and a pint. This is supposed to be a bloody celebration, not a wake."

Elissa watched Jo nibbling at the corner of her fruit scone. The café was emptying, shoppers heading for home with their parcels and string bags. Only an elderly couple and a trio of formidable, dark-clad matrons remained.

Elissa had thought that the crisp white tablecloths and sugary cakes of Pagnell's Tea Shop might cheer her friend and make it easier to tell her news without sounding cruel or gloating. But her courage had failed her, and she'd spent the last twenty minutes talking about nothing.

"It seems strange, doesn't it?" she said. "Think of all the cups of tea we've shared, but we've never been to a café together."

Jo added more butter to her scone. "You're right. This is a

first." She bit into it with relish. "But not the last, I hope."

Elissa glanced up at the clock. The place would be closing in fifteen minutes. "Jo –"

"Was there something you wanted to tell me?"

Elissa sighed. "Is it obvious?"

"You'd certainly never make a Mata Hari. You've been like a cat on hot bricks from the moment we sat down." Jo sipped her tea. "Not to mention that we've met every week at your house for goodness knows how long, and suddenly you disappear for over a week only to reappear with an invitation to Pagnell's. So I know something mysterious is going on."

Elissa rotated her cup in its saucer. "You're right. I do have something to tell you, and its good news. I just – I'm not sure how to say it, that's all. Without sounding terribly thoughtless."

"I can't imagine you being that."

As ever, Jo was full of light, bright comments and lively smiles, but Elissa could see the undertow of sadness she sought to keep at bay. The last thing she wanted to do was make it worse by parading her own good fortune.

She took a deep breath. Jo would have to know sometime. "About a week ago," she said. "Something rather extraordinary happened. Daniel Earshaw turned up on my doorstep."

Jo's eyes widened and she put down her teacup with a clatter. "My god. He's alive, after all this time?"

Elissa nodded.

"And you had no warning?"

"He wrote, but I never received the letter."

"What happened to him? Was he a prisoner?"

"He was. Hannah – his mother – was right all along. I was convinced that he was dead. And then – there he was, at my door, alive and well."

Jo rummaged in her skirt pocket for cigarettes. "Goodness," she said. "So it's true after all. The dead do come back to life."

"It does seem that way."

Jo lit up, much to the disapproval of the matrons in the corner. One of them called the waitress.

"And that's not all." Elissa lowered her voice. "He's been staying with me ever since. You remember his mother died? His house was sold and he had nowhere else to go."

"So you took pity on the poor lamb did you?"

"Well it wasn't only pity."

Jo's mischievous smile, her real, genuine smile, reappeared for a brief second. "Thought not."

"I'm going to marry him Jo."

"But Elissa that's wonderful!" Her voice rose and so did the matrons' eyebrows.

Elissa reached across the table and grasped her friend's hand. Jo looked so genuinely pleased that it broke her heart. The matrons, scandalised by so much naked emotion along with the smoking, rushed to pay their bill.

"I'm sorry," she said. "I hardly knew how to tell you."

"Why?"

"Because…well, I didn't want to parade my good luck when you…when you still…"

"Elissa you are a silly thing."

"I know."

"But a good and thoughtful friend."

"Will you come to the wedding? It's only a small affair, registry office, but I'd love you to be there."

Jo inhaled deeply on her cigarette. "I wouldn't miss it for the world."

Chapter 22

Elissa had thought that in the week since she'd given them the news her family might have come round to the idea of her marriage, but if anything matters were worse. At least her mother had softened towards Daniel. The loss of his own mother had brought out her compassion and she seemed prepared to forgive her daughter for springing a second marriage on them so precipitously. Not so, her father. Not so, Amy.

Her sister had been silent and morose all evening and her father kept up a constant interrogation of Daniel throughout dinner. What had he done before the war? What had he done during the war? What did he propose to do now? Most embarrassing of all, where was his father?

Daniel had borne it stoically enough, answering truthfully even about his father. He seemed to have expected this grilling. It was the first time she'd seen him wearing civvies, and the dark wool suit and starchy collar seemed to constrain him. His behaviour was formal and stilted, a performance for her benefit. It touched her that he was taking such pains not to upset her parents – much good that it did him.

As they gathered in the sitting room after dinner, her father recommenced his interrogation and Elissa realised that Amy had not spoken for nearly an hour.

"So," said her father to Daniel. "You have nowhere to live, I hear?"

"Not at the moment," he replied. "My mother's house had already been let when I returned from France." Elissa noticed his hands, which had been steadier over the last day or two, began to shake again as he put down his coffee cup.

"So she did not own your family home?"

"No."

Her father rubbed the side seam of his trousers with his left hand, a sure sign that a lecture was in the offing. "One should always own one's house if at all possible."

"Yes, I'm sure one should."

"And, being temporarily homeless, you propose to remain here do you, until you are married?"

"Edward, it's none of our business," said her mother, for the third time that evening.

"No, that's quite all right Mrs Haskell," said Daniel, "it's a fair question. I do own a property as a matter of fact. My grandparent's old farm. It's rather broken-down, but I was prepared to live there if there was no alternative. However, Elissa has been kind enough to offer me one."

Her father put down his coffee cup so that he could devote both hands to seam-smoothing. "And you think that's appropriate, do you?"

"In what sense?"

"Don't be disingenuous, Mr Earnshaw. You know exactly what I mean."

Elissa regarded them both with exasperation. The sharp, determined look in both sets of eyes, blue and grey, was alarmingly similar.

"Father –"

"Elissa, it has to be said at least once."

"No it does not. This is my house and I can invite whomever I like to stay."

Her father reddened. "You may not know any better Elissa, but *he* should."

"Are you implying," she said, feeling her own anger rise as she absorbed his full meaning, "that my moral education has somehow been lacking? And who do you think would be responsible for –"

"Elissa acted out of kindness to me," interrupted Daniel. "As she always has. She is the most warm-hearted person I have met, and that's why I love her. And why I'm honoured to marry her. There has never been anything shameful or unsuitable in her conduct to me. I've always assumed her greatness of character has been at least partly a result of her upbringing."

It was the longest speech he'd made all evening. Elissa was stunned, but not nearly as astonished as her father. His mouth worked, searching for a suitable response and she wanted to laugh – his sting had been pulled most effectively.

Her mother leapt into the breach. "Elissa tells me that you're a very accomplished musician, Daniel," she said. "Perhaps you would oblige us by playing something? We're a very unmusical family I'm afraid, but it would be a great treat for us to hear you."

Daniel took the hint. "Of course Mrs Haskell. Though I must warn you that Elissa is exaggerating my abilities." He raised his eyebrows at her as he moved across to the piano. Elissa had the sneaking suspicion that he had enjoyed her display of temper.

There were a few painful, silent minutes as he leafed through his pile of scores. She had the feeling he was deliberately taking his time, using the opportunity to calm himself down. Finally he dumped the whole lot back on top of the piano and began to play from memory. She saw how his shoulders relaxed as soon as he started. She recognised the piece – she'd heard him practising endlessly it these last days – the same gloomy, passionate Chopin Nocturne he'd played her that evening, that first time. On longer acquaintance, she liked it more, relishing its sudden changes of mood. She glanced at her father and could tell that he was impressed in spite of himself. Her mother was clearly enthralled, while Amy sat, head bowed, staring at her hands.

When Daniel had finished, her mother clapped and gushed and even her father managed a grunt of approval. Amy said nothing.

He swivelled on the piano stool to acknowledge the applause with grace, then he turned back to the keys. "And this is for my dear Elissa," he said. "I hope that in some way it makes up for my many shortcomings."

He played the piece she'd first heard that afternoon in Weir Street, over a year ago. The very first thing she'd ever heard him play. It was like a secret message, a reminder of what had brought them together. His customary intensity was modulated with a new lightness and elegance, and even she could tell that he had improved with practice. It was worth it, all this, she told herself. It was.

When he'd finished she smiled at him, encouraging him silently, but Amy stood up abruptly and blocked her view.

"I think I'll turn in," she said. "It's been a long day ." She smoothed out an invisible wrinkle in her skirt. "Goodnight, everyone."

Daniel spread out the blankets Elissa had left him and lay down in front of the fire. The piano sat mute and reproachful in the corner. His playing had been poor overall, though the Debussy was shaping up a little better. He'd allowed his anger to distract him in the Chopin. And now here he was alone, sleeping on the parlour floor. Elissa's parents had taken her bedroom, and she was in the spare room with Amy. Only right and proper of course. Tomorrow was Christmas Day, and they'd be going home on Boxing Day morning. One more day to be got through. Just a few more hours of keeping his temper, minding his words, biting back the replies. Then he could reclaim his place (he couldn't help thinking it was his rightful place) in her bed.

It would be all right in the end. Once they were married, her father would come round. He'd have to. The only one he was unsure about was Amy. Her, he couldn't read at all. Of course it didn't help that she wouldn't even look at him.

He heard a faint squeak and the parlour door opened a few inches. Elissa slipped through the gap and put her finger to her lips to shush him.

"What are you doing?" he whispered. "I thought you'd gone to bed."

"I was missing you." She pulled back the blankets and cuddled up next to him, her bare feet icy from the hall tiles. "Sorry about today."

He brushed a lock of hair back from her face, which was wearing a stubborn, set expression. He imagined her as a little girl, stamping her foot at her father.

"It's only to be expected."

"Well, *I* didn't expect it."

"Elissa, you are asking a lot of them you know. They didn't

241

even know I existed until a week ago and suddenly here I am, and you're marrying me. It wouldn't be so bad if I wasn't living here with you so openly."

"That's none of their business."

"Of course it's their business, they're your parents."

"That doesn't give them the right to tell me what to do. I'm a grown woman."

"No, but you can't expect them to be happy when you go against their wishes."

Her expression softened. "I suppose so. You're right, I know you're right. I just hoped they'd understand, that's all."

"They will. Give them time."

"You're so tolerant."

"It's really not that difficult. And it's worth it, to have you."

She kissed him on the cheek. "Thank-you for saying that." She leaned over him and brushed her lips against his mouth, then slid her leg between his.

"Elissa, you don't have to prove your loyalty to me."

"What do you mean?"

"You know very well." He pressed his forehead against hers. "Who do you think will get the blame if they hear us?"

She lay back against his shoulder with a sigh. "You will."

When Elissa slipped back into the spare bedroom, Amy was lying on her side facing the window, her shoulders hunched and tense.

"Where have you been?"

"To get a glass of water."

"Don't lie. You've been gone for ages."

"Amy –"

"You've been with *him*, haven't you? Don't think I don't

know what's going on. You couldn't even wait until you were married."

Elissa got into bed, pulled up the covers and turned away from her sister. "Go to sleep."

But Amy was not to be thwarted. "And how long has it been going on, that's what I'd like to know? You can't only just have met him. Makes me wonder if you were carrying on with him while Harry was still alive."

Elissa sat bolt upright, aware that she was being baited, unable to resist. "Amy, you know that's not true. If I didn't know better I'd say you were –"

"Jealous? Really? No Elissa, if I wanted to take a lover, I think I could do a little bit better than *that*."

Elissa noticed the tears shining in her sister's eyes. As usual, Amy thwarted anger by mitigating her meanness with victimhood.

"Don't be like this Amy, please," she said. "Give him a chance. Once you get to know him you'll like him, I promise you."

Amy sniffed, unimpressed. "As I recall you said the same thing about Harry. You didn't listen to me then either, when I tried to warn you."

"You never warned me about Harry."

"I did, Elissa, but you wouldn't listen. You're just the same now."

"I'm not. He couldn't be more different from Harry."

"That's true. But is he any better? You know almost nothing about him. And what about his *father,* abandoning the family like that? How do you know he won't do the same to you? He plays you a pretty little tune on the piano and you flutter your eyelashes and lose all power of thought."

Elissa could not help but remember Jo's response to her

news, so kind and loving. All she got from her own sister was vindictiveness.

"And he's a *shopkeeper's* son, Elissa."

"And I'm a schoolmaster's daughter. I didn't know you were such a snob."

"Bit of a comedown after Harry though, isn't it? Or perhaps the roughness is part of the appeal. Perhaps that's what's making you behave like a cheap little tart."

The long thread of Elissa's tolerance finally snapped and she hit her sister hard on the face. The sound broke the night-time quiet like a thunderclap.

Amy stared at her for an instant, her eyes wide. "You hit me!"

"Yes, and I'll do it again if you say another word."

Amy hunched over in her patented helpless-and-pitiful manner. "You're becoming cruel, you know. Is that *his* influence too?"

Elissa didn't want to hate her sister, but the emotion grew in her anyway like a stubborn weed. "I thought I'd –"

"Oh I won't say any more, don't worry. I won't speak of it ever again!"

"That will be a great relief."

Chapter 23

For most of the other people on the train it was an ordinary day. There they sat, reading their newspapers or paperback novels, looking out of the window, thinking with anticipation or dread of the day's work. Amid the drab of workaday clothes, Daniel felt like a peacock, dressed to the nines in his fine new suit, tie knotted too tightly, collar chafing his neck. After so long of the rough looseness of an army uniform he could not get used to wearing ordinary clothes.

Elissa gave him a sideways look, half-smiling. She thought he was nervous about the wedding. He took hold of her hand and laced his fingers through hers. She was wearing a new hat and a coat in some kind of soft, napped material. He liked the feel of it under the tips of his fingers. He liked the colour too, a deep pink that reminded him of her skin when she blushed. She squeezed his hand and turned to look out of the window as they entered the deep, tree-lined cutting that ran into Calderby station. Was she thinking of Harry, of her first marriage? Would she blurt out at the last moment that no, she could not go through with it, not again? Perhaps it had got too much, all this business with her family, and she was longing to change her mind. He knew that she hadn't spoken to Amy since Christmas Day. But then she turned back from the window, looked at him, and began to shake with silent laughter.

"What is it?" he said.

"You look completely terrified."

"Nonsense."

"Then why the expression of a lamb going to slaughter?"

"I have no idea what you're talking about."

"All right my darling, have it your way." She stood up as the train pulled into the station, her hand resting on his shoulder for balance. As they filed off the train amongst the clerks and typists, he bent under her hat and put his mouth to her ear.

"The only thing that frightens me," he whispered, "is that you'll change your mind."

"I would never do that."

"Sure?"

She swatted him gently on the cheek. "Of course I'm sure. I've never been so sure of anything in my life."

Elissa's parents were waiting for them at the registry office. They sat in an ante-room, a plush, carpeted affair with French windows overlooking a long, walled garden. They sat side by side along the wall and looked as if they were about to go to court to give evidence. Her father scowled but was polite enough in his greeting. There was no sign of Amy.

Elissa's friend Jo Kenyon arrived, dapper and smiling. She wore a matching coat and jacket, the sort of purplish colour that his mother used to describe as plum. She at least seemed happy for them – she gave him a kiss on the cheek and said that she remembered him from Garrett Hill. He left her with Elissa and escaped out into the hall for a last cigarette.

He scuffed about the hallway, smoking nervously, watching the entrance doors revolving in the chill January wind. He hoped Frannie and his wife would arrive soon so he would not feel completely outnumbered. They were his only guests; he hadn't invited the Ashworths, although he'd been tempted if only to witness the encounter between Elissa's father and Uncle William. He caught sight of his reflection in the long mirror opposite the revolving doors. It still had the capacity to ambush him. He was still thin, despite several weeks of good food and copious sleep, and in this light he looked old, agelessly old. Sometimes he felt that way too, as if he had been dead for a very long time and living was something he had forgotten how to do.

The door clicked and swished. He looked up smiling, expecting to see Frannie, but it was Amy, clad in a heavy black coat and broad-brimmed hat. She looked like she was going to a funeral.

"Hello," he said. "Glad you could come."

Her eyes were red – her nose too. A good hour's crying, at least. "It was touch and go for a while," she said.

"I can see that."

"Where's Elissa?"

"Through there." He pointed down the corridor that led to the waiting room and she walked away without another word.

"I'd be very grateful," he said to her retreating back, "if you didn't spoil it for her."

She stopped walking, but did not turn. "No," she said. "I'll leave you to do that at your leisure."

He watched her continue down the corridor until she was out of sight through the doors. In his mind he called her every obscenity he could think of, most of them learned from

Frannie. He had spectacularly failed with her and he could not understand why. At that moment Frannie clanged his way through the doors, as if summoned by his mental litany of curses. He was alone.

"Sorry," he said. "Am I'm late?" He was out of breath.

"No, there's plenty of time. Where's Kate?"

"She sends her apologies. We couldn't get anyone to mind the children."

He was sweating slightly, though it was cold outside. His suit – obviously pre-war – hung on him like a sack and he smelled of drink.

Do you mind it just being me?"

"Of course not. Come on, I'll introduce you to Elissa."

Back in the waiting room, Amy was sitting next to her parents doing her silent act and Elissa was talking to Jo. There was no sign that the sisters had even spoken. Behind him, Frannie hesitated.

"What is it?"

"Nothing. Nothing, old pal. Is that her?" Frannie seemed to be bracing himself.

"It's all right," said Daniel. "She doesn't bite."

"No. I'm sure."

Jo looked up as they approached. Her look turned to a stare and the colour drained from her face. Daniel looked behind him, wondering what she had seen, and realised that her gaze was fixed on Frannie. Frannie, however, was looking hard at his feet.

"Elissa," said Daniel, "I want you to meet my friend, Frannie Dwyer."

Elissa held out her hand. "Pleased to meet you, Mr Dwyer."

Frannie shook her hand quickly, his eyes shifting nervously.

"Likewise Mrs Ch – er –"

"Please call me Elissa."

"It's very nice to meet you. I hope you'll both be very happy." He let go of her hand and returned to examining his shoes with great interest. Jo was still staring. She recognised him obviously – but how could she possibly know Frannie?

"This is my friend Jo Kenyon," said Elissa.

Frannie had to look up then. "Hello Jo."

There was a long pause. "Mr Dwyer and I have already met," Jo said at last. Daniel thought that she was going to faint. "I'm sorry, would you excuse me for a minute?" She rushed away, hand to her face, disappearing through the door into the hall.

"What on earth's the matter with her?" he said.

Elissa ignored him. She was looking at Frannie curiously. "You've met Jo before then, Mr Dwyer."

"Yes, I've had that pleasure."

"So I hear." Her tone was icy. Daniel looked from one to the other of them. "I'd better go after her," she said. "It seems she's had a bit of a shock."

"I'll go," said Frannie. He looked as if he'd had a shock too – he had flushed an unhealthy shade of pink.

"I think I'd –" said Elissa, but he had already turned and walked away. Well!" she said. "What a *nerve*. Does he really think I'm going to leave her to his tender mercies?"

Daniel held her arm as she started after them. "Elissa, stay here."

"You don't understand."

"No I don't. And I'd like you to explain."

"I'm sorry, I didn't mean to be cruel Jo. Really I didn't. I thought it was for the best."

"Best for who exactly?"

She had run blindly to the far end of the walled garden, trying to put as much distance between herself and the building – and Frannie. She thought that the arched trellis would hide her, but he had tracked her with an unerring instinct.

"For everyone," he said. "I had a long time to think, all those months. I thought it would be better for you if I stayed dead."

"How nice of you to play God on my behalf."

She kept trying to turn away, but at every step he blocked her.

"I thought I'd already made you unhappy enough, you see. I was trying to make it easy."

"Easy! You think it was *easy* imagining you dead?"

"I didn't mean it like that."

For a few terrible moments when he'd first come in, she'd thought he was a ghost. He looked insubstantial enough. His solidity seemed to have drained away and he was all bone and bloodshot eyes.

"Did you think we were never going to see each other?" she said. "Calderby's not that big a place. You must have known this would happen sooner or later."

He thrust his hands into his pockets. "I didn't think you'd still be here. I thought you'd go back to your family after the war."

"Well I'm sorry to inconvenience you Frannie, but here I am and here I'm staying."

He stared at her helplessly. "I didn't think. I tried to do what was right. I didn't know what else to do." He leaned against the trellis, which creaked complainingly under his weight. He looked so defeated that a treacherous pity began to creep up on her.

"And are you happy?" she said. "Has it all worked out nicely for you? You told me your wife hated you, or was that another lie?"

"No, that's true right enough. I think she was quite content with me dead, to be honest. It proper took the wind out of her sails when I came back."

She laughed, a cracked, humourless cough. "Poor Frannie. You've managed to upset everyone's apple-cart, haven't you?"

"I don't think it's very bloody funny."

"Neither do I."

He was there, a few feet from her, alive after all this time. It hit her all at once like an avalanche, and she burst into tears. Tentatively he put his arms around her and she didn't pull away.

Janet was at her sister's in Southport, so there was no welcome committee when they returned home, and the fire in the sitting room had gone out. It did not seem an auspicious start. At least they'd finally got away from her parents, and from Amy.

Her quiet wedding had turned out to be a clamorous nightmare; Amy not speaking to her, her father glaring at Daniel all through the service, and, worst of all, Jo and that Frannie Dwyer. She'd seen them all the way through that meal at the Swan, that awful meal, watching each other and not speaking. But then the conversation had not exactly flowed. Her poor mother had made an effort, and Daniel had tried, but he was not a natural at polite conversation and the combined forces of her father and her sister had quickly silenced him.

She watched him resuscitate the fire with a poker. Sometimes she felt that everyone was conspiring against them. Even their friends had to bring their problems along to overshadow what was supposed to be *their* day. It wasn't fair. And what was she to do about Jo? They'd left together, her and that Frannie. Sneaking off, thinking no-one would notice.

"What is it?" Daniel was watching her.

"Oh, nothing."

"Don't 'nothing' me, Elissa. It's clear that you're upset."

"And why would I be upset? Hasn't it been a simply perfect day?"

He sat back on his heels, staring at the fire as if it were to blame. "I'm sorry that it hasn't turned out the way that you wanted."

"Oh, it's not you." She knelt down next to him on the rug and kissed him on the cheek. "It's nothing to do with you. I didn't mean to carp."

"Wait a minute," he said, pulling away. "My hands are dirty."

She watched him in exasperation as he took out a handkerchief to wipe the coal dust from his hands. "It doesn't matter, Daniel."

"I don't want to spoil your new dress."

"Oh, my new dress be damned!"

"I'm only trying to be –"

"I know, I know." It wasn't the dirt. She could see the tension in him, the way he crouched over the fire. The day had been spoiled for him too. "It's this business with Jo and your friend. I can't believe it."

"It was rather a surprise to me as well."

She unbuttoned her shoes and kicked them off. "You seem to be taking it calmly enough."

"What else can I do?"

"Don't you find it at all bothering?"

"I don't know. I've no idea what's been going on do I? You seem to know far more about it than I do."

"What's that supposed to mean?"

"You told me that you knew Jo was having an affair."

"Yes, but I didn't know it would turn out to be with your friend."

He loosened his tie and started to fiddle with his collar studs. "It had to be someone, didn't it? What difference does it make?"

"You haven't seen her these past months. You haven't seen how unhappy she's been."

He wrenched his collar free and flung it on the floor, along with the tie that she had chosen for him so carefully. "And you blame him for that?"

"Yes! Who else would I blame?"

"You don't know the whole story, Elissa. Neither of us does. But I met his wife, remember. I knew something wasn't right at home."

"Oh, and you think that excuses him, do you? You think that makes it all right to deceive her and ruin Jo's life."

"I didn't say that," he said with exaggerated patience. "And don't be melodramatic. Her life is hardly ruined is it?"

"Really? What kind of prospects do you think Jo has if she carries on with him? He's not going to divorce his wife is he? Not with two children and no money."

Daniel rubbed at the frown lines between his eyes. "You may be right, Elissa. But neither of us knows the whole truth. You only know what she's told you."

"Are you saying that she's a liar?"

"No. I'm saying that there are at least two sides to every story. You didn't see him with her, with his wife."

All at once, she did not want to be close to him. She hitched her skirt and stood up with as much dignity as possible. "You'll always take his side won't you? Whatever he does. Because he's your friend."

He stayed kneeling the rug. As her anger rose, he became increasingly quiet and distant. "I'm not taking his side. You must stop this, Elissa. You're behaving just like Amy. You've seen how she passes judgement on me. On us. You're doing exactly the same thing."

"Nonsense! It's not the same thing at all."

They stared at one other. He didn't understand. It was all an illusion; she had convinced herself that she loved him because he had come back from the dead. In his absence, she had remade him in the image of her lover. The shock of his return, the sheer, unexpected miracle of it had clouded her judgement and she had rushed into marriage with a man who was a stranger. Amy was right – it was Harry all over again. She had an overwhelming desire to flee. She must have glanced towards the door because he said:

"Don't go, please."

She opened her mouth, closed it again.

"You ran away from me once before Elissa, don't do it again. Shout and scream at me all you like, but don't run off, please. I can't stand it."

He knew. He knew what she'd been thinking. "I only want to help," she said. "I can't stand to see her so miserable."

He reached out and took her hand tentatively. "I know. But you may make things worse if you interfere."

The fire was blazing now. She sank back down onto the rug next to him and he held her gently, as if her anger had made her fragile. She twined her stockinged feet around his.

"I have to do *something*," she said.

"You are doing something. You're being her friend, her loyal friend."

"I suppose so." She sighed. "But that doesn't seem like much."

"Elissa, you underestimate yourself. Your friendship counts for an awful lot, as I have good cause to know."

His physical presence calmed her, made her feel safe. That was no illusion. It was real in a way that it never had been with Harry. "I'm sorry if I was cross with you. I thought that you didn't understand."

"I don't. You're a mystery, Elissa, and I'm going to have great fun unravelling you."

She prodded him gently in the ribs. "How can you be so light-hearted about it?"

"I'm not. I'm pretending. Really I'm terrified."

At three o'clock that afternoon, nearly two years since he had last crossed her threshold, Jo unlocked the door of her flat to admit Frannie once again. As he looked around her little room, she could not help but be touched by the fond glances he gave her chairs, her rag rug, her folding table and her photographs, as if he were reacquainting himself with old friends. He looked at everything but her.

Jo knew that she did not have it in her to hate him. She wanted to, badly. But instead she was left with a wrenching sense of sorrow at how worn and unwell he looked. The cuffs of his shirt were grubby and frayed, and when he took her hand his skin felt hot and damp as if he were running a fever. She could still smell last night's drink on him. No, she didn't hate him, but neither did she feel much in the way of love.

"Do you want tea?" she said.

"Only if you do."

"Do you want it or not?"

"I…Yes. Please."

"I'll put the kettle on then."

He was afraid of her now, she could tell. Not of her exactly, but what she might do. Secretly, she relished it. Yes, she thought, you feel it, you suffer. See how you like it.

She lit the gas ring, watching the flame flicker from blue to orange as it licked the sooty base of the kettle. On the side of the kettle was a slight dent where she had dropped it one morning last winter, half asleep, as she'd dragged herself up in the dark to get ready for her shift at Garrett Hill. In the uneven groove, a thin line of soot had gathered and she'd never bothered to scrub it clean.

"Jo?"

She did not want to turn round. She did not want to see him standing there, just as he had all that time ago, in the same spot, looking the same. Except that he wasn't the same. She could see, could feel, the difference.

"It'll be ready in a minute," she said.

It was his silence that made her turn around. He had gone back to sit in the chair and slumped forward, head in hands. He made no sound, but his shoulders were shaking as he tried to smother the emotion that racked him. He was crying. She had seen a man weep before – more than once, these last years – but still it shocked her. She went to him.

"Don't be sad Frannie," she said, standing over the chair. "Please don't be. You're alive, that's the important thing."

She scarcely knew how to offer him comfort. She reached out tentatively and touched the top of his head, her fingers sinking into his thick, uncombed hair. Quick as a whip he clutched her, both arms about her waist, and buried his head against her stomach. Her knees gave way a little.

"I thought it was the proper thing to do, you see," he said, into her skirt. "The right thing. I never expected to live and when I did, I was determined to put things right. I wanted to let you go. I know it sounds daft, but it was for you as well. I promise you, that's the truth."

A secret part of her was angry. How dare he cling to her and justify himself? She patted his head, awkwardly. She wished he would let go. Touching him still made her giddy with longing, but she no longer welcomed the sensation.

"I believe you," she said. "I believe that you meant well." She didn't know what more to say. His presence was still a magnet to her, but she understood him more clearly now. She could see how he was sad and a little pathetic. Had he been like that before? She wasn't sure. He seemed so changed.

He released her and leaned back in the chair. "You can't forgive me can you?"

"I don't know."

Perhaps his cruelty had simply nullified her feelings. Or perhaps she'd never loved him at all, simply got drunk on lust and loneliness. It was all too sudden, too soon, and she needed time to think.

He tried for a nonchalant shrug. "Can't say I blame you."

"You've no right to blame me for anything." The words were out before she could stop herself. Her anger was bubbling up from a deep well. She sighed, trying to shake it off. "I think you'd better go, Frannie."

She could see in his eyes he hadn't been expecting that. She noticed a brief flicker of calculation.

"I've only just come."

Obviously, he'd thought that now he'd penetrated her

sanctuary, he'd be able to worm his way back into her affections without too much effort. She struggled to keep her voice calm and even.

"I need time. I thought I could talk with you calmly, but I can't."

She stood back from the chair, out of reach. He took the hint and stood up. "Can I come back and talk to you again? Soon?"

She found a weak smile. "You know where I live."

"How about tomorrow?"

"You must give me a few days. You were dead, and now you're alive. I can't simply switch my feelings on and off in a moment."

"I'll call round next week then."

"I'd appreciate it if you'd send me a note first."

"Don't worry, I'll be discreet."

He'd said that to her before, when they'd first met. It tripped very easily off his tongue. "It's not your discretion I'm concerned about."

Again she wondered, as she had wondered back then, if she was just one of many. Her shame deepened; she had been such easy prey.

"I assume you're not going to go home and tell your wife about me?"

He could not look her in the eye.

"I thought not. Well, come back next Saturday. Same time. Unless I hear from you to the contrary."

"Thank-you Jo. I won't let you down."

It's a little late for that, she thought. "Goodbye Frannie."

And he was gone, clumping down the back stairs and out into the yard. She didn't follow him. She could still smell him in the room, the sour odour of sweat and drink. She flung open both windows onto the street. Even the acrid air of Calderby smelt sweet by comparison.

Chapter 24: April 1919

Elissa turned her collar up against the rain and darted from tree to tree in pursuit of shelter. The stream was gushing at full spate and the shingled path ran with water. Lately she'd begun walking into Calderby, following the path she'd taken that day with Daniel – was it already a year ago? The path ran downstream along the valley and into the narrow, back ways of the town, through cramped alleys at the back of grimy terraces. It wasn't pretty in its final stages, but she didn't mind. Walking helped her think, and it worked off her frustrations. Not that she was unhappy, far from it, but her life had been turned inside-out these past years and it had been harder than she thought to settle. The peace she'd longed for still seemed to elude her.

Sometimes she took walks further afield, spending long afternoons among the hills and valleys around Luddenridge, exploring as she'd never had time to do during the war. Once her time at Garrett Hill had ended, she had nothing to fill her days with but being a wife – and being a wife, however much she loved her husband, was no longer enough. She had tasted something different and she wanted more. She must do something. She repeated it, again and again, like a chant. She *would* do something. She could feel it, like the rumble of a train in the distance. She did not know what it was, not yet, but it would be something, and soon.

She twisted the wedding ring on her finger, remembering her other ring and its fate. She would never have believed, the night when she'd flung Harry's ring into the garden compost (it was still there for all she knew), that eighteen months later she would be married again to an utterly different kind of man. One who, like her, was not content with an easy life.

The path forked away from the stream and widened into a rutted lane. She turned right into the alley that ran along the back of Foster's Mill, skirting the smoky, industrial heart of Calderby. She emerged at the head of Market Street, emerging into a sudden bustle of shoppers and trades-people. Jo lived in a cold water flat two stories above a haberdasher's shop. The entrance was at the back and Elissa cut through the narrow, cobbled alley to a lane behind the shop-fronts. She wondered if Jo was ever afraid, coming back here alone after dark. What had she done all those nights they'd worked at Garrett Hill? She was ashamed to think that she'd never thought before of her friend's safety.

As she unlatched the gate, she looked up to see Jo waving from the window of her eyrie. The back door was open and she let herself in, climbing the rickety stairs to meet her friend on the landing.

"You're just in time for lunch," said Jo.

The flat opened into a sitting room with a curtained-off kitchen area in the corner. There wasn't much furniture apart from two armchairs by the fire, a gate-leg table and a heavy sideboard, but the fire had been lit, the table set and the room was neat and welcoming. Elissa's eyes were drawn to the framed photographs that lining walls. Most were of seascapes

– rocky beaches, jagged cliffs and grey, metallic sea – but there were a few of Jo's family.

These she explained to Elissa; the family group of her and her brothers as children, held still by determined parents, the posed, individual portraits of her and her brothers, and one or two of her brothers in uniform that she'd taken herself at the beginning of the war.

"Steak and kidney pie," she said, luring Elissa away from the photographs, "with mashed potatoes and carrots. I hope that's all right. I bought the pies fresh from the butchers this morning so they should be edible."

"It smells delicious."

Elissa sat down at the table as Jo produced two steaming plates, the small, cylindrical pies surrounded by creamy mash and delicately sliced carrots. Jo was modest about her cooking skills. She was creative and resourceful, and Elissa envied her ability to conjure up delicious feasts from nothing. She'd always been at best an indifferent cook, and had quickly surrendered to Janet's expertise when she'd moved to Luddenridge.

Jo watched her tuck into the rich, spicy pie. Her face was strained, her eyes shadowed. Elissa wondered if she was worried about money. She had confessed a month ago that she was running short.

"Are you feeling well?" Elissa said. "You're looking a little pale."

Jo smiled wearily. "Just tired."

"Have you heard anything yet from your father? About the shop?"

Jo scooped up a forkful of carrots and mashed them in with her potatoes. "He seems to have gone off the idea. I did remind him that the notion of opening a photographic studio in Calderby came from him, but apparently the lease on the shop runs for another year, and even then I don't think Mr Stansfield has any intention of moving out."

"Oh. That's a shame."

"I suppose I could always look at renting another property, if I can find somewhere cheap. And of course if I can persuade my father to change his mind."

"Why don't you let me help?"

Jo paused, astonished, with a forkful of pie halfway to her mouth.

"It's the ideal solution. I've been thinking for some time that I need a worthwhile project. I would be happy to be a partner in business with you."

"Is that what it would be? A business partnership?"

Elissa realised she hadn't thought this through. It had simply occurred to her, and she had spoken. "Yes, why not? I would like to back you Jo. I believe in you. I don't know quite how it would work, but that doesn't matter. I trust you."

"Elissa, I truly appreciate your confidence in me. But you're my friend and I don't want anything to spoil that."

Elissa reined in her enthusiasm. It had come clear to her; the thing she'd been chasing on all those walks. As she'd told Jo, she needed a project. What better than her own business?

"Why don't you take a little time to think about it?" she said. "There's no rush."

Jo laid her fork carefully down on her plate. "I'm sorry, Elissa. I haven't been entirely honest with you." She clasped her hands together under the table. "I've actually...I'm think-ing of leaving Calderby. Moving back home to my parents."

This was a bolt from the blue. "May I ask why? You seemed

so determined, so sure you wanted to stay."

"I know. But…things are proving more difficult than I thought."

Jo was studiously avoiding her eyes and Elissa knew there was more to this than a recalcitrant father. Jo seemed afraid, and she had never known her friend to show fear of anything.

"What's really worrying you Jo? I hate to think you're suffering in silence about something. I'm your friend, and I can still keep a confidence even if I'm a married woman these days."

Jo finally met her eyes. "You remember what I told you, about what happened on your wedding day?"

"That man Dwyer? You said you'd asked him not to bother you any more."

"I did, that's true. But he didn't do what I asked. He did bother me again. In fact, he continues to bother me on a regular basis."

Elissa's stomach tightened. It's what she'd suspected all along.

"I try to stop him. I tell him not to come back, but…I feel so sorry for him, Elissa. He gets into a terrible state."

"You mean he gets drunk?"

"Yes, but that's not all of it. He's a haunted man. He's not how I remember him, and I get so confused because I'm not sure if my memories are false, or if he's simply changed."

"Jo, you owe this man nothing."

"I know, but I…it's hard to turn him away. It seems so cold. All I do is talk to him, give him some food and a cup of tea, and then send him home. I don't let him stay. You must understand, Elissa, I'm not in love with him. I'm not sure I ever was. I've been the most terrible fool."

Elissa understood, better than Jo could ever know. "You're not a fool, my dear, you've just been cruelly used. Now he's trying to mop up his troubles with you and it's not fair. It's not your burden to carry."

"You're right. But what can I do?"

"This may be my own selfishness because I don't want my friend to go away, but I don't think you should leave Calderby."

"Elissa, he's started coming around at night, shouting outside my door if I don't let him in. I'm afraid. My neighbours are already wondering what I'm doing here all alone. It won't be long before I'm the scarlet woman of Calderby."

"Why don't you come to stay with us for a few days? It'll give you some time to think things over, decide what you want to do."

"I don't want to impose."

"Nonsense. We'd love to have you."

"But Daniel...he and Frannie are such good friends."

"Don't worry. Daniel won't tell him you're there, I'll make sure of that."

Frannie took a last look at the outhouse roof before turning away to light his cigarette. The tip burned from red to orange as he inhaled.

"Place is nearly a ruin. You're wasting your time if you ask me." The words mingled with an exhalation of smoke, attenuated by contrary gusts of air. It was a stiff, bracing day up on the tops and spring seemed a long way off.

"I disagree," said Daniel. "There's life in it yet. I know it needs a lot of work – "

"It needs a fair bloody fortune. All of the slate needs

replacing, for a start."

"I know, and most of the inside walls need replastering, and the brick repointing. Maybe even a new damp course. I do realise what's involved."

Daniel watched his friend for further signs of interest or impatience.

"Are you sure it's sound? Structurally, I mean."

"Of course." He wasn't, not yet. He wasn't sure about any of this, but he was not going to let Frannie see his doubt.

Frannie sniffed and wiped his nose on his sleeve. "I think you're mad," he said, "but if you decide to go through with it, I don't mind giving you a hand. Weekends like."

Daniel ground out his own cigarette with the tip of his boot. This was it – the opening he'd been waiting for. He had to put this in exactly the right way or Frannie would not bite.

"Now you mention it, I'd be very grateful for your help," he said. "The problem is, I'm going back to college soon, and that, along with the teaching, is going to take up most of my time."

Frannie eyed him askance.

"So I thought that you might like to take charge of it for me. Be my supervisor, if you like. As a favour."

"You thought that, did you?"

"I'd pay you of course."

Frannie stared at him. Daniel had the sense that his friend was looking right through him, not seeing him at all.

"It's very kind of you old pal, but it seems a little like I'm the one being done the favour."

Damn him, why couldn't he just accept the offer with good grace? It wasn't as if he had many other options.

"I was thinking that it went both ways. You'd be doing me a great service in that you'd be saving the house. If I leave it another year it'll be too late. And of course once it's done, you'll be first in line for renting it out if that's what you want. A place for you and your family. A proper home, fresh air and space for the children –"

Frannie silenced him with a heavy hand on the shoulder. "Don't push your luck, Dan."

"All right. But will you think about it?"

He nodded, then stalked off across the yard. Daniel knew better than to follow. That Frannie hadn't said no immediately was a miracle, but also an indication of how desperate things had become. The old Frannie would never have countenanced such a scheme – he would have scoffed at it as charity.

He watched his friend lean on the gate and light another cigarette, surveying the expanse of moorland behind the house. In some ways it was an ideal solution; help his friend, save the house. He could always rent it to someone else if Frannie didn't want it. But something about the idea did not sit right with him. It seemed a two-dimensional thing, sensible on paper, but when confronted with the gloomy reality all he felt was hopelessness.

Worse, he wondered if what Elissa had told him about Jo Kenyon had in some subtle way transmitted itself to Frannie. Was he acting differently towards his friend? He'd found it hard to hide his dismay – the Frannie he knew, sure and indomitable, was not a man to go troubling women who didn't want him. But then the Frannie he thought he knew was not an adulterer either. Elissa was right – they had to do something about this. He had to at least try.

A few thick droplets of rain splattered onto his face and arms. The clouds hung so low that they almost seemed to touch the moor. He watched Frannie hanging over the gate, looking out into space. Best give him time to see sense. See this for the chance it was.

Daniel retreated inside to the musty back kitchen and brushed the worst of the coal dust and grime from the range. It was stuffed with fresh coal and newspaper, but despite his precautions the coal was damp from its long sojourn in the outhouse and gave off puffs of acrid smoke as he lit the paper around it. By the time he'd got the fire going, the rain was coming down hard. Frannie appeared on the back doorstep, collar up against the wet.

"It's bloody freezing out there," he said, removing his cap and wiping water from his face. "Have you got that thing lit yet?"

"Just about. I've a flask of Bovril in my knapsack if you want some."

Frannie squatted down by the range, stretching his hands towards heating metal. Daniel joined him, pouring Bovril into tin cups.

How many times had they sat together like this, in how many places? In barracks, huts, dugouts, sodden holes in the ground. As soldiers, as captives. They'd had nothing and shared everything. The scales had always balanced. Yet somehow, however little there was to go around, Frannie had always given more. It was the essence of him. Now Daniel had to find a way of giving something back in return.

But Frannie was not going to make it easy.

"Your offer's very kind, old pal," he said, blowing into the cup of hot Bovril, "but building work's not really my line. And anyway, I've a prospect of a new job come Monday. A proper job." He laughed humourlessly. "Church's Mill. Can you believe it? Bloody Church's."

"Frannie –"

"So I don't want to hear no more about it."

There it was again, the harsh, red-eyed glare. Daniel had the sense that something within his friend had fractured. He didn't want believe it. Not Frannie. Frannie was indestructible.

"What was he called?" His glare had lost its focus and he stared into the range, seeing beyond the sputtering coals, beyond the dim and dusty kitchen, into a different world.

"Who?" said Daniel.

"You know, the youngster with the cake. Do you remember, that bloody Simnel cake? Tasted like sawdust. Whatever happened to him?"

"You mean Denny Wade?"

"Denny! That's it. Denny Wade. He was a funny one."

"He's dead."

A long pause.

"Is he?"

"Don't you remember?"

Frannie stared at the glowing, shifting shapes among the coals, as if the real answer were there.

"'Sfunny," he said. "I could have sworn that…" He rubbed the back of his neck and, with a visible effort, tore his attention from the fire. "Well. Never mind. Dead is dead. Now I think we need something a bit stronger than Bovril, don't you?"

269

Chapter 25

I t was after midnight when Jo gave up trying to sleep. She had been in bed for two hours, staring wide-eyed at the ceiling, her tired mind running in circles. She would make some hot milk with honey – sometimes it helped her sleep. She swung her legs over the side of the bed and reached for her shawl. Her suitcase stood next to the dressing-table, packed and ready. In the morning, she was to go to Luddenridge, stay the week with Elissa and Daniel.

It was meant to be a respite, a space to think, but she wondered. There was the inescapable fact that Daniel Earnshaw was Frannie's best friend, and his loyalties would surely be torn. Jo did not want to create conflict so early in her friend's marriage – there was no point in both of them being unhappy. Besides, she feared she was just delaying the inevitable. She didn't want to abandon Elissa, but deep down she had already made up her mind to leave Calderby.

She fumbled for her slippers in the dark, not bothering to light the bedside lamp. Tying her shawl around her, she crept downstairs. The moon, just past full, shot stripes of cold light up the stairwell from the back door. The night was warm and the rain that had drenched the promise of spring all week seemed finally to have stopped.

She had just reached the landing when she heard the latch lift on the gate outside. She froze. He had not been here for over a week now, and she'd begun to hope he would not be back. But here it was, his characteristic, insistent banging on the back door. She crept down the stairs. She didn't even consider not answering – she knew he would not give up until he'd woken half the street. She heard the sound of slurred muttering from the other side of the door as she unbolted it.

"Please be quiet," she whispered to the shadow that was blocking the moon, "you'll wake the neighbours."

"Damn the neighbours," said Frannie, pushing past her none too gently. He staggered up the stairs and lost his footing, falling to his knees with a clatter. The banister creaked a complaint as he hauled himself up. She followed him, staying silent, watching him stumble into the dark sitting-room. She lit the gas as he fell into his usual chair by the fire. He watched her move about the room, turning up the gas, raking the coals. Finally she faced him. He was flushed and red-eyed, looking up at her defiantly like an errant child.

"Aren't you going to kiss me?"

She was filled with a cold, hard rage. "You're lucky I opened the door to you. I'll make you some coffee and then you must go home."

"I don't want any coffee."

She tied her shawl tighter. "Then what do you want?"

His eyes were dark and wide. She had the uncanny feeling that he wasn't seeing her at all, but someone else, some imagined enemy.

"I thought I might find a welcome here," he said. "Thought you'd be glad to see me."

"I've told you, I don't want you coming here, especially at

271

night. I thought I'd made myself clear."

He laughed loudly, baring his teeth. "Why'd you let me in then?"

"Because I knew you'd start shouting and cursing if I didn't."

"You think you know all about me, don't you?"

"I don't know you at all Frannie. But it's what you did last time you turned up in the middle of the night – or are you too drunk to remember?"

"Bloody hellfire," he said. "You're starting to sound just like my fucking wife."

"Well maybe you should go home and talk to her then."

He looked at her sideways, trying to reconcile her with the Jo he remembered.

"Maybe I will," he said. But he didn't move. He turned his head to stare into the fire until his eyelids drooped. Jo knew that if he fell asleep now she would be stuck with him for the rest of the night. She coughed loudly.

His head jerked up. "I saw Dan today," he said abruptly.

"I know." She said it without thinking.

He leaned forward in his chair, suddenly awake. "Oh do you now?"

"Elissa mentioned it this morning."

"And what else did she mention?"

"Nothing."

"Had a nice little talk about me did you?"

"No, we've got more important things to discuss."

"Tell you about her nice little charity scheme did she? Her neat and tidy plan for getting me out of the way. Cos I bet she put him up to it, the tight little bitch."

Jo's hands balled into fists. "Don't you dare talk about her like that!"

"Oh shut your bloody trap. The sun doesn't shine out of her backside you know."

"And what would you know? You know nothing about her, though she's the wife of your best friend. You might at least make an effort to like her. Daniel is doing his utmost to be a friend to you, and all you can do is insult his wife."

"Not to her face I don't."

"Ah well, that's all right then. Why don't you let him help you Frannie? It's not a weakness you know."

"You don't know what you're talking about. I don't want his —"

"Charity? Is that what you think it is? Someone tries to give you a helping hand you throw it back at them by calling it charity."

"You've got no idea."

Without realising it, she had inched forward across the room. Now she was standing over him. "You're just scared," she said. "You can't cope on your own and you won't accept help, so all you do is run away and hide at the bottom of a bottle. You hang around here like a pathetic lost dog even though I've told you I don't want to see you. I've tried to be nice, Frannie, because I cared about you once, and I'm worried about you. But now I'd be quite happy if I never saw you again."

"Shut up!" He leaped out of the chair, gripped her shawl and tightened it around her neck. "Don't you say another word." His voice had gone very quiet and his eyes were empty. For the first time, she was afraid of him.

"Or what?" she said, "What are you going to do? Hurt me? I'm not your enemy."

She looked deep into his eyes, pitting all the force of her will against him, but there was nothing to fight. All she saw was emptiness. There was a great big dead space inside him, swallowing him up like a tumour. It shocked her. His eyes flickered and he let go of her, took a step back. He knew. He knew that she'd seen him.

"Frannie," she said, as gently as she could. "There's no shame in it you know. We all need help sometimes."

He didn't reply. He turned his back on her and walked out of the room without a word. Her stomach felt like it was full of cold lard and she was shaking from head to foot. She heard his boots on the stairs, and the back door creaking open and shut, then a few seconds later the gate. Then he was gone, and she sank down onto the chair in relief. It was done. She knew that this time he wouldn't be back.

Sometimes he couldn't breathe and when that happened he had to get away. There were too many people and there were the people that weren't people but shadows, getting harder to pretend that he didn't see them. Even Jo could not make it better, though she had once. Once he thought she might be the making of him, not any more.

It was gaining on him. No way to stop it. Jo had made it stop once. She had made him want and it was good to want, but now he could not feel anything, like there was a barrier between him and everything else. He was shut away in another place and he could not find his way back. He might try to find it, now he was out in the air, away from all the people. All the noise and the people. How could they stand it?

Here was the bridge and some stairs. He knew this; the canal path. He knew where it went. Home. Was it home? It was dark, but he would remember soon. He would just keep walking.

But there they were again, the shadows. Sometimes they spoke. Sometimes they were angry, and he couldn't blame them. They had no-one to look out for them now. They were all gone, scattered every which way. He could not hold them together any more.

That day on the ridge he'd held them together. They'd all been ready to break that day. What was it called, that place? He could never remember those strange foreign names. That particular day it hadn't been raining. One of the few days in that long summer and autumn when it hadn't been raining. The show was over, they'd been told, at least for now, and they'd been sent to clear up.

So many. He couldn't believe it. Scattered, littered, a whole blanket of them, half buried in the churned waves of earth along the gentle rise of the ridge. And the smell. Young Marlow had been sick. And the grey, the colours. The green, the purple, the blue and the black. The shiny, rotten, stinking black.

They'd identified the bodies from their tags, if tags could be found, or from pay books or personal items or insignia. A lot of them had been Highlanders. He'd written down the names and numbers on a map, noting the location of the body, or whatever part of the body it was that they'd found. Then they'd buried them, each and every one. The ones that were too far gone to bury in one go they'd collected together in sacks. Jesus, the pieces, all in sacks, like harvesting root vegetables it was. He'd done that once as a boy. Where had that been? Not here, not Calderby.

Where was he? He had to walk, clear this fog out of his head. Yes, there it was, the canal. He would follow it home. It was clear, the water was clear and dark, and the sky was dark too.

He couldn't tell where one ended and the other began. He couldn't tell. The water was nice. It moved slowly in a line of ripples, grey against the dark. He followed the water, the path and the water. He looked into it for a while. The faces were there in the water and they swayed beneath him and then they disappeared and he saw the moon and the stars again.

The water was on his skin, thick and heavy. Cold. He didn't like the cold, but he would probably get used to it. He'd got used to worse. Things had turned over somehow – the water was above him. How was that possible? He could not breathe his nose was full of something. He kicked out, but there was something gentle around his legs, soft but firm. It held him and would not let go. He went down into thick darkness, but the cold was not so bad now. No sense in struggling. There was time there was always time.

Jo woke with a jolt. She was curled up in the chair by the fire. The fire had died, and she was filled with a sudden, inexplicable terror. She had been dreaming of struggle and darkness. The clock on her mantelpiece showed ten minutes after three. She had slept for over two hours.

She walked to the middle of the room, surveying every wall, every surface for answers. Something was wrong. Her scalp tingled and her heart beat a rapid tattoo against her ribs. In the room, nothing had moved. The gaslight hissed under its mantle. She'd turned it down low and the light flickered in an uneven rhythm. She rubbed her eyes. The dream was receding, but her fear would not subside. She was driven by a powerful urge to run, to search, to uncover whatever it was that had awoken her.

She went up to her bedroom and dressed quickly in a heavy

woolen skirt, cardigan and walking boots. Back in the hall, she pulled on her old Mackintosh and a beret. In the mirror, her face looked chalky and wild. None of this made sense, but she had to do something. She had only felt like this once or twice before in her life, but she had learned to trust such feelings and follow them. She ran out into the soft chill of the night and hoped that this time she was mistaken.

As she crossed the bridge over the canal she remembered how she'd walked there with Frannie two years ago. The back of her neck prickled. He had come this way tonight, she knew it.

She descended the steps into the bridge's shadow. It was starkly lit by the moon, but the canal path below was dark. She felt her way slowly, sensing the trampled earth of the path, keeping the oily thread of water to her left. She had no idea what she was doing here, but she walked on anyway, taking one step then another, wound in like thread on a bobbin.

After a few hundred yards the canal curved to the right and the path widened. The moonlight penetrated a little further and she could see the grassy path, illuminated dull silver-grey like a photographic negative. Further on, a dark, humped shape floated among the weeds at the edge of the canal. It looked like a sack of old clothes. As she came closer, the thing shifted in the canal's invisible currents and something white and obscene rose to the surface. At first she thought it was a dead fish. Then she realised it was a hand.

She wanted to turn back, she wanted her bed and oblivion, but she had to go on. She had to know for sure because she could not trust her eyes. She could not believe it was him. He could not be here, floating dead in the canal, his body curved as if embracing the water. She stumbled back, her mind rushing away, then sank onto her knees and retched acid bile into the wet grass. She had given herself to him with such abandon, such a sense of lightness. He had been so full of life, and he had filled her with it too. How had they come to this dark place?

For in that moment some movement in the water had turned him and she had seen his face and she had seen that the emptiness in him had won. His dead, black eyes were full of it as they reflected the moon.

Chapter 26

Elissa woke to find Daniel gone, but he often got up in the night so she did not worry. Then she heard his voice from downstairs, soft, placating, and puzzled, and there was another voice too, rising and falling in sharp, panicky waves. It was Jo. She sat up, fully awake now. What was Jo doing here in the middle of the night?

From the landing she could see the light in the hall below. She leaned over the banister to see Daniel standing in the doorway, struggling to hold on to a distraught Jo.

"What is it?" she called. "What's happened?"

Jo's face was pulled tight in a rictus of pain, her face wet with tears. She wore no hat and her hair flew loose in wild, snaking waves. When she saw Elissa, she ran across the hall towards her.

"Oh god Elissa, please, I don't know what to do. I didn't know where else to go."

Elissa ran down to meet her at the bottom of the stairs, enveloping her in a tight hug. Jo was hot and cold all at once, her body heaving, fighting for breath.

"Jo, you're all right now," she said, "you're safe. Tell us what happened." She looked across at Daniel. His face was set hard and in his eyes she saw a hollow fear.

"He's dead." Jo broke off, overwhelmed by a racking sob. "Oh god, I can't – I found him but it was too late."

"Who? Who's dead Jo?"

"Frannie," said Daniel quietly. "I think she's saying he drowned in the canal."

"No, surely not."

"She says she found him."

Jo sagged against her, drained and limp. "Come on Jo," she said. "Let's get you warm."

"I'm going down there," said Daniel. "I have to know."

She nodded. He disappeared upstairs to get dressed and she led Jo into the sitting room where the fire was banked up for the night. She pulled an armchair close to the grate and sat Jo in it, then raked the fire until it roared. She had to keep Jo warm or she might go into shock. Her friend was mute and unresponsive as a rag doll.

"Jo?" she said. "I'm going to fetch you a blanket. I'll be back in just a moment."

She met Daniel in the hall, pulling on his army overcoat. "Are you going to the police?" she whispered.

"She says she's already done that," he said. "I've no idea how she got here. She must have walked. She was calm for a minute and then she just…collapsed."

Elissa could see the terror, dimmed and controlled in his eyes. She squeezed his hand tight. She wanted to say to him, please don't go, you don't have to. But she knew that he did.

"Come back as soon as you can." She embraced him quickly and turned away, not looking back when she heard the front door slam. A churning, selfish fear began to take shape. *Please don't take him too*, she prayed.

From the bridge, Daniel saw policemen gathered like crows around something shapeless on the canal path. Walking, running the two miles from Luddenridge to Calderby, he had denied it to himself, wavering between disbelief and numb terror. Frannie could not be dead. He had seen him only this afternoon, and he had been – well, he had not been fine exactly. But alive, and not about to contemplate suicide.

Four policemen in uniform stood over the body, one writing in a notebook, while another, presumably a plainclothes man, knelt at his side, touching various parts with delicate care. Daniel wanted to shout at him to stop, to leave his friend in peace. For it could not be denied – it was Frannie.

Lying on his back, arms spread in supplication, he lay open-eyed and sightless on the path, pale as a deep-sea fish.

One of the policemen saw Daniel and moved to intercept him.

"Step back please, sir," he said, holding up the flat of his hand as if directing traffic.

"I knew him," Daniel said, his voice choked and wheezy. He said it again, louder. "I knew him. He was my friend."

The policeman looked him up and down as if measuring him up as a suspect. Daniel closed his eyes, opened them again. Frannie was still lying there, still dead.

"Can you give me his name sir?" said the policeman. "There's nothing on the body to identify him."

"Francis Dwyer. He lives in Canal Street. Number twenty-three."

The policeman scratched down the details in his pad. "How did you know he was here?"

"Jo told me. Miss Jo Kenyon. I'm assuming she's the one who called you?"

281

The policeman cleared his throat. "Kenyon is it? A young lady came to the station, told us the place then disappeared," he said. "She didn't leave her name. We'd like to know her whereabouts if you can help."

And the implication was that there'd be trouble all round if he didn't.

"She's at my home. Forty, Hill Road, Luddenridge. My wife is looking after her. As you can imagine she's rather distressed."

The policeman raised his eyebrows. "And what exactly was her relationship to the deceased?"

"You'll have to ask her that," snapped Daniel.

"Oh I will. And your name is?"

"Daniel Earnshaw."

The man scratched in his notebook. "And you were this man's friend you say?"

"Yes."

"When was the last time you saw him alive?"

"This afternoon. I mean, yesterday afternoon."

The man's questions were intolerable. Daniel knew he was thinking that Frannie had killed himself. That he had taken the easy way out and jumped into the canal. He wanted to shout at the man, grab him by the scruff and shake into him that it wasn't true. It was an accident, and that was that. Frannie would never have taken his own life.

Daniel wished he had never come. He knew that the questions would keep on coming, and all the time over the policeman's carrion-black shoulder, the plainclothes-man in Homburg and overcoat crouched over his friend, while the four other policemen stood like sentries. And there on the ground there was Frannie, or what had been Frannie, eyes open to the sky.

Elissa sat with Jo, curled around her in the chair, and held her as she cried. She gave her whisky to drink and drank some herself. Jo would be quiet for a while, then thrash and cry again, but slowly, as the whisky and the warm fire took effect, her breathing softened and Elissa thought that she had finally fallen asleep. But then she sat up and said:

"It's my fault he died."

Elissa disentangled herself from the blanket so that she could look her friend in the eye. "How could it possibly be your fault?"

"He came to me last night. He was drunk and he made me angry. I told him to stop pestering me. I told him I never wanted to see him again."

"Jo that doesn't mean – "

"I know, but it was the last straw for him, I could see it in his eyes. I saw for the first time how…fragile he was. He fooled us all."

Elissa chafed her friend's icy hands, trying to warm them. "You mustn't think like that Jo, really you mustn't."

"You don't understand. I can't help it."

"I do understand, better than you think. For a long time I blamed myself for Harry's death. I came to hate him, and the last time I saw him I told him I hoped he'd never come back. I thought in some insane way I'd conjured his death. Guilt and grief twisted me, and I felt cursed."

"Yes, that's exactly how I feel. Cursed." Jo didn't seem to have heard anything but that one word. She slipped out of the chair and perched on the rug in front of the fire. "Frannie wasn't the same when he came back. He was like a ghost. As if he was never really here at all." Her voice was calmer now, and firm. "I think the war made him into something else. It killed him, just as surely as if he had died on the battlefield." Jo spread out her fingers and then snatched them close into a fist. "It reached out and took him, just like that."

She looked up at Elissa, tears in her eyes. "We think the war's all done and we're home safe. We think we've survived and now we can carry on with our lives and forget all about it. But it's always going to be just behind us, over our shoulders, ready to drag us back and make us suffer. Somewhere the war is still being fought, and it'll carry on, forever. It'll never really be over. Not for us."

By the time the policeman let Daniel go, after several pages of notes and half an hour of sharp, relentless prying into details that were none of his business, Calderby had sprung to life. A colourless dawn leeched grey mist over the streets and the canal, and as he climbed the stairs up to Bridge Street, the shops were opening and the road was filling with carts and motor vans. An ambulance had pulled up on the kerb, waiting for its load.

The trains were running now and he caught the early-morning stopping service to Luddenridge. But he wasn't ready to go home yet. Instead, he turned right out of the station and took the Raistrick road that twisted uphill, out onto the moor. He marched up the slope, double-time, moving one foot in front of the other, just as he had through all these years of war, always with Frannie somewhere near, chivvying, guiding and protecting.

He couldn't get the picture out of his mind; Frannie's body, grey and soaking, uncannily pale, dumped like a pile of weed

284

on the canal bank. It was an accident, not suicide, that's what he'd told the policeman. He would never believe that it was suicide.

This was all wrong. Frannie was supposed to be here, keeping him company, sharing the memories that he was now condemned to guard alone. This man, who had saved his life on so many occasions, had not allowed him to return the favour. He couldn't help but feel it as a betrayal. There were things about him that only Frannie knew, things that he would never tell anyone, not even Elissa.

He crested the hill and turned left onto the grassed-over track, the ground hard despite the recent rain. A cold month had held back the spring, windy days and nights chilling the seeds in the ground. But yesterday's downpour and the gathering warmth of this sunny morning were stirring the life of the season. Below and behind him, the valley opened up in a wide "V" towards Calderby, its floor lush and green. Brown, seamed rocks stood lumpily out of the hillside and the fields gathered together like drawn threads as they receded towards the town. Calderby squatted and smoked in the distance, a dark, amorphous lump of brick punctuated by chimneys.

It was one of those strange mornings where the sun is filtered and funnelled through cloud to create an unnatural effect, casting a luminous green over the grassy slopes of the valley. In contrast, the shaded stone of the walls and the spiked shadows of trees were bleached light brown, like the sepia tones of a photograph. He reached the end of the track and leaned against the garden wall. Frannie should be here, living in this house, working, thriving. He didn't deserve to die, it wasn't fair. But then none of it was fair. It made no sense; almost everyone he knew was dead, a long, endless litany of names with Frannie at the end of it. Why had he, of all people, been left behind?

In one of the sudden changes of mood he remembered so well from childhood, the clouds shifted apart and sun spilled over the valley. The house shone, caught in a wash of sunlight, its dank, collapsing roof and crumbling walls vanquished for just an instant. Light and shadow moved across it in waves, pulses of illumination that made it appear to be breathing. In the light, all the faults were flattened and he could no longer see decay, but beauty and possibility.

But it was a cheat, an illusion. It had been fooling him all these years, miring him in memories and old, dead dreams. The house's flaking paint, rotting timbers and crumbling stone had held him fast to winter. The sun reached him now, spreading across his hands and face. The light penetrated the skin of his hands and his blood responded to the heat. Life flooded his limbs like venom.

He had to make a new world and be ruthless about it or he too would join the ranks of the dead. Maybe not now, or tomorrow, or even next year, but in the end the ghosts would claim him. He had to cut everything away. A flash of sun reflected in one of the upstairs windows like white fire, and all at once he knew what he had to do.

By the time she had put Jo to bed in the spare room, the sun was fully up and Janet had arrived to start the cleaning. Elissa did not tell her the full story – just that Jo had come to stay with them earlier than expected. She went upstairs to dress and was shocked to discover from her bedside clock that it was after nine. Daniel had been gone for four hours. She dressed quickly, and when she looked up from brushing her hair at the dressing table, she noticed a spiral of black smoke rising from the top of the moor.

She dropped her brush and ran to the window. There was no mistaking it. The smoke rose from the exact place on the horizon that had drawn her eyes so often this past year – the distant outline of his family farm. All those months before Daniel had come back to life at her front door, she had stared at it mournfully, regretting what she had said and had not done.

When she ran out onto the landing, she found Jo standing in the doorway to the spare room, fully dressed.

"I thought you were asleep."

"I couldn't. Is anything wrong?"

"I...I'm not sure. The farm is on fire."

"Farm?"

"Daniel's family's place. I can see it from my room."

"He's not back yet?"

"Jo, I'm sorry. I have to go. I'm worried about him."

Jo followed her down the stairs. "I'm coming with you."

"Nonsense, you're not well."

"Let me help, Elissa, please. I'll go mad if I stay here alone."

Elissa took Jo's Macintosh from the hook in the hall and handed it to her. "Very well then, wait for me outside. I'll just tell Janet we're going out."

She ran as far as she could, but the climb was steep and she had to slow to a walk halfway up the hill. Jo kept pace with her without complaint and the only sound was their panting breath. As they reached the top of the moor the plume of smoke widened and darkened and an acrid smell of burning reached her. By the time they'd got to the turning off the main road, grey flakes of ash blew past on the breeze, sticking to her face and hair.

The house was in flames and it roared like an animal. The windows glowed a devilish red, and as they approached the front door tumbled off its hinges and crashed to the ground, a tongue of flame licking over it into the air.

"No," she whispered. One word, all she could say. "No no no." She scrambled down the grassy track, trying not to breathe the bitter smoke. Jo grasped her arm to hold her back, but she shook free. She was not going to lose him, not again. She had sworn it.

A timber crashed inside the house. It was a skeleton now, dying, the fire dancing within it in a terrible imitation of life. He could not be in there, he must not be.

"Come on," said Jo. She had managed to get hold of Elissa's arm. "Let's go around the back. I think that's where he might be."

She led Elissa over a break in the garden wall on the right of the house. The outbuildings were not alight yet, and they managed to slip into the back yard without mishap. The smoke was thick here though, and they could see only a few feet.

"Daniel!" she cried. "Where are you?"

The smoke swirled around them, acrid and choking. The house popped and crackled and roared.

"There he is," said Jo, pointing, and the smoke lifted for a second to reveal him sitting on the wall a few yards away, cool and calm as you please. He was actually smoking a cigarette.

Elissa rushed over to him. "Daniel! Didn't you hear me calling?"

His eyelids flickered as if he were waking from a doze. He looked at her, he smiled. His face was smudged and dirty, but he didn't seem hurt, apart from a red weal on the back of one hand.

"Are you all right?"

He took her hand. There was something disturbingly euphoric about him. "I found a tin of paraffin in the shed."

She wanted to shake him. "You stupid, stupid man. Why did you do it?"

"Don't worry Elissa, I wasn't trying to do away with myself. It just seemed the right thing to do. I'd no idea it would burn so *well*."

Elissa laughed, fighting hysteria. "Your inheritance is going to be nothing but a few stones and some rather large lumps of charcoal."

"Good. It's the past. It'll drag me down if I let it. It had to go." His words had a kind of logic, but also an edge of madness. "That's what we have to do," he said. "Burn the past. You'll help me, won't you Elissa? We have to make a new world."

"What kind of world?"

"I don't know." His eyes were wide and blind, just as when she'd first met him, that same look of emerging from a dark dream.

"I don't know."

About the Author

This story is fiction but was inspired by an incident in my family history. It is my first novel, though I've been writing for almost as long as I can remember. I have been fascinated by the tarot for many years and have published two decks: *The Quantum Tarot* (with illustrator Chris Butler) and *The Universe Cards*. I'm currently working on a new speculative-historical novel series, to be published in 2025. I live in an unfashionable part of south London with my partner and the inevitable cat.

Printed in Great Britain
by Amazon

45462780R00169